"I'm not walking up there buck naked!" Honey screeched.

Gideon didn't answer.

"I said I'm not walking up there without a stitch of clothes on," she called.

"Fine. That snake'll probably decide to crawl out once it gets dark." He twisted his head, slanting her a grin.

"Don't look at me," she snapped, moving her arms to cover herself as much as possible.

"Aren't you forgetting something?" he asked.

"What?"

"I've already seen just about all there is of you, bright eyes. Who do you think got you out of your wet clothes a few nights ago?"

She sniffed. "You're no gentleman to remind me of that."

"I never claimed to be...."

Dear Reader,

When Honey Logan sets out to prove to her banker father that she is capable of working at his bank, she winds up handcuffed to a notorious bank robber in *Forever and a Day*, the sequel to Mary McBride's bittersweet Western romance, *The Fourth of Forever*. Don't miss this delightful new story from this talented author whose last two books have gotten 5★ reviews from *Affaire de Coeur*.

Author Miranda Jarrett continues to entertain audiences with her series of stories based on the adventures of the infamous Sparhawks of Rhode Island. Her latest, *The Sparhawk Bride*, is the story of a young woman kidnapped on the eve of her wedding.

Unicorn Vengeance, a tale of destiny and intrigue, is the third book in Claire Delacroix's trilogy featuring a family whose sons bear the mark—and the curse—of the ancient kings of France. And *Heart of the Hawk*, the second book of this year's March Madness author Elizabeth Mayne, is the heart-wrenching medieval story of a woman who refuses to marry without love and a man who has vowed to never love again.

Whatever your taste in historical reading, we hope Harlequin Historicals will keep you coming back for more. Please keep a lookout for all four titles, available wherever books are sold.

Sincerely,

Tracy Farrell
Senior Editor

Please address questions and book requests to:
Harlequin Reader Service
U.S.: 3010 Walden Ave., P.O. Box 1325, Buffalo, NY 14269
Canadian: P.O. Box 609, Fort Erie, Ont. L2A 5X3

MARY McBRIDE

Forever and a Day

Harlequin Books

TORONTO • NEW YORK • LONDON
AMSTERDAM • PARIS • SYDNEY • HAMBURG
STOCKHOLM • ATHENS • TOKYO • MILAN
MADRID • WARSAW • BUDAPEST • AUCKLAND

ISBN 0-373-28894-8

FOREVER AND A DAY

MARY McBRIDE

can't remember a time when she wasn't writing. Before she turned her talents to fiction, her poetry was widely published in "little" magazines and college quarterlies.

Her husband is a writer, as well. "It's wonderful," she says. "I have my own live-in editor and proofreader. The only problem is our combined libraries are threatening to crowd us and our two boys out of the house."

They live—and buy bookcases—in St. Louis, Missouri.

For Leslie, again

Prologue

New Mexico Territory—1884

Race Logan had about as much use for trains as he did for bank robbers. Both seemed bent on his ruination. The Atchison, Topeka and the Santa Fe had muscled him out of the freight hauling business some years ago. And now, after he'd turned his hand and his considerable fortune to banking, that new endeavor was threatened by a gang of desperadoes who kept slipping through the bumbling grasp of the territory's lawmen.

He couldn't decide which he hated more—railroads or thieves. He guessed it didn't make much difference anyway since the Bankers' Association had outvoted him on this harebrained scheme that had him here—three miles from Lamy Switch on the short line between Albuquerque and Santa Fe—waiting for the 3:45 and a damn convict from the Missouri State Penitentiary.

The dun mare beside him lifted her nose from a
bramble of snakeweed now and pricked her ears. Only
seconds later Race could feel the ground begin to
tremble beneath his boots. Right on time, blast its oak-
burning heart. He dashed his cigar down and ground
it to dust with his heel while he squinted into the distance.

Up till then it had been a clear and bright summer
afternoon. But the big black locomotive coming down
the line seemed to carry a weather all its own. Bad
weather, Race thought as he watched gray smoke swirl
from its stack and hover like a storm cloud against the
high green backdrop of Glorieta Pass. The massive
engine thundered past him while the brakes squealed
and shot sparks, slowing the train just enough for a
man to leap through a billow of steam and to land like
a cat, despite leg irons and wrist cuffs.

The train picked up speed again, spitting enough
cinders in its wake to blind a man as well as choke him.

Race Logan muttered a curse as he groped in his
vest pocket for the keys they'd forwarded from the
prison in Jefferson City. The warden's accompanying
letter had been blunt. He remembered it word for
word.

Dear Mr. Logan,
    Over my strenuous objections, the governor of
Missouri has directed me to transport Mr. Gideon Summerfield to New Mexico Territory and to
remand the prisoner into your custody.

In my considered opinion, you and your business associates are making a grave mistake by
taking the law into your own hands. In light of
your friendship with the governor, however, I
wish you well in your endeavor, misguided as I
believe it is.

The prisoner will remain shackled during
transport. Enclosed please find the appropriate
keys, and be advised that once they are used, you
will be seeing the last of Gideon Summerfield.

                              Harmon Sadler, Warden
                       Missouri State Penitentiary for Men

With that warning in mind and an oath on his lips,
Race strode toward the prisoner through the lifting
steam, ready to unshackle him, only to discover one
loose cuff already dangling from the man's wrist.

The convict squatted down. "Are you Logan?" His
glance cut toward Race briefly before he turned his full
attention to the leg irons.

Race barely had time to respond before the man
straightened up, jingling loose chains in his left hand
as he extended his right in greeting.

"Gideon Summerfield," he said. Then he cocked
his head toward the disappearing caboose. "Figured
it was best not to get folks all riled up on the train.
Let's hear your plan, Banker, and then I'll tell you
whether it'll work or not."

While Race spoke, the prisoner sifted handfuls of
earth between his fingers, his gray gaze following the
dust as the wind blew it away. Probably hadn't felt ei-

ther—earth or wind—in years, Race thought. Good. The man had eyes like a wolf. Cold. Cautious. Calculating. He was suddenly and oddly glad his only daughter was a thousand miles away, vaguely relieved that by the time she came home from school, this business would be done. He hoped.

"How long?" Race asked him now.

"Couple weeks, I'd guess. Three. Less than that if I'm real lucky. But I'll bring them in, Banker. You can count on that." He brushed the dust from his hands and glanced up. "Whose damn fool plan is this, anyway? Yours?"

"The Bankers' Association," Race grumbled. "Outvoted me seven to one. We're not like Texas, Summerfield. We don't have an outfit like the Texas Rangers. Dwight Samuel and his gang just keep picking our banks clean and then falling through the cracks between the local law agencies."

"So you got yourselves a thief to catch a thief," the convict stated in his flat Missouri drawl.

"I guess you could look at it that way." Race Logan folded his arms and pinned the man with his own icy stare. "We don't want any unnecessary trouble. No bloodshed. I want that understood from the start. I won't have any innocent people getting hurt."

"It's your party, Banker. You best tell your associates and all those *innocents* of yours not to get on the dance floor once the band starts to play."

"Our people all know what to expect. Just stick to the plan, Summerfield. I don't think I have to remind you that every hope you have for a parole depends on it."

"Well, then." A sudden grin slashed across the convict's taut lips. "You'll be wanting to hang on to these, Banker." He gave the leg irons and wrist cuffs a jingle before tossing them to Race. "Just in case."

Chapter One

Race Logan's daughter yanked on the heavy bank door as if she meant to tear it off its hinges. Warm noon air gusted into the lobby with her, riffling papers and the top page of the tearaway calendar on the wall. The elderly teller glanced over the rims of his glasses—first at the date, then at the high hands of the regulator clock and finally at the young woman who stood there tugging off her gloves.

He plucked off his spectacles, put them on again and gulped. "Miss Honey!"

"Hello, Kenneth." By now she had whisked her porkpie hat from her head and was stabbing the pins back into the velveteen confection.

"Aren't you...shouldn't you be...?" Kenneth Crane crooked a finger under his tight collar to make room for his Adam's apple as he swallowed hard and loud. "I thought you were east...at school."

Honey Logan sniffed in reply, an eloquent proclamation that not only was she no longer east, but she was very much here and intended to remain.

"Y-your father's not here," the teller stammered. "Actually no one is supposed to be here this afternoon. Only... only me." His eyes sought the calendar once more, then jerked to the clock. "You see, Miss Honey, any minute now we're expecting... we're going to be..."

"Just go on with whatever you were doing, Kenneth," Honey snapped as she moved toward the paneled oak door that separated the president's office from the lobby of the bank. If the fussy old teller tried to stop her, she was prepared to jab him with a hat pin.

"But, Miss Honey..."

She slammed the door on his protest. For a minute Honey leaned against the smooth oak surface, breathing in the familiar fragrance of the dim, cool office, letting it fill her senses. Leather. Her father's Cuban cigars. The pungent, clean scent of ink. Or was it money? She'd never been entirely sure.

Her gaze lit on the vacant swivel chair behind the massive oak desk. Its tufted leather bore the impression of Race Logan's wide shoulders. "Daddy, I'm back," she whispered. "And I'm staying, whether you like it or not."

She tossed her hat onto the horsehair sofa, then crossed the room and plopped into her father's chair, kicking it into a spin that ended abruptly when her foot collided with the safe.

Staring at the huge black vault with its embossed faceplate and brass combination lock, Honey remembered the day it had arrived on the back of a mule-drawn wagon. Was it ten years ago? Eleven? It seemed like yesterday, but she couldn't have been more than nine or ten then. She remembered how the sun had blazed on the gilt letters—Logan Savings and Loan. Most of all, she recalled the way her fingers had itched to turn the big brass dial and the way her heart had swelled with pride to see her name—Logan—in such bold, beautiful letters. So beautiful. So important. So... responsible.

For the past few months she'd been toying with the notion of changing her name, and the sight of the imposing vault convinced her now. She was indeed going to take back the name with which she'd been christened—in memory of her mother's first husband, Ned Cassidy, who had died the day she was born. It was a name as sober and imposing as the iron safe before her. "Edwina." She said it softly, savoring the feel of it on her tongue. Just heavy enough. Like oatmeal or one of her mother's Christmas fruitcakes, neither of which she particularly cared for, but the name had a gravity that was infinitely appealing.

"Honey." She had Race Logan to thank for that. He couldn't abide anything that smacked of the Cassidys, back then or now, and when he'd come back from the war to discover he had a daughter who had a Cassidy name, he'd tricked her into naming herself by asking "What's your name, honey?" She'd given the obvious and parrotlike response and had been Honey Logan ever since. Well, if she'd named herself once, she thought, she could certainly do it again.

She swung the chair full circle and gazed thoughtfully at the desk top. Her father's distinct, almost stern penmanship covered an assortment of papers there.

The little oval tintype of her mother gazed calmly from its place beside the crystal inkwell.

They were going to kill her. For the first time since her abrupt and unannounced departure from Miss Haven's Academy in St. Louis several days ago, Honey felt her courage wavering. She swallowed in the hope of drowning the butterflies that were beginning to flutter in her stomach. Bankers didn't suffer from butterflies, she reminded herself. Bankers didn't succumb to doubt and dread. They were tough and strong. Like her father.

She glanced at the gold lettering on the safe again. Bankers were, above all, responsible. And that was exactly what she intended to be. Unless, of course, her father killed her before she got the chance.

Heaven knew Race Logan was capable of it. And although her father didn't say much about that aspect of his life, Honey had listened to her Uncle Isaac spin stories over the years about her father's legendary exploits as a wagon master on the Santa Fe Trail. The moral of most of those stories, however, wasn't about murder. It was about hard work and responsibility.

Honey had taken those tales to heart. There was nothing she wanted more than to follow Race Logan's example. But while she craved responsibility, her father merely wanted her to be safe and secure—preferably in his own house, on a high shelf in a glass box whose key rested comfortably in his vest pocket. Having just spent the past two years in a glass box called a finishing school, Honey had decided she was indeed finished—with glass boxes.

But how in the world was she going to convince her father? The mere mention of the word *responsibility* now was guaranteed to bring a dark scowl to his handsome face and his voice would surely thunder like God Almighty's when he proclaimed, "Don't talk to me about responsibility, young lady. Not after you walked out of school the way you did."

Well, she hadn't walked out, Honey thought now. Not exactly. It had been more like storming out. She hadn't wanted to attend Miss Haven's Academy in the first place, but her father had insisted. Then, after nearly two years of trying to please him by applying herself diligently to the study of music and literature and the domestic arts, Honey had had enough of arias and sonnets and delicate stitchery. She yearned to accomplish more.

Longing to follow in her father's footsteps, she had at last approached the academy's directress about her wish to pursue a new and individualized curriculum. But after Miss Euphonia Haven's palpitations subsided, the woman had sniffed indignantly and had informed Honey in no uncertain terms that the study of higher mathematics and finance was *unsuitable for young ladies*. So Honey had packed her trunks and taken the first train home. Unsuitable! She'd show them unsuitable!

This was her rightful place. Honey shifted in the big leather chair, aware of the way the back and seat had been molded by her father's solid frame and how the leather on the arms had been nearly worn away by his sleeves. She was, after all, his eldest child. Didn't she deserve the opportunity to be his heir? Surely she could convince him.

If not, perhaps her mother could. Tiny Kate Logan had gone toe-to-toe with her strapping husband more than a few times over the years on her daughter's behalf. Honey smiled wistfully now, remembering the last time her mother had come to her rescue by engaging her father in an all-out bidding war for a supper basket he was determined to keep from any and all of his daughter's young suitors. Although her mother had won, Honey hadn't enjoyed the fruits of the supper basket or the victory all that much. The beau in question had turned out to be little more than a fawning fool. The first of many.

On the other hand, her mother might not help. Not long after that bidding war and giving birth to her fifth child, Kate Logan had announced her unconditional withdrawal from the fray.

"I'm tired of being in the middle all the time," her mother had said. "You look like him, you think like him, and sometimes you're even more bullheaded. You two Logans can butt heads for a while without me between you. I swear, Honey, you and your daddy have just plain worn me down." True to her word, Kate had even abstained from the battle over finishing school, leaving Honey to lose it on her own.

But she wasn't going to lose anymore. She was here, her fanny planted firmly in Race Logan's big chair, and here she was going to stay.

Holy hellfire! Couldn't anybody see that she was bright and eager and willing to work hard to prove

herself? Didn't anybody understand that she needed
to prove she could be a trustworthy human being?

Apparently not, Honey thought glumly. She was
just going to have to show them. And that was why she
had come directly to the bank after getting off the
train. She planned to be here—in the bank—working—when her father returned from his noon meal.
She was going to show him what a valuable asset his
daughter was—how diligent she could be—how trustworthy and, dammit, just how responsible.

Yanking open the bottom desk drawer, intending to
stow her gloves there, Honey found herself gawking
instead.

"What in the world...?" she murmured at the sight
of chains and an odd metal contraption, which she
lifted, cautiously, by one end. Wrist cuffs! How odd.
Now why would her father have a pair of wrist cuffs
in his desk drawer?

Curious, she fit the circlet of steel around her wrist
and stared at it while a shiver rippled the length of her
spine. What a horrible, ugly thing it was. A bracelet
for a desperado. Jewelry for a thief.

A sharp rap sounded on the door just then. Honey
jerked upright, and the cuff clicked closed.

"Miss Honey," Kenneth Crane called through the
door. "I must speak with you. Now."

"I'll be right out." Honey tugged at the steel
bracelet. Damn! All she needed now was for Kenneth
to see what a fool thing she'd done. He'd promptly tell
her father, and then she'd be lucky if Race Logan
didn't clamp the other half of the wrist cuffs to a
doddering old *dueña*, a chaperon who would never let

Honey out of her sight. Or worse, to his own thick wrist.

She tried unsuccessfully to slide the steel over her hand.

"Miss Honey," the teller called again, rapping once more for emphasis.

"Just one confounded minute, Kenneth."

Honey could hear his footsteps retreating to his post behind the teller's window as she glared at the shackle on her right wrist. If looks alone could melt steel, the metal would have dissolved right then. But it didn't. She was stuck and she knew it. Like a rat in a trap.

As she rose from the swivel chair, the empty cuff clanked against the desk. "Damnation!" she muttered. She'd just have to keep her hand behind her back until she could find somebody with a hacksaw to get her out of this fool thing. Maybe she could bribe her brother, Zack, to... No. Zack could keep a secret about as well as a parrot, and nothing would delight him more than seeing his trouble-prone sister cuffed like a common thief. She'd just have to seek elsewhere for help. In the meantime, though, she was going to carry on with her plan to be right here, hard at work, when her father returned from lunch.

The lobby was still empty, thank heaven, when she sidled up behind Kenneth, her right hand concealed in the pocket of her skirt, her lips forcing a cheerful grin.

"I'll help you count those greenbacks, Kenneth."

The elderly teller spun around at the sound of her voice. He threw up his hands helplessly, and suddenly greenbacks were everywhere—sliding off the counter, slithering along the floor, settling under Honey's skirts.

Oh, for heaven's sake, she thought. The man was as skittish as a colt in a storm. He had just tossed about a thousand dollars like a handful of confetti, but if her father walked in now, Honey knew very well just who would get the blame.

"Get a grip on yourself, Kenneth," she snapped, crooking her knees and lowering herself to the floor to gather as much currency as she could one-handed.

The aged teller seemed to melt beside her. "You . . . you're not supposed to be here, Miss Honey. Please. Nobody else is supposed to be . . ."

Boot heels clomped on the opposite side of the counter, followed by the distinct sound of iron clearing leather. And then a deep, whiskey-rich drawl.

"The name's Summerfield."

What little color remained in Kenneth Crane's face drained away. His Adam's apple somersaulted in his throat as he mumbled something unintelligible, then crumpled into a dead faint on the floor beside Honey's knees.

"*Gideon* Summerfield?" she exclaimed.

Gideon contemplated the pretty face that had bobbed up from behind the counter like a windflower after a warm spring rain. The blue-green eyes that bloomed big and round with surprise. The moist petaled lips that forgot to close completely after speech. The dark tendrils of hair that framed her face, then spilled over her shoulders and couldn't quite conceal a breathless, ample bosom.

After five years in prison, the sight of a female—pretty or otherwise—windflower or weed—was enough to snap every nerve in his body. And the sight of this particular female jolted him like white-hot lightning. For a dizzying second, he didn't know where he was...or why.

"*The* Gideon Summerfield?" The blue-green eyes blinked and the petaled lips quivered.

He wrenched himself from the empty-headed bewilderment. For crissake! If he wasn't careful, Gideon thought, he'd be on his way back to Jefferson City in leg irons and steel bracelets. No woman in the world was worth that.

"That's right, sweetheart. And now that you know who, let's move on to why." He leaned against the counter, edging the barrel of his pistol between the brass bars. "Hand it over."

Honey wasn't sure which terrified her more—the Colt or the deadly, gunmetal gray of the eyes that were narrowed on her face. Gideon Summerfield! If what she had read in the papers was true, this man wouldn't hesitate to pull the trigger. Frank and Jesse James. Cole Younger. Gideon Summerfield. Dwight Samuel. The names rolled through her mind like a funeral march. They were cold-blooded killers, all.

Her knees were knocking together beneath the counter as Honey raised her hand, still clutching some of the bills she had gathered from the floor. "Here." She shoved them beneath the brass grille. "Take these."

The gunmetal gaze dipped to the crumpled banknotes, then swung back to Honey's face. A tiny grin played at the corners of his mouth as Gideon Summerfield tipped back the brim of his hat with the muzzle of his gun.

"Must be all of twenty dollars there," he drawled.

That amused expression only chilled her more. "Just...just take it and get out. I won't scream. I promise. I won't even tell anyone you were here."

His grin flashed wider. "Hard to make a living robbing banks at twenty bucks a throw, wouldn't you say?"

She stood there just staring at him now, her turquoise eyes big and bright with fear, her lips pressed together to still the trembling, her chin tilted that defiant little notch.

Something twisted in Gideon Summerfield's gut then. What the hell kind of a man was Race Logan to leave a windflower to face this situation alone? The girl was terrified, and rightly so with the cold barrel of a Colt pointed at her young heart. Logan no doubt had figured a defenseless flower would cause the least trouble, provoke the least amount of violence from the jailbird. But, dammit, didn't the banker have any inkling how frightened this little teller would be? Didn't he care?

Gideon cursed himself for his own misguided sympathy. What good would it do anyway? Most likely just land him back in a dank five-by-eight cell in Missouri. Hell, the little bank clerk would survive this fine, even wind up with a doozy of a tale to tell her grandchildren one day.

"I'm not going to hurt you," he said brusquely. "Let's just get this over with. Hand over the money."

"No."

He stared at her in disbelief, not certain he had heard her right. "This isn't a Presbyterian social, darlin'. I wasn't asking you to dance. I said hand over the money."

Her chin came up another notch. "No."

"You're playing this out for all it's worth, aren't you, sweetheart?" He thumbed back the hammer of his gun as his eyes narrowed to steely slits. "The money. Now."

Honey was about to tell him no again when Kenneth Crane rose shakily behind her.

"I—I'll get it for you," he stammered.

"Much obliged." Gideon's eyes remained on the windflower, whose pretty face had puckered indignantly at the old man's words. There was as much fire in her eyes now as fear.

"Kenneth, don't you dare..." she began, then fell silent when the tip of Gideon's pistol touched her chin.

His words were directed to the teller, who was heading for the paneled oak door of the office, but his gaze skewered Honey. "I appreciate your compliance, mister. I'll appreciate your speed even more."

"Kenneth!" Honey wailed.

"Shh. Hush up, sweetheart. It'll all be over within a minute or two. Nobody'll blame you for this."

Honey glared at him. "A lot you know, you... you..."

His lips quirked into another grin and one eyebrow lifted rakishly. "Thief?"

"No-good, degenerate snake!"

Gideon Summerfield laughed out loud. "Plenty of folks would agree with you, darlin', but none of them would have the vinegar to say it to my face." Gray eyes skimmed her face, her throat, the lace frills on the bodice of her dress. "Vinegar," he murmured huskily, "and lace and honey. Sweet, warm honey."

"I'm not afraid of you."

His gaze jerked up to her face and the remnants of his smile disappeared. "You should be," he ground out from between clenched teeth, thinking if she had even a glimmer of the fire blazing in him right now this little girl would run screaming from the bank, whether he held a gun on her or not.

"Well, I'm not." What she feared right now was facing her father's rage when he discovered his bank had been robbed while his daughter was in it. If she had ever hoped to impress him with her responsibility, this incident would dash those hopes irreparably. He'd never let her even visit the bank again, much less work in it.

Damnation! She wanted to reach across the counter and just choke this desperado for the way he was messing up her plans and her life. Her hands clenched into fists at the thought, and then Honey realized she was still wearing half of the wrist cuffs. The legal half. Jewelry for a thief. Now, if only...

Kenneth Crane came out of the office, lugging a large canvas bag by its leather handles. "Here... here it is," he said as he shuffled toward Summerfield on the public side of the counter.

Ignoring the gun, Honey scurried around the counter. Then, just as Gideon Summerfield extended his hand for the bag, Honey reached out and clamped the empty cuff around his wrist. At the sound of the click, her eyes blazed victoriously and her mouth settled into a smug line.

"Oh, Lord," breathed Kenneth Crane, appearing to wither inside his suit.

Honey flicked the teller a disdainful look. She had expected that from the fainthearted wretch. From Gideon Summerfield, on the other hand, she expected curses and a battle royal with fists and fingernails and feet. She stiffened her body in preparation.

He did curse—a soft, almost whispered expletive that seemed more prayer than oath—and then he shook his head just before his free arm circled Honey and he hoisted her onto his hip.

"Put me down," she shrieked. "Kenneth, for God's sake, don't just stand there gawking. Do something."

"Oh, Lord," the teller moaned. "I don't know what to do."

It was Gideon Summerfield who answered him with a growl. "I'll tell you what to do, fella. You tell your boss to be a whole lot more careful about who he invites to his parties."

Then, with the money bag in one hand and a flailing Honey in the other, he walked out the door.

Chapter Two

"Here now. You drink this, Miz Kate. It'll put them roses back in your cheeks."

Kate Logan gave Isaac Goodman a weak but grateful smile as she took the proffered glass, then drained it.

"Better?" Isaac raised a grizzled eyebrow, watching her shiver slightly after swallowing the brandy.

She nodded. "What are we going to do, Isaac?" she asked the bear-size former slave, who had been her husband's partner on the Santa Fe Trail as well as her own dear and trusted friend for so many years. "What in the world are we going to do?"

Kenneth Crane had come and gone from the rambling adobe house just off the plaza. The bank teller—chalk faced and trembling on the verge of tears—had told them of Honey's return and her unplanned involvement in the planned robbery. But the news that had left Kate pale and weak had had the opposite effect on her husband. Race had exploded. His curses had thundered through the house, and even now the pounding of his footsteps and the sound of slamming drawers and doors shook the oak floors and the thick adobe walls.

"*We* ain't going to do anything," Isaac answered, angling his head toward the hallway in the direction of Race's resounding curses. "'Neath all that thunderation, I suspect Horace is working out a plan. He'll get her back, Miz Kate. You know he will."

Kate's hands fluttered in her lap. "I'm so frightened for her, Isaac. She's out there all alone."

The black man eased himself into the chair beside hers. He sighed as he reached out his one good arm to pat Kate's trembling hand. "Well, now, she ain't exactly alone, is she?"

Kate threw a dark glance at the beamed ceiling. "I almost wish she were. Whatever was that child thinking, leaving school without permission and then clamping herself to an outlaw like Gideon Summerfield?"

"She wasn't thinking." Race Logan's voice reverberated off the thick walls of the parlor as he stomped across the threshold. "Your daughter hasn't used her head once in her life as far as I can tell. It's the Cassidy influence on her. Goddamn moon-faced people who couldn't find their way out of a privy without a map and a torch."

Isaac Goodman grinned and settled back in his chair. The mere mention of the Cassidy name always guaranteed a good ten minutes of fireworks between Race Logan and his wife. Twenty years ago in Leavenworth, Kansas, a pregnant Kate had married Ned Cassidy in desperation when she believed Race Logan had abandoned her. It never seemed to matter that the sickly, round-faced storekeeper had died before Kate's child was born or that she'd never loved him anyway. Truth and logic never seemed to count for much when Race got heated up. Nothing could light a fire under him like the name Cassidy. And nothing could light up Miz Kate like Race. Isaac looked at her now—anticipating her fiery reaction. He wasn't disappointed.

Her green eyes flashed like emeralds. "Your daughter inherited the Cassidy fortune, Race, not the Cassidy blood. It's your hot blood that runs through her veins and your hard head on her shoulders. If she quit her schooling and clamped herself onto some cutthroat you hired to rob your bank, the Cassidys have nothing to do with it. Honey's pure Logan." She paused only long enough to catch her breath. "And just what do you think you're doing, strapping on that gun?"

Race glared at her, then gave his belt a yank to settle the holster against his thigh. "What does it look like, Kate?" he muttered as he bent to tie the leg strap.

"It looks like you're leaving me again." Kate's voice quivered and tears brimmed in her eyes.

Race straightened up from anchoring his sidearm. For a second his big hands hung helplessly at his sides. "Katie." His voice was gentle now. "Look at me, love."

Her lids lifted to find warmth and solace in his lake-colored gaze.

"I won't be gone long. I promise you." He bent on one knee and grasped her fidgeting hand, then pressed it to his lips. "Only long enough to find her and bring her back."

"Don't go alone," she pleaded. "Can't you organize a posse? Since Summerfield is supposed to have robbed the bank..."

Race's mouth tautened.

"Too many eager guns in a posse," Isaac said. "Horace'll do fine by himself, Miz Kate. Besides, there ain't no stopping him now. Leastways nothing comes to mind."

"That's right, partner," Race said, straightening up and shooting the old man a hard look. "Can I count on you staying put and keeping an eye on Kate and the boys for me?"

Isaac grinned. "I'm getting too old to go traipsing off after you, Horace. But you might want to remember that you ain't getting any younger neither. You're carrying about twenty years that convict ain't even seen yet."

"He took off with my daughter, Isaac."

The older man slowly raised an eyebrow. "From what that pale, shaky teller of yours observed, Horace, didn't sound like the man had much choice."

Kate rose from her chair and moved close to her husband. Touching his arm, she could feel the tension that hardened his muscular frame. It didn't matter what Isaac said. Race was done listening. Rage and determination emanated from his body like pure heat, and she knew from experience that the combination made her husband a dangerous man. In twenty years, his hair had silvered some and his face had a few more weather marks, but his temper was still a fearsome thing. Gideon Summerfield, God help him, wouldn't be the first man Race Logan had killed.

* * *

Stupid. Stupid. Stupid. Honey chastised herself for the hundredth time. *Dumber than a post.* That was what she should have cuffed him to. A post. A rail. Something permanent rather than five and a half feet of portable female. Gideon Summerfield had carried her out of the bank, then had slung her up onto his saddle like a sack of potatoes, swinging himself up behind her and jamming his heels into his big roan gelding. They'd been riding hard ever since. Two hours. Maybe three. Honey wasn't sure. Her sole certainty was her own damn blasted stupidity. That, and the outlaw's hot breath on the nape of her neck and his iron grip around her middle.

She had spent the first hour screaming and cursing and railing over her shoulder at him, catching glimpses of the hard set of his mouth and the steely cast in his gray eyes. The outlaw remained silent, soaking up her ravings like a sponge. After that—hoarse, exhausted, expecting at any moment to be yanked from the saddle then flung to the ground and raped—Honey settled into a grim and wary silence as Santa Fe fell farther and farther behind them. Ahead there was nothing but sky and sage-dotted hills.

And it was so damn hot, Honey thought she might melt like a stick of butter. After two years in St. Louis she had forgotten just how fiercely a June sun could blaze in the territory. It wasn't helping any, either, having a man's chest—as hard and hot as a stovetop—rubbing against her shoulder blades and his breath like the blast of a furnace on her neck.

"Stupid," she hissed, this time out loud.

Gideon Summerfield's hand twitched on her rib cage. His other hand pulled back on the reins. "Yup," he said as he slid to the ground, jerking her right hand along with his.

All of Honey's senses sharpened in self-defense. "Stop it. What do you think you're doing?" she squealed as he hauled her down from the tall horse.

"Answering nature's call." He began walking toward a low-growing juniper, towing Honey along at arm's length.

"You're not," she said. "I mean, you…you can't."

Gideon Summerfield continued toward the bush. "Lady, I can and I am."

"But we're…I'm…there's no privacy," she wailed.

He halted. "You should have thought of that before you decided to be my Siamese twin, sweetheart." Saying that, Gideon Summerfield reached to unbutton his fly.

Honey twisted her head in the opposite direction, closed her eyes and her ears as well. She had been prepared to deal with rape, with a violent assault on her person. But not this. It was an assault on sheer decency. Mortified, her face burning, she began babbling.

"Stupid, stupid, stupid. What was I thinking? That you'd just hand back the money and accompany me to the sheriff's office? What a dolt. What a fool. I'd have been better off if you'd just shot me. Left me for dead on the damn bank floor. Or cut my arm off and left me for the buzzards ten miles back. I'd have been better off—"

"Are you done?" he drawled.

Honey blinked. "Oh! Are you?"

He buttoned his pants. "Your turn, sweetheart."

"I should think not," she said with a sniff.

"Suit yourself." He started back toward the horse with Honey stumbling in his wake.

But this time it was Honey who halted, digging her heels into the dry ground, resisting the pull on her wrist. "I demand to know where you're taking me, Mr. Summerfield. Where, and what your intentions are."

Gideon gritted his teeth. His intentions, for chrissake! For the past couple hours his intentions had been at war with his baser instincts as he held this lush package of female in his arms, as he breathed in the sweet, clean scent of her hair and made himself dizzy contemplating the delicate shape of her ear and the pale, smooth curve of her neck. He looked into the blue-green defiance of her eyes. Then he reeled her in by flexing his arm.

Honey collided with the toes of his boots, the solid wall of his chest. "Don't," she snapped, trying to twist away.

"Don't what?" Gideon's lips just brushed the crown of her head. "Don't breathe in your woman scent? Don't touch you? What?" He slid his fingers into the wealth of her hair, then clenched a fistful of the dark silk, pulling back, tilting her face to meet his. "Don't kiss you?"

Honey stiffened beneath his gaze. "Don't act like a brute, Mr. Summerfield."

His eyes roved slowly over her face—saw the spark of fear in her eyes, the hectic color on her cheeks, the defiant twist of her sensuous mouth. This *brute,* he thought, hadn't touched another human being in five years except to give or receive punches, except to clap his hand on the hard shoulder of a convict in front of him to shuffle down a corridor in lockstep. He'd felt the cold stone floor of his cell, the icy metal of his cage, the sting of leather, the clout of wood. And this *brute* was dazed now, dizzy with the touch and smell and sight of sweet flesh and moist lips. He didn't want to possess her so much as blanket himself in the softness of her, lose himself in the womanliness and purity of her, warm himself in her essential fire.

They were in the middle of nowhere with only scrub and dust, a weary horse and a hot blind sun for witnesses. She was his for the taking. And Gideon Summerfield, *brute,* hard and hot and wanting her, let her go.

His teeth were clenched so hard he could barely form the words. "Don't worry, bright eyes. You're not my type." It wasn't so far from the truth, after all. The women in his life had been whores for the most part, professional or not so professional. There had been a lady or two along the way, more curious than amorous, more interested in bedding a notorious thief than making love to a man. Not like this lady, though. Young as she was, her quality ran deep. More quality than he could handle at the moment.

When he eased his hand from her hair, Honey straightened up and smoothed the folds of her skirt, keeping her head down to hide the hot flush that had spread like wildfire over her cheeks. "I should hope not," she snapped. "And I'd like an answer to my question. About where we're going. And when you plan to let me go.''

The sooner the better, she thought. For one heart-stopping moment, she had thought he was going to kiss her. But then he didn't, and rather than relief, Honey had felt a vague and bewildering disappointment. She didn't want this desperado to kiss her. Most assuredly she didn't.

She raised her chin and gave him the most scathing look she could muster. "When *do* you plan to let me go?"

His mouth hooked into a lazy grin and he lifted their joined wrists. "Let you go? Hell, I thought I was your prisoner, bright eyes."

"That isn't very funny, Mr. Summerfield."

"Gideon," he said.

"I beg your pardon?"

He shrugged. "Look. Why not call me by my Christian name as long as we're going to be cuffed together for a while." He slanted a meaningful glance toward their wrists. "And you might as well tell me your name while we're at it. Doesn't make a whole lot of sense keeping up such niceties when we're going to have to be answering nature's—"

"Edwina," she said sharply, cutting him off.

An odd smile touched his lips. "Doesn't suit you."

"Neither do you, Mr. Summerfield."

He hung his head in mock surrender, and as he did a lock of hair fell across his forehead. For the first time, Honey noticed its rich color. Nutmeg? No. More like cinnamon. It looked warm and spicy where it curled over the collar of his shirt. There were glints of gold wherever the sun touched it.

"Edwina," he murmured now, making the name sound antique, if not downright crotchety. "You got a better last name?"

Still contemplating his hair, Honey was about to reply with the truth, but suddenly and thankfully refrained. If he knew she was the daughter of the owner of Logan Savings and Loan, there was no telling what this desperado would do. Even if he did have spice-colored hair and such an engaging, lopsided little grin. "Cassidy," she said.

He lifted a finely shaped hand to touch the brim of his hat. It was a gesture Honey found most men performed awkwardly, like gawky little boys. But this outlaw managed it with the ease and grace of a man who had spent his past few years in a palace rather than a prison.

"Pleased to meet you, Miss Edwina Cassidy. We'd best get on our way now." He slid his gaze toward the shrubs. "You sure you don't have to..."

"I'm quite sure, Mr. Summer—"

"Gideon," he corrected as he swept her up into his arms and carried her toward the grazing horse.

After he settled behind her, Honey angled her head over her shoulder. "You never did tell me where we were headed, Mr... um, Gideon."

He slid an arm around her waist, fanning his fingers out on her midriff. "Didn't I?" He urged the big horse forward with a nudge of his heels, then added with a deep-throated chuckle, "Fancy that."

* * *

"We need a room." Gideon's voice was a low rumble as he approached the desk clerk. Miss Edwina Cassidy slept soundly in his arms while he attempted to keep his own right hand as well as hers hidden in the folds of her skirts.

The gangly young clerk eyed him blandly, suppressing a yawn. "You and the missus?"

"That's right."

The boy let out a knowing little snort, coupled with a wink. Since the small hotel on the main street of Cerrillos was the front half of a dance hall, Gideon suspected the kid had seen women taken up to rooms every which way—awake, asleep, alive or dead drunk.

"That'll be four dollars, in advance," the boy told him now.

Gideon shifted the little bank clerk's deadweight so he could dig into his pocket. "Here's five," he said, flipping a gold coin onto the counter. "Make sure we get some hot water and clean towels."

"Yeah. Sure thing." The boy pushed a brass key toward him. "Up those stairs and down the hall on the right," he said, angling his head in that direction.

"Dance hall stay open all night?" Gideon asked him.

The boy looked at the sleeping female, shifted his gaze back to Gideon's face, then winked again. "All night. All morning. All the liquor you can tuck away. All the women you can—"

Gideon cut him off. "You want me to sign a register or something?"

"Dad-blast, I almost forgot." The boy dipped a bent-tipped pen in an inkwell and passed it, dribbling, across the stained counter. "Just scribble anything," he mumbled. "It don't matter."

Slowly, with his left hand while balancing his sleeping cuff-mate on one hip, Gideon printed his name, then turned the book so the boy could read it. "How's that?"

"Yeah. Sure." The boy's bored, half-open eyes skimmed the page, then widened and bulged. "Its fine, Mr. Summerfield." His throat crackled as he attempted to swallow. "It's just fine, sir. I'll be sure and get those clean towels for you. Hot water, too. Anything else I can do for you, sir?"

"Nope. Towels and water will do fine. Much obliged." Gideon shifted the soft burden in his arms, then headed up the stairs, all the while feeling the boy's amazed gaze on his back. Five years in prison, he thought, hadn't dimmed his reputation all that much. Good thing, too. He was going to need every bit of it to accomplish what he had to do.

The room was small and spare and no doubt flyspecked, but to Gideon's eyes anything with four walls and a bed was sheer heaven compared to iron bars and a wooden pallet. He closed the door with his foot, then lowered the sleeping woman onto the mattress.

She didn't wake, but Gideon hadn't expected her to. The ride from Santa Fe had been long and hard. Twelve hours in the saddle under a relentless sun. He'd offered her his hat, but she had refused with a proud stiffening of her shoulders and a cluck of her tongue that told him pretty clearly where she thought he could put his hat. She had ignored him for the most part, staring ahead, stewing, fretting, plotting Lord only knew what as her teeth worried her lower lip.

By moonrise, though, she hadn't been able to fight exhaustion anymore, and her proud chin had dipped wearily onto the high-buttoned bodice of her dress. Gideon had tucked her head onto his shoulder and pressed his cheek to the soft fall of her hair, easing back on the reins and slowing the big roan to a lullaby walk. He wasn't in such a hurry for cold revenge that he couldn't savor the warmth of Miss Edwina Cassidy for a quiet little while.

He sat beside her now, watching as the light from a three-quarter moon glossed the dark tangle of her hair. With his free hand, he reached to smooth it away from her sunburned face, thinking maybe he could scare up some vinegar to take some of the sting out of that delicate skin. Lord knew his own was smarting from the harsh New Mexico sun.

Sighing, he reached in the pocket of his shirt and withdrew a quill toothpick. While his mouth twitched in a grin, it took him all of a minute to jimmy the lock on his half of the cuffs. It took him a tad longer, though, to wrestle the limp lady out of her rumpled dress.

"Stupid," he muttered softly as he felt the dampness of her underskirts. Damn stubborn female would have let her insides explode rather than lose her confounded dignity. Only total exhaustion and sleep had finally relieved her.

With a gruff curse, Gideon proceeded to strip her of the wet underthings. He swore again when he discovered she wore a combination. Corsets and drawers came off easy, but these damn one-piece garments were hell on a man in a hurry, or one with a decent purpose and trembling fingers such as his were now while they worked the buttons down the front then slipped the soft cotton from her shoulders.

Moonlight silvered the pale skin beneath his fingertips and gleamed in the deep valley between her lovely breasts. Their crests bloomed like roses in a night garden. As he beheld her, Gideon realized he wasn't breathing. His mouth had gone dry as sand, and his hands had clenched into tight fists as his leaden, shuttered gaze failed to respond to his wish to turn away. His lips moved soundlessly, once again damning the banker for planting this innocent flower in his path. It was more than a sane man could stand.

Almost more. Gideon stood up and stared at the wall as he whisked the garment from her hips and legs and tossed it into the sodden pile beside the bed. He folded her gently into the bed linens then and raised her arm to clamp his half of the cuff onto the iron bedpost.

"Sleep tight, Miss Edwina Cassidy," he murmured. He gathered up her clothes and walked softly out of the room.

The string band stuttered in the middle of its tune when Gideon pushed through the batwing doors into the dance hall. He felt the keen appraisal of every eye in the smoky room, and he heard the telling shift in the rhythm of everyone's breathing, the way voices stilled a second, then softly rose again as he crossed to the bar.

A perverse pride welled in the back of his throat, and his gut tugged a little as he thought of so many other rooms he had entered with his cousins—with Jesse and Frank and Dwight. The young desk clerk had done his job just right. The word had been spread. The name of Gideon Summerfield had gotten around. And its magic was still there. But it wasn't magic, as Gideon well knew. It was fear that was rippling through the room. It was the rush from the wings of the angel of death.

"Name your poison, Summerfield," the bearded bartender said.

Gideon leaned an elbow on the carved sweep of walnut and lifted a boot onto the rail. "Rye, if you've got it, otherwise anything'll do."

As the barman turned to retrieve a glass from the wall behind him, Gideon surveyed the dimly lit room. A dozen men. A sprinkle of whores, including the one who was sashaying toward him now.

"You're a hell of a long way from Clay County," she purred, fitting her hip against his, slipping her fingers between the buttons of his shirt.

"You, too, darlin', judging from the sound of you." Gideon immediately recognized the flat border state drawl. He tried to ignore her inquisitive little hand as it traced over his belly. He tried and failed to ignore the tightening in his groin.

"Born and bred in Liberty," she said. "How 'bout you?"

"Colton."

"Never heard of it."

Gideon's mouth twitched. "It wasn't much, even before the Yankees burned it. I'm looking for somebody from home. Maybe you can help me."

"Maybe." She slipped a button on his midriff to allow her hand freer, warmer access.

Gideon reached back for the glass on the bar top, tilted his head and downed the liquor in a single swallow. He tapped the empty glass on the counter, raising an eyebrow to signal a refill. "And one for the lady," he drawled, returning his gaze to the painted, fine-handed redhead.

"Who're you looking for, honey?" she asked him, angling her blue-lidded eyes up to his. "Other than me, of course."

"My wife," he said in a low, level tone.

The redhead blinked. "Word is you've got one of those upstairs right now."

Word, thought Gideon, traveled fast. Good. "I'm looking for my first wife. The one who walked out on me." He narrowed his gaze on the whore's curious face. "With Dwight Samuel. You know him?"

Her expression seemed to melt. Only two bright dabs of rouge remained to color her suddenly pallid face. Her red mouth opened, hung slack for a moment, then snapped closed.

Gideon sipped his drink. That was answer enough for him, he thought. "Dwight get to Cerrillos often, does he?"

She eased her hand from his shirt and took a small step back. "I don't know nothin'. I don't want to know nothin'."

He caught her wrist in an iron grip. "Tell him I'm looking for him." His lips sliced into a grin. "Do that for me, sugar, will you? Tell my cousin I'm looking to join up with him again."

Chapter Three

Honey woke slowly. Like a lazy fish, a languid swimmer rising to the surface of warm, dark water. At first she thought she was back at school in St. Louis, but then she remembered her long train ride back to New Mexico. This wasn't her room, though. She wasn't home. Where in the world...? Then her mind broke through the murky barriers to reality.

"Oh, Lord!" She moved to sit up, but steel clinked on iron, and the metal cuff bit into her wrist. "Hell and damnation," she muttered.

Unable to sit up, she lay there, taking bleak inventory of her situation. The last thing she remembered was staring ahead at the rough, moonlit contours of the hills, trying to ignore the dull ache in her bladder, trying desperately to stay awake. Obviously, she thought now, she hadn't. The ache was gone, and she shuddered to even think about that. She shuddered, too, at the feel of the scratchy linens against her skin.

Gideon Summerfield had left her—naked as a jaybird—cuffed to the bedpost. The idea of that desperado taking off her clothes was enough to set her blood boiling, but even worse at the moment was the thought that he had escaped with the bank's money.

Lifting her head, Honey searched the moonlit room, then breathed a small sigh of relief when she saw the canvas sack leaning against the washstand. Thank heavens. If the money was still here, she still had a fighting chance to get it back for the bank. But her sense of relief was fleeting. If the money was still here, then so was Gideon Summerfield. And she was hooked to the bed like a fish on a line. A naked fish at that.

Jerking on the steel cuff did nothing but hurt her already bruised wrist. With her free hand, Honey tossed the covers off, then clambered up on her knees. If that damn bandit had opened his half of the cuffs, then surely there was a way...

A key scraped and turned in the lock on the door. Honey dived beneath the covers just as light from the hall wedged into the room. She held her breath while the door clicked closed and the bolt shot home.

Her wildly pounding heart was crowding the breath from her lungs now. She made a fist of her free hand beneath the covers. If he so much as touched her, she thought, she'd claw his eyes out. She'd rip his flesh with her teeth. She'd...

The sound of water splashing into the washbasin sidetracked her panicky thoughts. Then came the soft rustle of fabric, followed by more splashing. Honey opened one eye and peeked over the covers.

The moon seemed to sculpt his broad, wet shoulders and cast in dark pewter the cords of his neck. Silvered water streaked down his ropy arms. He shook his head, sending quick beads of diamond water into the air. As he started to turn, Honey caught a glimpse of the hard-carved muscles on his chest before she squeezed her eyes closed again. She didn't dare let him know she was awake. No telling what he might do. Worse, she'd die of shame if he knew she'd been watching him with such outright curiosity.

She swallowed, then gritted her teeth, hoping he hadn't heard the dry contraction of her throat, which had sounded loud as a thunderclap to her.

She heard the clink of his belt buckle, the pull of leather against cloth, and the dull thud of his heavy holster settling against the bedpost. The mattress dipped under his weight then, and Honey held her breath. She lay so still she could feel her heart crashing against her ribs.

Gideon exhaled wearily as he pulled off his boots and let them drop on the floor. The sponge bath hadn't done much to clean up his mood, but it beat being hosed off with icy water once a week. He hated being dirty almost as much as he hated being locked in a cage. What he wanted, he thought, was a hot bath in a big copper tub where he could sink to his chin, breathe in the rising steam, close his eyes and let every muscle and nerve relax.

A bed was the next best thing. Although sharing it with the little bank teller wasn't his idea of the perfect way to relax. Maybe he should have spent an hour or two with one of the girls downstairs, he thought now, just to take the edge off. But it hadn't seemed worth it at the time. Their dull eyes dispelled the promises of their warm hands.

Anyway, right now sleep was nearly as compelling as loving. Good God, he was tired. Sighing roughly, he eased back on the mattress and closed his eyes.

"Don't you come one inch closer or I'll scream. I swear I will."

Eyes still closed, Gideon grinned. "No, you wouldn't."

"Just try it and see."

He levered up on one elbow, gazing down at her stubborn little mouth, the moonfire burning in her eyes. "Is that an invitation, Miss Cassidy?"

Her eyes widened fearfully, but her voice stayed level and brave. "You wouldn't dare."

"You're right," he growled as he lowered himself back onto the mattress. "Go to sleep, bright eyes. You're safe."

Honey rattled the chain hooked to the iron bedstead. "You don't expect me to sleep like this, do you?" she hissed.

"Hush."

She rattled the chain once more, and kept up the racket until Gideon rose with a muted curse. Five years in prison had made him remember only the fair part of the fair sex; he'd clean forgotten how irritating they could be without half trying. And this one was trying. He retrieved the quill pick from his shirt pocket, jimmied the lock, then clamped the steel bracelet over his left wrist and clicked it closed. "Happy now?"

"Thrilled," she muttered.

"Good." Gideon dug his shoulders deep into the mattress. "Close your eyes, Ed. It'll be morning all too soon."

She was quiet a moment, listening to the cadence of his breathing. "What are you planning to do?"

"Sleep."

"I mean tomorrow." She raised both hands in a gesture of frustration, tugging his arm up along with hers.

Gideon wrenched back his hand. "I'm planning to be dead on my feet tomorrow if I don't get ten minutes of shut-eye. Now hush."

Honey was quiet another moment, until she couldn't keep still or stand the suspense any longer. "Where are my clothes?"

His silence was nearly palpable, like the quiet before a storm, like fire working its way along a fuse. Honey expected an explosion, but instead she felt the muscles of his arm relax and heard him release his breath in a long sigh.

"They're being washed," he answered quietly.

"Oh." She was sorry she had asked. She was mortified, and grateful for the dark to hide the color staining her cheeks. Her voice, so strident before, quavered now. "You . . . you must think—"

"I think," he said, cutting her off, "that you're as stubborn as a weed. Now go to sleep, will you? Or at least just keep that pretty little mouth of yours closed."

But she couldn't sleep. Honey lay there for a long time, wide-awake, listening to the sound of Gideon Summerfield's deep and even breathing. She shifted slightly onto her side to watch the rise and fall of his muscular chest, to study the soft hair that thinned as it neared his belt line, to feel the warmth that radiated from his arm where it touched hers.

A week ago, under the watchful eye of Miss Haven and her staff, Honey wasn't permitted to promenade with beaux or to have tea alone with a gentleman caller. Now here she was—naked as the day she was born—sharing a bed with a notorious outlaw. The preposterousness of the situation brought a wild little giggle to the back of her throat when she probably ought to have been screaming for help.

But she wasn't afraid of Gideon Summerfield, even when reason told her she should be. The man had had ample opportunity to do whatever he pleased with her, and the fact of the matter was that he had conducted himself as a gentleman. She remembered the moment on the trail this afternoon when she had thought that he was going to kiss her. But he hadn't, and there had been that surprising little quiver of disappointment inside her, like air being let out of a balloon.

Honey tilted her head now, the better to peruse his profile in the moonlight. He wasn't bad looking. In fact, Gideon Summerfield was decidedly handsome. There was strength in his face—from the firm line of his jaw to the deep slashes that parenthesized his mouth to the slight hook of a nose that had undoubtedly been broken once or even twice. But, strong as they were, his features possessed a certain vulnerability now that he was sleeping, now that those gunmetal gray eyes were closed.

His hand twitched. His closed lids fluttered. Honey wondered what sort of dreams a desperado had. Was he planning more robberies? Figuring out how to spend his ill-gotten gains? Somewhere, deep in his sleep, was he lining up innocent bank tellers like tin ducks in an arcade, taking aim and shooting them one by one? Was he...?

His hand twitched again, jingling the chain that linked them, and then—slowly, warmly—his big hand slid over hers and closed. Honey's heart shifted perilously and her breath snagged within her chest. From beneath her lashes, she watched as his lips parted in a soft, almost desolate moan. Perhaps, she thought, it wasn't a dream at all inside his head, but a nightmare. Perhaps it was Gideon Summerfield who was the target....

He rolled to his left, casting a heavy arm across her, bringing his face just inches from her own. "Cora," he murmured in a voice thick with sleep and need. "Hold me. I'm so cold. So goddamn cold."

Without even thinking, only responding to the husky plea, Honey slipped her free arm around him. Slowly she spread open her hand, over smooth skin, over sleek muscle. She smiled softly. Some desperado, she thought, adjusting her vision to study the face so close to hers.

His breath mingled with hers. Soap. A hint of whiskey. The pure male fragrance she recalled from snuggling in her father's arms and burying her face in his neck. Aside from him, she'd never really been this close to a man before, even though she'd had more than her share of beaux. It seemed they were always in someone's shadow, though, or under someone's watchful eye. When they kissed her—and few had ever dared—it was always brief, fleeting, tentative.

Her eyes focused on Gideon Summerfield's lips, wondering what they would feel like against her own. Even in sleep, there was a hardness to his mouth. Could such a hard mouth kiss softly? Honey wondered. She moved closer. Then closer still, until her lips felt the warm flutter of his breath.

A deep groan issued from him, and before Honey could shift away his mouth had claimed hers with a warm urgency that sent tremors through her. His lips were softer than she'd have dreamed as they covered hers. His tongue was warm and gentle as it explored, then delved. She moaned helplessly as waves of pleasure surged through her, as new feelings were born in her along with strange and bewildering urges.

It was Gideon who broke the kiss, sighing, shouldering more deeply into the mattress. "Hush, darlin'. Hush, Cora," he murmured against her wet mouth. "Sleep now." His hand slid beneath the covers to settle firmly and protectively over Honey's breast. "Sleep."

Sleep! She couldn't breathe. Her entire body was thrumming and her mind was snapping like a telegraph wire whose messages were positively scandalous. What was she doing in bed with a bank robber and enjoying it? Honey closed her eyes and clamped her lips together, shocked at her behavior, stunned and surprisingly warm beneath Gideon Summerfield's big, gentle hand. But sleep? She might never do that again, she thought. And who in the world was this Cora?

When she woke, the room was golden and warm with sunshine. The light of day revealed a tawdriness in the room she hadn't been aware of the night before. Above her head, the ceiling was cracked and peeling. The wallpaper was patterned with stains and poorly rendered roses, all of them stuck to the wall at a queasy tilt. There was a scuffed wooden dresser with a missing drawer, a cracked mirror and a chipped pitcher and bowl. It was the worst-looking room Honey had ever been in. And to think last night, lying in the outlaw's arms in this bleak iron bed, it had all seemed quite elegant.

The outlaw, she realized dully, was gone. The handcuffs were gone, too. And so was the canvas money bag from Logan Savings and Loan. Honey groaned. Then, after casting a woeful look down at her exposed bosom, she groaned again. What was she supposed to do now?

And what was that red-and-black satin concoction draped over the foot of the bed. He didn't expect her to wear that, did he? She rolled her eyes toward the ceiling. Well, all in all, she supposed, it was better than wearing handcuffs and a sheet.

After she had gritted her teeth and pulled it on, the dress turned out to be nearly a perfect fit, even if it did leave little to the imagination in the vicinity of her chest. Honey glared in the mirror over the dresser, tugging at the rigid stays in the bodice, then watching the weight of her breasts drag the satin fabric down once more. Good Lord, she'd be glad when she got her own civilized clothes back. She'd be even gladder when she got her father's money back, which was what she was aiming to do.

There was a hairbrush beside the pitcher. She scowled at it viciously enough to kill any critters that might be lurking in its bristles, then dragged it through her dark, tangled locks. After a sigh at her less-than-fetching reflection in the mirror, Honey stalked to the door.

She pulled it open and walked smack into an enormous plaid shirtfront.

"Well, now, ain't we in an all-fired hurry to find another man." The rough voice assailed her ears as the breath that carried it assaulted her senses.

Honey pushed both hands hard against the greasy flannel. "Get out of my way."

"Hold on there, sis. You don't have to go all the way downstairs looking for your next poke. I'm right here. And right ready, too." Saying that, the huge man grabbed Honey's wrist and plastered her hand, palm side down, against the front of his trousers.

A little squeak of shock broke from her throat, and then Honey Logan did the only thing she could manage to think of in the name of decency and in the way of self-defense. She squeezed—hard.

"Lemme go, you she-devil," the giant howled. He raised his hand to strike her.

"You do that and you're a dead man."

Coming from the stairwell, Gideon's voice was low and lethal, the devil's own. At that moment, though, to Honey it sounded better than any choir of angels.

The big man twisted his head toward the warning. "What's this little bitch to you?" he grunted, his arm still poised to loose a powerful blow.

"She's my wife."

The arm came down, and now the giant's voice was closer to a sob than a howl. "Well, hell, fella, your wife's got my..."

"Let him go, Edwina," Gideon commanded.

It was only then that Honey realized her hand was still clamped like a vise on her assailant's private parts. She wrenched it away immediately, allowing the man to retreat at an awkward lope down the hallway, nodding curtly to Gideon as he passed.

Honey crossed her arms and sagged back against the wall, closing her eyes briefly, trying to absorb the liquid shaking that had begun in her knees. Gideon covered the distance between them in two long strides.

"You're going to get one of us killed if you're not careful, bright eyes," he admonished her in the same lethal tone he had used a moment ago.

Honey's eyes flashed open. She was prepared to burn him alive with a look of hot and righteous indignation, but when she saw the glint of cool amusement in Gideon Summerfield's eyes she felt a sudden and uncontrollable urge to giggle. She clapped her hand over her mouth, trying to stifle it.

Gideon grinned, briefly. Then his gray eyes clouded. "Lucky for you I just happened along."

Suppressing the remnants of her laughter, she raised her chin into his somber face. Whatever she had intended to say escaped her momentarily as she caught a whiff of shaving soap and spied the tiny nick beneath his ear. He'd had a shave and a haircut, too. Yesterday's shaggy cinnamon locks barely brushed his collar now.

The sight set off a swirl of butterflies in her stomach. But when she noted that that collar was attached to a clean and apparently brand-new shirt, Honey squelched the confounded fluttering inside her. New clothes cost money, and she had a pretty good idea where it had come from.

"Thank you for rescuing me, but it really wasn't necessary, I assure you."

"I could see that, Ed," he drawled, shifting his hips lazily and leaning a shoulder into the wall. His mouth slanted into the smallest of grins. "You had the, um, situation pretty well in hand by the time I came along."

The color that suffused her cheeks forced her to avert her eyes. Where she'd be right now if Gideon Summerfield hadn't come along just when he had, Honey didn't even want to consider. But then again, he didn't have to treat her like a helpless, witless child either.

"What have you done with my money?" she snapped, going on the offense.

"*Your* money?"

She glared up into his face. "I suppose you think it's yours now that you've stolen it from decent, law-abiding, hardworking people."

He chuckled softly. "Possession is nine points of the law, bright eyes."

"And what about me, Mr. Summerfield? Do you believe that you possess me as well?"

His slate gaze skimmed her face, then lowered to the black lace edge of her skimpy bodice. "Nope. I just think you need a little looking out for, at least as long as you're filling out that dress the way you are."

She tugged up on the red-and-black satin. To no avail, she realized. "Well, don't look, dammit."

"Hard not to."

The sudden and unbidden thought that this man had undressed her made Honey's heart begin a brisk, panicky tattoo. Had those dark pewter eyes caressed her then as they were now? And—the thought shocked her—had they liked what they had seen?

"Are you hungry?" he asked her.

"What?" For all the images skittering through her brain just then, Honey barely heard him and could only vaguely comprehend his meaning.

"Come on." He nudged himself away from the wall, towered over her a moment, then curled his fingers around her upper arm. "Let's get some food in you and then we'll see about getting you back to Santa Fe."

Honey pulled away. "With or without my money?" she demanded hotly.

"Without. You'll be lucky to get back there with your virtue, let alone your life."

"I'm not leaving without my money." Honey crossed her arms and widened her stance.

"Fine with me, lady." Gideon threw up his hands. "When you find it, you let me know. I'll be down the street eating breakfast at the café." He turned on his heel, stalked down the hallway and left her standing there.

"Fine," she called after him, shaking a fist for emphasis, even though he couldn't see it. "I hope you choke."

She was going to get that money back if it was the last thing she ever did. She'd hand that canvas sack to

her father, proving once and for all, beyond the
shadow of a doubt, just how capable and responsible
she was. He'd be so grateful as a consequence he'd
probably trade in his desk for an enormous partner's
desk, then install her in a big leather chair right across
from his. She smiled wistfully at the prospect.

Beneath her crossed arms, Honey's traitorous
stomach churned and growled. She'd find that canvas
sack if she had to turn the hotel and the whole town
upside down. In the meantime, though, steak and eggs
and steaming coffee was beginning to sound like a
king's ransom. Starving to death wasn't going to accomplish anything anyway, she thought.

She gave another quick upward tug to the red-and-
black bodice of her dress and trotted down the stairs
in Gideon Summerfield's wake. She'd find the
money—right after breakfast.

Chapter Four

The big plate glass window in the café was thick with grit, inside and out, but still Gideon could see across the street where the lady in the skimpy red-and-black dress was facing off against a young prospector. The boy looked to be about seventeen, thin as grass, and just about as green. Gideon didn't see a need to intervene—yet.

He sipped from his mug of coffee as he continued to gaze out the window. Lord, she was a beauty. The morning sun blazed like wildfire through her deep mahogany hair. Her skin—plenty of which was showing—was smooth as cream. Her legs—and plenty of those showed, too—were long and slim. From this distance he couldn't see the color of her eyes, but he figured they must be burning like blue flames, judging from the cowed stance of the young prospector. The poor kid looked as if he was about to use his shovel to dig himself a hidey-hole right there on the planked sidewalk.

Gideon felt his mouth slide into a crooked grin. Edwina. The grin got a little more lopsided. Ed. A hell

of a woman, he thought. One of these days that little
bank teller was going to make some man's life pure
heaven—and sheer, unadulterated hell—on earth.

He'd had a brief taste of her heaven this morning,
waking as he did with his hand curved over her lush,
sleep-warm breast. He was surprised he hadn't awakened her the way he had wrenched his hand away, then
bolted from the bed feeling like a kid caught raiding
the candy jar. Not candy, Gideon thought now. There
was no candy that had ever filled his hand the way her
firm flesh did. More like sweet, ripe, sun-warmed
fruit. Like late summer apples. And just as dangerous in their allurement, for this was no Garden of
Eden and he had already fallen farther than Adam had
ever dreamed.

His grin hardened into a scowl. He was going to fall
even farther, too, as soon as he located Dwight Samuel. The plan, as the banker Logan had outlined it,
was to lure his cousin and former partner into a
doomed bank robbery. The reward for that betrayal
was supposed to be Gideon's parole. But Gideon had
other plans, and the only reward he sought was revenge. After that, it didn't make much difference what
happened. He planned to cross the border into Mexico with enough money to see him through however
many days remained in his sorry life.

Now through the dirty window he watched the little bank teller tossing her proud head, slashing the
young prospector with the sharp tilt of her chin,
dashing the boy's hopes for good as she sashayed away
from him toward the café. Gideon held her in his gaze
while his breath changed rhythm, his heart suddenly

pressed hurtfully against his ribs, and the rest of him grew heavy and hot with desire. There was no denying that he wanted her. And there was also no denying that there was no room for Miss Edwina Cassidy in his plans.

She shot through the café door and strode to his table, standing there, haughty and a little breathless, glorious in her ire, a lady demanding her due. Well, not from him, he thought. He was glad she was riled because that anger would serve her as a weapon now. It would help see her through. Because he couldn't. He tamped down on his natural inclination to rise to seat her, and instead slid his foot to shove out a chair.

"Have a seat," he said almost gruffly.

She sat, her spine stiff as a rod, her legs tucked primly to the side, her slim ankles crossed.

"Want some coffee?" he asked, taking a sip of his own, foolishly believing the hot liquid would somehow douse the hotter flames rising inside him.

Honey bit her lower lip. She was dying for coffee, but Gideon Summerfield always made her feel so contrary she almost told him no. "Yes. Please."

He signaled the lumpish Mexican cook, who seemed loath to leave his griddle to approach their table.

"Coffee for the lady," Gideon told him. He angled his head toward the sizzling griddle. "And we'll each have a plate of whatever it is you're fixing back there."

"*Huevos,*" the cook said.

"Whatever," Gideon replied. Then, after the cook had turned and shuffled away, he looked at Honey. "Do you speak Spanish?" he asked almost sheepishly. "What the hell did I just order?"

"Rattlesnake," she snapped. "I hope you like it."

He swallowed, hard, and drummed his fingers on the table. "Yeah. Oh, sure. How's it fixed?"

"With onions usually. Or sourweed. Sometimes they mix in frogs' eggs." She shrugged. "It depends on the cook."

Honey had to bite the inside of her cheek to keep from giggling as she watched the outlaw wince and cast a quick, suspicious glance toward the kitchen at the back of the café.

"Pretty tasty, is it?" he asked. "You eat it often?"

Honey fashioned her sweetest smile. "Oh, my, yes. It's considered quite a delicacy, even out here where rattlesnakes are so prevalent."

The cook brought Honey's coffee. *"Algo más?"* he asked Gideon, whose brow was furrowed now and whose voice cracked just slightly when he replied, *"Huevos,* huh?"

The Mexican smiled and bobbed his head affably. *"Sí, señor. Huevos."*

Gideon nodded and, with a soft sigh, lowered his worried gaze to the tabletop.

"No más, gracias," Honey told the cook. When the man left, she sipped her coffee. Between sips, she smiled sunnily at her nervous breakfast companion.

Good, she thought. She didn't mind making him uncomfortable one little bit. It pleased her enormously to watch Gideon Summerfield sweat. The man had been much too cool and controlled behind those ice gray eyes. He deserved a little spoofing, in Honey's estimation. Then, quite suddenly, she remembered the night before, when he had turned to her in his sleep, pleading for warmth. *So cold. So goddamn cold.*

"Who's Cora?" she asked him now.

His gaze shot up from the stained oilcloth that covered the table. "What?"

Honey managed a casual tone. "I asked you who Cora is." She'd never seen such a surprised or bewildered expression on anyone's face, which piqued her curiosity to the extreme. The man could barely put two words together when he tried to speak.

"What . . . ? How do you . . ."

She sipped her coffee again, then shrugged indifferently as she set the cup back on the table. "It's just that you mentioned her name in your sleep last night. I was merely wondering who she was."

A muscle worked furiously in Gideon's cheek and his teeth seemed clenched so tight, Honey despaired that he would even get a word out.

But he did.

Two words. A harsh, hard-bitten phrase.

"My wife."

And now it was her turn to feel bewildered. Stunned, actually. His answer had struck her like a blow and sent her thoughts reeling. Why the fact that this man had a wife should have any impact at all on her feelings was a mystery to her. Honey drew in a sharp little breath. "Oh."

He just sat there then, silent as a stone, staring out the window.

"Where . . . where is she? Cora. Mrs. Summerfield, I mean," Honey inquired, her voice lower now, bereft of its former sunny lilt. "I don't believe you've ever mentioned where you're from."

"Missouri."

"Ah."

Her comment met with a blank wall of silence, but Honey was determined to claw her way over it.

"Then she's back there? In Missouri?" It wasn't all that easy, she decided, posing questions to a stone. "Whereabouts? I know something of the state because my fath—" She broke off in the middle of the word, reminding herself that Gideon Summerfield wasn't the only one at the table who had secrets. She had one or two of her own.

"I have some relatives—distant ones—who used to live in Westport. Near Kansas. On the border, isn't it?"

He offered no comment, but nodded slightly, leading Honey to presume he had at least heard her. "Gideon," she persisted, "I asked you where . . ."

"I don't know," he snarled, his steel gaze at last leaving the window and finding her face.

Her eyes widened. "You don't know where your wife is?"

"That's right."

"Well, I don't understand that at all. It would seem to me . . ."

He raised a hand to silence her. "Look. She took off after I went to prison. End of marriage. End of story."

Not by a long shot, Honey said to herself. "So you're still married, then. Legally, I mean."

"What difference does that make?"

Honey sat a little straighter. "It doesn't. I'm just curious." It wasn't a total lie. She was curious—intensely so. But she still didn't know why it did indeed make a difference whether or not Gideon Summerfield was married.

"Well, don't be," he said just as the cook put a plate of scrambled eggs and fried peppers on the table in front of him.

"Huevos, señor," the Mexican announced proudly.

Gideon glared at the plate, then extended the dark look to Honey. "Rattlesnake," he muttered, shaking his head.

One corner of her mouth lifted in a grin. "I said I *spoke* Spanish. I didn't say I spoke it well." She picked up her fork and proceeded to taste the delectable, familiar food.

Gideon devoted his complete attention to his breakfast. Honey enjoyed their companionable silence until her appetite was satisfied. Her curiosity, however, remained ravenous.

"How long ago?" she asked, slanting her fork across her empty plate.

"How long ago what?"

"When you went to...you know..." Why, she wondered, was it so difficult for her to say the word? She already knew he was a criminal, for heaven's sake. She'd met him at a bank robbery, hadn't she?

Gideon put his fork down now like a man who'd just lost his appetite. "Prison," he said. "That's English, bright eyes. Not your blasted, misconstrued Spanish."

"Prison." She repeated it if only to prove that she could. The word, however, seemed to stick in her throat.

"Five years ago," he added as he pulled the quill pick from his shirt pocket and settled it in the corner of his mouth.

"Why?"

"I got caught," he answered bluntly. "Why else?"

"Robbing a bank?"

Gideon eased back in his chair, tipping it onto the two back legs. "More or less," he replied, then worked the quill to the center of his lips, preventing further conversation.

He hadn't been robbing the bank, he thought bleakly. Not that time anyway. For a year and for the first time in his life, he'd been on the right side of the law. He'd married Cora, more out of high hope than hot affection. He'd taken up tenant farming with something like a vengeance, planting oats and corn and wheat till his hands were blistered and his back nearly broken. When he wasn't being a farmer, he was being a carpenter and a bricklayer, fixing up that down-and-out tenant property till it looked like a real home. All the while, he'd bowed and scraped to the local authorities till his forehead was nearly rubbed raw. Trying. Trying for once to do right.

Hell, he'd been living so clean he practically squeaked, when his cousin, Dwight Samuel, had shown up one afternoon at his little hardscrabble farm just east of Sugar Creek. Dwight had called it quits with Jesse and Frank, forming his own ragged gang of cutthroats and thieves. The trouble was he couldn't trust a single one of them, and he needed a man to watch his back.

A fool was what Dwight had needed, Gideon thought now, and a fool was just what he'd found. Dwight had played on his sympathy. His cousin had played him like some kind of fiddle, to the tune of old times, past crimes committed in the name of the Confederate States of America and William Clarke Quantrill, old loyalties and long-lingering hates.

"Family," Dwight had said finally. "I helped raise you, Gid. You owe me."

A dubious debt, Gideon had thought. His cousins had raised him to ride fast, shoot straight and steal. Still, they had taken him in when there was no one else to look out for him. And dubious or not, it was a debt.

He remembered Dwight laughing as they rode into Liberty the following day. "Hell," his cousin had said, "this bank's been robbed so many times, I expect they'll just hand over the money right quick and breathe a sigh of relief to see us ride out."

But they hadn't. The bank had been robbed so many times they were bound and determined not to let it happen again. The tellers had been armed. Half the town had been on the alert. Gideon had been holding the horses outside when Dwight had come flying empty-handed out the door, gunsmoke billowing at his back.

"They're all dead. Shot down like dogs," he'd yelled. "Let's get."

Dwight had leapt on his horse, grabbing the reins from Gideon just as hot metal had torn through

Gideon's thigh, and then a bullet in the shoulder had pitched him into the dirt of the street.

"They get you?" his cousin had yelled down at him.

Gideon only remembered raising a bloody hand. "Pull me up. I can ride."

Dwight's horse's hooves had danced perilously close to Gideon's head as the robber had peered down at him. "Hell. You're dead, too. Sorry, cousin," he'd said, then slashed his heels into the horse and was gone.

A feminine voice cut through Gideon's reverie now. He looked at the woman across the table, almost surprised to find her there, startled to discover himself alive and breathing.

"Which was it?" she asked him now, her eyes brilliant with curiosity. "More or less?"

"More," he said, thinking it had been more than he'd ever bargained for. Enough to land him in the state penitentiary when he recovered from his wounds.

Her head tilted fetchingly. She raised a hopeful eyebrow. "It wasn't a case of mistaken identity or anything like that, was it?"

Gideon laughed in spite of himself. She was so young, so unspoiled. He appreciated her innocence and her willingness to believe in his, even though he wasn't worthy of it. "I was guilty, Ed," he said.

Her optimistic expression slackened a moment, hope withering in the harsh glare of fact. "Oh," she said.

He grinned. "Disappointed?"

She shook her head vehemently.

"Yes, you are," he said with a sigh. "You're like most females. You want to make a man better than he is. Change his past to suit your own sweet notions. If you can't change his past, then you set out to change his future." He slanted back in his chair and crossed his arms, eyeing her with amusement.

But she didn't appear to be amused, either by his views on the opposite sex or by his evasions. "Is that what Cora tried to do?" she snapped.

A bitter laugh broke from Gideon's throat. "Hardly. Cora had enough trouble with her own past to waste her time worrying about mine."

"Did she rob banks, too?"

"She was a whore." The words came out more harshly than he intended, causing the little bank teller to flinch and drag in her lower lip. Gideon leaned forward. "Forget about Cora, will you? She took off five years ago, and I haven't given her a second's thought since then."

"Yes, you have." Her voice was quiet and firm. "You turned to her for warmth and for comfort last night in your sleep."

He probably had, Gideon thought mournfully. But he wasn't going to admit it to this little girl just to satisfy her overblown female curiosity. "What I turned to," he growled, "was a woman in my bed. Any woman."

"You spoke her name," she insisted. "You said—"

Gideon shoved back his chair. "I don't give a rat's ass what I said. All right? Will you just stop?" He stood up and dug some bills out of his pocket, then tossed them on the table. "Come on."

Honey rose slowly to her feet, shoulders stiff, chin tilted. "Where are we going?"

"To catch the ten o'clock train." Gideon slung his arm around her and propelled her out of the café before she could respond.

The tracks ran north and south at the edge of the little town, and by the time Gideon had pushed, pulled and bullied Honey in that direction, the locomotive was already getting up a thundering head of steam. He clamped his hands around her waist and lifted her onto the platform of the last car, then vaulted up behind her.

Honey, who had been muttering under her breath all the way from the café, shook the red-and-black flounces of her short skirt now. "I can't ride on a train dressed like this. What'll people think?"

The look that Gideon gave her was a clear indication of what *he* was thinking. His lips were poised somewhere between a smile and a leer. His gray eyes sparked over her bodice as he stepped closer to her, forcing Honey to edge backward until her shoulders were pressed against the rear door of the train. Honey felt like a spring lamb in the grim shadow of a famished wolf. When she opened her mouth to protest his nearness, she could only squeak.

"They'll think you're beautiful, bright eyes," Gideon said. He lowered his head to kiss her, doing what he had wanted to do from the first minute he'd laid eyes on her in the bank, allowing himself this taste of heaven now, knowing this was all he would ever have of her. And while his mouth claimed hers, Gideon slid his arms around her and worked his fingers into the red satin sash at the back of her waist.

Stunned by the warm assault, Honey's first instinct was to push him away, but when her hands made contact with the hard press of his chest, when his heartbeat surged against her open palm, when he breathed, "Kiss me back, darlin'" against her rigid lips, she was lost. Almost against her will, she found herself relaxing in his embrace. And, as if they had a will of their own, her lips parted in invitation to his warm, seeking tongue.

Dizzy now, and trembling down to her toes, Honey dimly realized she wasn't breathing. When she wrenched her mouth away to take in a great gasp of air, Gideon didn't release her. And he didn't stop kissing her, only now those kisses were burning across her cheeks, along her jawline and down the length of her neck. When his lips brushed over the exposed swell of her breasts and his tongue blazed a sizzling trail in the crevice between them, Honey sucked in another gulp of air.

Gideon moaned softly against her wet mouth. "Ah, Ed. Lord, honey, I wish . . ." He drew in a breath, filling his lungs with the sweet scent of her, while reminding himself that wishes were useless things for a man like him. If wishes were wings, the jails would be empty and the sky would darken with convicts.

He raised his head, studying her dazed expression, reveling in the flush of color his kiss had brought to her pretty face. He couldn't imagine ever wanting a woman more than he wanted this one, now, this minute. "I wish..." he began, then fell silent at the choked sound of his own voice.

Her huge, luminous eyes glowed with a strange mixture of desire and curiosity and fear. Her lips glistened from his kiss. "What?" she whispered. Her sweet breath riffled against his cheek. "What do you wish, Gideon?"

He merely shook his head with his arms still around her, their gazes locked.

Honey could feel his hands moving along the back of her dress, tugging at the sash. For a moment she thought he was going to undress her, and to her own bewildered amazement, she found herself yielding to those hands, to the will of this man who seemed to paralyze her own will while he drugged her senses.

There was a deafening rumble then, followed by the long ear-splitting blast of a steam whistle. The train jolted forward. And Honey was jolted to her senses.

"Stop that," she snapped. She stiffened in his embrace. "Get away from me."

Gideon stepped back. He eased his arms from around her, widening his stance and locking his knees to absorb the swaying motion of the train as it began to slowly pick up speed. He smiled down at her now, then bent for one last taste of her lips.

"It would have been a little bit of heaven, Edwina Cassidy. You and me." He sighed, and then his face hardened. "Well, hell. You take care of yourself now. So long, bright eyes."

He gave a brief glance to the ground that was beginning to blur beneath the moving train, then took another step away from her and launched himself over the metal rail of the platform.

Wide-eyed, too stunned to react, Honey saw him land on bent knees between the rails, then watched as he straightened up, grinned devilishly and blew her a kiss.

"Gideon," she yelled. He was leaving her! The thought hit her like a lightning bolt. And like the inevitable thunderclap came the realization that he was getting away with the money.

Like hell he was, Honey thought. If he could jump from a moving train and land like a damn cat, then so could she. But when she took a step toward the railing, something promptly jerked her back.

Honey reached both hands frantically behind her for a moment, then shook her fists toward the outlaw's receding form.

"Damn you, Gideon Summerfield, you no-good, lying, snake-tongued thief!" she screamed.

The whole time the desperado had been kissing her senseless, he had also been tying her sash to the rear door of the train.

Chapter Five

Gideon paused in the lobby of the hotel, his eyes lingering on the batwing doors of the saloon at the back. It was early afternoon, but already he could hear the chink of bottles against glasses, the slap of cards, the rough harmony of male curses and throaty female laughter. The tightness in his gut pulled in another notch. Too easy, he thought. It would be too easy to push through the doors, down the liquor to put out the fire that was burning in him, take a woman upstairs to douse the other flames.

He wished...

Forget it!

With a brittle curse, he headed for the stairs, took them two at a time, then slammed the door of his room behind him. Before him there, on the bed, all prim and pressed, were the little bank teller's clothes. The dress was laid out—its skirt fluffed out and the sleeves set primly at each side—as if waiting for Edwina Cassidy to take shape inside. He focused on the pristine white lace of the dainty underclothes carefully folded there, ready to be lifted and fleshed out. Gideon's mouth went dry.

His eyes slanted to the mirror. "You're one sorry case," he told his gaunt, dusty reflection. Pretty sad when the mere sight of feminine smallclothes bashed a man's heart against his ribs and dried his tongue like so much jerky. But it wasn't the clothes, and he knew it. It was the woman who had worn them. The little windflower who had gotten in his way, thanks to the banker's indifference.

But Edwina Cassidy was gone. Gideon grinned in spite of his sullen mood as he pictured her shaking her fists at him from the back of the speeding train. She'd have jumped. He had known that instinctively. That was why he'd hitched her to the door with a succession of half-knots and slipknots that would take her a good ten minutes to undo. He hoped. Hell, his fingers had been shaking so bad while he was kissing her it was a wonder he hadn't tied himself up right along with her.

He sighed. By now she was probably hunkered down in a seat, still mad as hell. He could almost see her, staring out the window, gnawing on her lip, attempting to conceal her lush bosom while she tried to figure out what to do next about the stolen money. But once she got back to Santa Fe and once she discovered nobody at the bank held her accountable for the loss, the tiny teller would calm down and go about her business as if nothing had ever happened.

Probably in a week she wouldn't even remember him. Some young storekeeper or cowhand would walk into the Logan Savings and Loan to make a deposit, take one look at the little teller's sea-colored eyes and hand his damn heart right over the counter along with his money. Probably in a month or two...

A sudden rapping on the door obliterated his thoughts. Gideon's hand rested on the butt of his gun as he called, "Yeah? Who is it?"

"Angie."

He opened the door in response to the feminine voice, then leaned against the frame, looking down at the redheaded whore from Missouri. From home. It flashed through his mind that here stood a kind of answer to his needs, and he wondered why it suddenly seemed to matter that she wasn't the *right* answer. When he finally spoke, his voice was as taut and barbed as wire. "What do you want?"

The whore's mouth twitched in quick disappointment, then smoothed out to resume its customary, half amused, half bored expression. "There was a man downstairs asking after the girl," she said. "Just thought you'd want to know."

Angie shrugged then and turned to go, but Gideon's hand flashed out to catch her arm.

"Who?" he growled.

"Said his name was Logan. That's all I know. Said he was looking for a girl, about twenty, about my height." She lowered her voice. "He mentioned your name."

"What did you tell him?"

She glanced at her arm, where his fingers were compressing her pale flesh. Gideon followed the direction of her gaze. He released her, cursing under his breath as he saw the crimson imprint that would soon turn black-and-blue. He closed his eyes briefly. "Sorry," he said through clenched teeth.

"Hey. Don't worry about it, Missouri." Angie gave her head a little toss. "I've been treated worse."

Ashamed because he had bruised her, unaccustomed to apologizing, Gideon simply stared at her. The whore's mouth tilted into a small, fleeting grin.

"A lot worse," she added. "And don't worry none about Logan. He was looking for her, not you. I heard you'd put the girl on the northbound train, so that's what I told him. He was out of here so fast it like to made my head spin. Seems to set great store by the girl."

That was obvious, Gideon thought. It was obvious, too, that the banker had much more than an employer's interest in his little teller if he had followed her all the way here.

Well, hell, what natural man wouldn't? If Miss Edwina Cassidy worked for him, Gideon would open the bank early and toil late just to keep her in his sights. Why should Race Logan be any different? Still, it didn't make any sense when the man had allowed her to face a hard-bitten bank robber all alone.

Angie nudged him with her hip now, reminding him of her presence. Her voice was husky, her words curling up like smoke. "You need a little something to distract you from all those troublesome thoughts, Missouri?"

He did. After five years in prison, he very much needed something, someone. But not this, not her. Gideon smiled as he traced his finger lightly over the discolored flesh of her upper arm. "Maybe later," he said softly. "I appreciate the information." He winked now. "And the invitation."

She stopped him as he was digging into his pocket for a coin. "It's on the house," she said. "That and anything else you might be needing. I'll be downstairs if you change your mind, Missouri."

He watched her going down the hallway, one hand trailing provocatively along the wall. He saw her add an extra little twitch to her backside when she started down the stairs, as if to tell him what a damn fool he was and to demonstrate just what he was missing. Not that he needed it pointed out. Not when every nerve in his entire body was screaming what an infernal idiot he was.

With her lower lip snagged between her teeth, Honey glared at her own reflection in the train window. Hugging her arms more tightly over the indecent bodice of her dress, she had managed to build up a head of steam to rival that of the locomotive that was carrying her relentlessly north. To Santa Fe. Home. Empty-handed. And dressed like a dance hall delight.

Well, she was lucky she was clothed at all, she thought now, after practically having to take her dress off to untie the knots that Gideon Summerfield had rigged. After that, she'd had to pound on the door for ten minutes before the conductor reluctantly opened it. The man had even had the nerve to ask her for her ticket. When she'd told the officious little man just what he could do with his precious tickets, the conductor had taken her by both elbows and hustled her to the only empty seat in the last car.

"I'll deal with you later," he had told her before turning to the woman in the rear-facing seat across from Honey, doffing his cap and profusely begging her pardon for the inconvenience.

"It can't be helped, I suppose," the iron-haired matron had sniffed, drawing up her overstuffed, pigeon-purple bosom. "Trash *will* travel."

Honey had started to inform the battle-ax just who this piece of trash was, but—after an initial and indignant "excuse me, madam"—she had slumped into silence while her face fairly burned with embarrassment and shame. It had suddenly occurred to her that if the woman did indeed know who she was, her reaction might be exactly the same.

There were women in Santa Fe—big, pigeon-breasted paragons of virtue and their nervous, sparrow-faced sisters—who looked at her mother the same way this matron was looking at Honey now. Along with references to trash, people whispered the name that had followed Kate Neely Cassidy Logan across a thousand miles and twenty years. "Kate the Gate." Never to her face. No. And certainly never anywhere around Race Logan. But it happened.

Honey remembered an afternoon when she'd been about seven or eight years old when her mother had returned in tears from a lemonade social, followed a short while later by a fire-breathing, bruised and battered Race Logan. Her Uncle Isaac had taken Honey aside and had tried to explain to her that day about her mother's unfortunate and undeserved reputation.

"See, your mama grew up poor, Miz Honey. So poor she didn't always have shoes to put on her feet. And sometimes folks with nothing else to do, they make up stories about pretty, shoeless girls. Miz Kate didn't have nobody back then to protect her. Not till your daddy came along."

"I'm glad I'm not poor," Honey remembered saying as she had cuddled within the circle of Uncle Isaac's one arm. "And I'm glad I've got you and my papa to protect me."

She sighed now, watching the rough landscape pass outside the window. Between the two of them, they had probably protected her a bit too well. One of the reasons her father had sent her away to school was to shield her from the gossip that continued to circulate around Santa Fe. To shield her and to see that she acquired the polish and the fine veneer that her mother had never possessed.

Some veneer, she thought dismally as she glanced down at her outrageously exposed bosom. The gossip about Kate the Gate would pale after Honey the Whore arrived home, half-naked and empty-handed.

"No. Absolutely not," she muttered, earning a sniff and grimace of disgust from the matron sitting across from her. There had to be a way to get that money back and redeem herself. After all, the train was barely a half hour out of Cerrillos, no more than ten or fifteen miles away from that rat, Gideon Summerfield. She could still go back. She could still recover the bank's money. She could . . .

The train's whistle shrilled and the brakes squealed as it chugged to a rumbling halt. All the men in the car began to grumble and consult their watches while the purple-swagged woman Honey had christened Mrs. Pigeon leaned her bulk toward the window and peered out with a sour expression on her face.

"Why are we stopping?" Honey asked her.

"I'm sure I wouldn't know."

When Mrs. Pigeon withdrew from the window, Honey took her place. "Oh, Lord," she breathed, seeing exactly why the train had come to an unscheduled, screeching halt in the middle of nowhere. Race Logan!

Her father's favorite horse, a dun mare named Jonquil, stood waiting patiently beside the tracks, dipping her graceful head to a bunch of broomweed. Honey didn't see her father, though, which only meant one thing. He was probably already on the train.

She lurched to her feet, stepping on Mrs. Pigeon's toes as she moved quickly into the aisle, not even bothering to apologize as she rushed for the rear door, whisked up her satin skirt and clambered over the rail. Once down on the ground, Honey slunk along the side of the train until she reached the quietly grazing mare.

"Hello, Jonquil," she said softly, reassuringly. "You remember me, girl, don't you?"

The horse lifted her head, snuffling, nodding, and Honey reached out to stroke the mare's velvet nose while moving slowly to her flank. After a nervous glance over her shoulder, she wedged her foot in the high stirrup, then grabbed the saddle horn with both hands to haul herself up. Leaning down to grasp the reins her father had dropped, Honey patted the horse's slick yellow gray neck and whispered, "I know you're tired, Jonquil, but you and I are going for a quick little ride.''

In the parlor, Kate was lighting a lamp against the oncoming darkness when she thought she heard Race. By the time she had picked up her skirts and rushed into the front courtyard, her husband was slamming through the tall wooden gate in the adobe wall that separated their house from the street. He closed it with such force that the gate bounced on its frame and swung open again. Tethered just beyond it, Kate caught a glimpse of a flea-bitten, one-eared mule.

She tried not to laugh, but she couldn't help herself. ''That's about the sorriest excuse for transportation I've ever seen. What are you doing riding an old, broken-down mule, Race?''

He reached back and pulled the gate closed with a curse. Then he just stood there like a lightning bolt, trying to decide where to strike.

''Your daughter stole my horse,'' he howled.

Kate pressed her hand to her heart and breathed a sigh of relief. ''Well, at least that means she's alive and well.''

''Only until I get my hands around her neck,'' he snarled as he brushed past Kate into the house.

She glanced heavenward, with quick thanks and grim frustration, before turning and following in her husband's wake.

Just inside the door, Kate encountered her oldest son, Zack. The seventeen-year-old's angry face was a dark mirror of his father's.

"What's Papa so sore about, Mama? He nearly bit my head off and all I did was ask him about Honey."

Kate reached out and smoothed a lock of dark hair from his forehead, accustomed to her role as buffer between her volatile husband and their children. "Just stay out of his way for a while, Zack." Her mouth quirked now into a grin she couldn't quite suppress. "Your sister stole Jonquil right out from under Papa's nose."

The boy's turquoise eyes, so like his father's, widened as his breath whistled through his teeth. "And he let her live?"

Still smiling, Kate nodded. "Apparently," she said. "Apparently Honey's very much alive."

It was only much later, in the quiet darkness of her bedroom, that Kate allowed her worries to unfold in her heart. She ached for her daughter—the beautiful child who longed to be praised for more than her beauty—the headstrong young woman who yearned to be released from beneath her father's protective wing, to spread her own wings and take flight.

It was so for all their children, she thought now. Honey. Zack. Creel, at twelve, and ten-year-old Aitch were already bristling under their father's protectiveness. Even Baby Neely, only three, was learning to shake his fist in his papa's adoring face. The only one who seemed to have escaped Race's steadfast, loving grip was their adopted son, Cass.

When it came to seventeen-year-old Cass, Race seemed to forget his enmity for anything Cassidy. He forgot that Kate had married Ned Cassidy when she'd despaired of ever seeing Race again. He forgot that her sister-in-law, Althea Cassidy Sikes, had done her level best to bring both Race and Kate to ruination, or that it was "that cold bitch" who'd given birth to the boy who had become his fair-haired favorite, the boy who was now back East studying hard so he could one day take his father's place at the bank.

"Now that boy's got a head on his shoulders," Race would say. Or, "Cass is the only thinker in this litter of hotheads we've spawned, Kate."

What Race kept conveniently overlooking was the fact that his natural children were perfect copies of himself. All of them. They had his dark hair and his beautiful turquoise eyes. They had his bearing and his intelligence. But most of all, their children had his hot blood and his mulish streak.

Kate sat up in bed now, punched the pillows into a pile behind her and lay back with a sigh. For undiluted stubbornness, Honey was probably the worst. Kate supposed it was because she was the first and the only female child. Race's protective cloak had smothered their daughter ever since he'd come home from the war to discover her existence.

Kate's fingers worried the thick braid of red-gold hair at her shoulder and she frowned, trying to recall something Isaac had said not so long ago when she had been grumbling about Race's tyrannical ways.

"He don't know no other way to love, Miz Kate," Isaac had said. "Just like he never knew any other way to work except to do it all hisself." The old man had grinned slyly then. "Strikes me, too, that it's just

Horace's way of doing for you by taking pure care of your babies.''

She knew, in the depths of her heart, that what Isaac said was true. For her sake, Race was "taking pure care.'' Somehow—and particularly with Honey—he was trying to make up for all that had been missing in his wife's young life. Kate had never had anyone to truly take care of her until Race had blown into her life like a wild, hot wind on that Fourth of July when she was seventeen.

The night her daughter had been conceived, she reminded herself now. "Honey," Kate whispered into the darkness. "First you walked out of school, then you clamped yourself onto a vicious criminal. What in the world are you hoping to prove except maybe that you can get yourself hurt without anybody's help?''

The bedroom door opened slowly, slanting light from the hallway across the bed. Kate's breath caught when she saw Race's tall, sturdy frame silhouetted there. Even after twenty years—despite quarrels or sorrows, trials or mere aggravations—her husband still managed to take her breath away.

He stood there quietly, leaning against the frame, until she raised an arm toward him. Then he closed the door behind him and walked to the bed. Kate scooted over to make room for him.

When he stretched out beside her, sighing as forlornly as she'd ever heard, Kate could feel the tautness of every muscle in his big, familiar body.

"Race," she whispered. "Let somebody else..."

"Don't fight me, Katie," he answered, his voice gentle despite his words, his arms moving to surround her. "Just love me, darlin', and sleep close."

He'd close his eyes, perhaps, but he wouldn't sleep tonight. Not a minute. And tomorrow, unless the Lord Almighty could somehow prevent it, Race would saddle up a fresh horse and ride off once more after his daughter and Gideon Summerfield.

God help us all, Kate thought as she slipped out of her nightgown and curved her body against the man she loved more than her own life.

Dawn was just glimmering in the window when Kate and Race were awakened by Zack's shout.

"Papa! Mama! Hurry! Something's wrong with Uncle Isaac."

Race stepped into his long underwear on the run and Kate didn't even bother with her robe, but simply wrenched her cast-aside gown over her head before following her husband down the dark hallway. When she reached the kitchen, Race was already kneeling on the floor beside Isaac. Kate struck a match and lit a lamp.

Young Zack's face was pale. His turquoise eyes were huge and glistening with tears. His voice, normally deep and defiant, trembled now, as did his hands. "Uncle Isaac fell, Mama. We were standing here talking about Honey and how somebody ought to do something about getting her back, when his legs just plain folded." The boy's voice broke. "I don't know. Maybe it was my fault. We were arguing. I said Papa ought to have gone back last night, instead of coming home, but Uncle Isaac..."

Kate clasped an arm around her distraught son as she looked down at Isaac Goodman's huge, crumpled body. "Hush, Zack," she said softly. "Race?"

"He's breathing, Kate." Race twisted his face toward their son. "Zack, you run get Dr. Cullen. You pound on his front door and if he doesn't answer, then go around back and pound on his bedroom window. Tell him it's an emergency." Race dragged in a breath before he continued. "You tell him your father said for him to get over here yesterday, if not the day before."

"Yes, sir." Zack pivoted and shot out of the kitchen.

Sinking to her knees beside Race, Kate curled her shaking fingers around Isaac's thick wrist, closing her eyes as she felt the solid pulse. "Isaac?" she queried softly.

Race shook his head somberly. "Let's get him to bed," he said. He slipped one arm beneath the big man's shoulders and another under his knees. "Come on, partner." He picked the bear-size man up gently, effortlessly, as if he were carrying a slumbering child to bed.

Kate scurried ahead to Isaac's room, just down the hall from theirs, where she folded the linens back to allow Race to lower Isaac onto the mattress. Together they covered him and stood, side by side, gazing down at the motionless body of the man who had been, for both of them, a father and a friend.

"Where's that damn doctor?" Race muttered.

Kate lifted her hand and smoothed it across his back. "It's only been a few minutes. He'll be here."

Moments ago in the kitchen, Race's voice had been strong, stern with command. Now he sounded bleak, bewildered. "What is it, Katie? Isaac's never been sick a day in his life."

"I don't know, love. He's well over seventy. Sometimes..." Now Kate's voice failed her momentarily as she fought to contain both her tears and her fears. "Zack will be back with Doc Cullen soon. I'm sure there's something he can do."

"By God, there better be," her husband whispered.

There were footsteps rushing down the hallway then, and Zack burst into the room.

"I got him, Papa," the boy said breathlessly just as Samuel Cullen, plaid shirt stuffed into his trousers and his black bag in one fist, followed him into the room.

"Kate. Race. What the devil is...?" No sooner had he spoken than he glimpsed Isaac laid out on the bed. The doctor snapped open his bag and elbowed all three Logans out of his way. "When did he take ill?" he asked, and knelt beside his patient.

"This morning," Kate answered.

"Just keeled over," Zack put in.

"He hasn't been sick a single day in his life, Doc," Race said. "What do you think it is?"

Cullen was holding Isaac's thick black wrist now. "Pulse seems strong," he murmured. Then he leaned forward to pry up one wrinkled black eyelid, after which he cocked his head and put his ear close to the old man's face.

Race and Kate exchanged anxious glances.

"Is he dying, Doc?" Zack whispered.

"Hush," his mother said. "Let Doc Cullen do his job, Zack."

The doctor sat back on his heels now. "That's a fine suggestion, Kate. All of you get out and give Isaac and me some breathing space."

"I'm staying," Race growled.

Kate tugged at his arm but her husband didn't budge until Samuel Cullen glared at him and muttered, "Fine. Then I'll go, Race. Don't know why you sent for me, anyway, if you're such a competent physician."

The doctor braced his hands on his knees, preparing to rise, when Race sighed.

"All right, Samuel. But only for a minute. We'll be just out in the hall. And I'm warning you, if that old man dies and I'm not with him, I'll nail that black bag of yours as well as your hide..."

"He knows, Race," Kate said, curling her arm through his and leading him out into the hall.

"Shut that door behind you, too," the doctor called.

Kate felt as if she'd been standing out in the hallway for days, although it had only been ten or fifteen minutes at the most. Race had been pacing back and forth, cursing the doctor up one side and down the other and calling him a "damn quack" so often that Kate had finally felt compelled to remind her husband that that damn quack had helped bring four of their babies, quite robustly, into this world. She would've reminded him about the time Honey had been so sick with pneumonia, only just then Samuel Cullen came out of Isaac's room, shaking his head. To Kate he seemed more baffled than sad.

"What is it, Doc?" she quickly asked.

"Well..." He scratched his head, looked from Kate to Race and then back. "I can't say exactly. Could be his heart. Could be just his age. But it's grave. Awfully grave."

Behind her Kate heard Race's breath hitch and his big shoulders bump against the wall.

The doctor gazed down and busied himself with the latches on his medical bag. "There's nothing I can do." He shook his head again. "I'm sorry, Race."

Kate thought it odd that their longtime caretaker so assiduously avoided looking in their eyes, but she decided that Sam had concluded one or both of them might cry if he met their worried gazes. Or perhaps that he would.

"How long does he have?" Race asked, his own choked-back tears evident in his rough voice.

"Hard to say, Race. Could happen any time. Or then..." The doctor shrugged. "I just can't say."

Kate saw him to the door, and when she returned Race was standing with his head bowed beside Isaac's bed.

At the sound of her footsteps behind him, Race whispered wetly, "I can't just go and leave him like this. Not after all these years, Kate. Not after all Isaac's seen me through. I can't just up and go."

"Then don't," she said. "Stay."

Race dragged in a deep, rough breath, letting it out with a curse. "What about Honey? What am I going to do about my little girl?"

Kate leaned her head against his arm. "She's not so little anymore, Race." She sighed. "Who knows? Maybe this is the Lord's way of letting her find her own way home."

Chapter Six

Honey rubbed her hands up and down her bare arms. Thank God the sun was up, she thought. She had spent a long, chilly night in the little alleyway beside the livery stable in Cerrillos, her eyes rarely straying from the front door of the hotel. Unless Gideon Summerfield had wings, he was still in there. And when he came out, she was going to follow him—to the ends of the earth if need be—until she got her money back.

Her money. That was how she thought of it now. Not her father's, or the bank's, or the citizens' who had made their weekly deposits. Hers. It sure as hell wasn't Summerfield's.

"Poor Jonquil," she murmured to the mare, who stood quietly beside her. While lying in wait for Gideon, Honey hadn't dared unsaddle the animal, although she had sneaked into the livery stable for a bag of oats after everyone was gone. "Lucky Jonquil," she muttered now. Honey herself hadn't had a bite to eat since her meal in the café yesterday morning. Her stomach rumbled now as if responding to her thoughts, and she crossed her arms tightly to still the gnawing pangs.

Her eyes felt gritty from lack of sleep. When she hadn't been watching the hotel door, she'd been looking up and down the street, fully expecting to see her father kicking up the dust on a borrowed mount or else just stalking her on foot. The thought almost made her laugh. She was stalking Gideon. Her father was stalking her. The three of them were like an angry little parade. The banker. The thief. And the...? What was she, Honey wondered, other than cold and hungry and so tired she could hardly see straight?

She lifted her gaze to the window of Gideon's room. The room where he had slept in a bed all night. Damn him! Well, she hoped he was as cold as he'd been the night before when he had turned to her in his sleep.

The thought stirred a peculiar flutter in the pit of her stomach. She sniffed disgustedly, ascribing the butterfly to her ravenous hunger. It certainly wasn't thinking about that snake-tongued scoundrel. A married scoundrel at that. And one who'd lost track of his wife.

She scooted closer to the side of the building as the morning light began to bring the main street of Cerrillos to life. Two prospectors ambled by, leading their pack mules out to the edge of town. A milk wagon clattered past. Soon the shades went up on the bank across the street. At that precise moment the hotel door opened, and Gideon Summerfield walked out.

The butterfly in her stomach surged once more, and this time Honey put it down to pure excitement, rather than hunger. It certainly wasn't the way the outlaw stood on the planked sidewalk with his long legs slightly parted or the way he shifted his lean hips as he adjusted his gun belt. Or the way he rolled his broad shoulders as if to work out a kink in a muscle. And she'd be damned, she thought, if she'd allow herself to react at all to the way the cool morning sun seemed to tip his cinnamon hair with gold. It wasn't him she was glad to see, she told herself. What made her glad was the prospect of seeing him lead her to that canvas sack stuffed with money—*her* money—from Logan Savings and Loan.

She flattened herself against the wall while his eyes scanned the street. His horse was probably right here at the livery stable, she thought. After he crossed the street, she would ride Jonquil around back and wait to follow Gideon when he rode out.

But he didn't cross the street. Instead he walked slowly, almost lazily, up the sidewalk to the bank. He paused in front of the door a moment. Honey watched as his lean body tensed, as he flexed the fingers of his right hand before gliding his gun from its holster, as he strode into the bank.

My God, he was going to rob it! Honey's first instinct was to yell for help. Then she clamped her lips together. No. Let him rob it, she thought. Let him get away with another big fat sack brimming with cash. She'd follow him just as she had planned, then, instead of recovering a single bag of money, she'd get two. Her victory would be twice as sweet. She leaned back against the livery wall, smiling.

It wasn't long before he sauntered out of the bank as casually as a shopkeeper who'd just deposited the day's receipts. He was strolling along as if he didn't have a care in the world—only the canvas sack he swung in his left hand. Free as a bird, she thought disgustedly, with nobody shouting alarms from the bank, or firing shots at the robber, or taking off in hot pursuit. It was as if nobody cared.

In fact, as Honey watched in amazement, she saw someone peek from the bank window, then disappear into the dark interior. Well, it was probably a teller like Kenneth Crane, she thought. Too weak-kneed to do anything but hand over the bank's money and then quiver and cower behind a wall.

Fine. Wonderful. It was all the better if nobody else pursued him. Then there wouldn't be anybody to tell her to go back or to get out of the way. When she recovered the money—and she *would* recover the money—two sacks now—there wouldn't be anybody else trying to share the praise or claim the glory. And best of all, her father would know there was no one else to credit for such persistence and responsibility. Only his daughter. By God, she'd make him proud if it killed her.

Gideon Summerfield walked into the livery stable, just as she had predicted. Honey scrambled to her feet.

"Let's go, girl," she said, and clambered up onto Jonquil's back.

Gideon swiped off his hat, ran a sleeve across his forehead, then squinted ahead into the late-afternoon sun. "Damn little mule," he muttered. She had been following him all day, through the rugged gullies and canyons west of Cerrillos. Twice he'd ridden a big circle around her while she just kept plugging along, obviously believing he was just over the next ridge. Her relaxed posture in the saddle made Gideon wonder about the young woman's sanity. Didn't she know she was lost?

And why the hell was she following him anyway? He knew it was Logan's mare she was on, remembering that fine piece of horseflesh from when the banker had met him at the train, so Gideon surmised that Logan had caught up with his little teller somewhere along the line yesterday. What he couldn't figure out, though, was why, instead of giving herself over to her employer's protection, Miss Edwina Cassidy had stolen the man's horse.

Hell, any woman impulsive enough to shackle herself to a bank robber probably would steal the bank president's horse if she thought it would help her get the stolen money back. But if she was following him in hopes that he would lead her to the canvas satchel, she was wrong. Dead wrong.

Lost, too. And still dressed like a damn whore. Lucky for her he had folded up some of her respectable clothes and stuffed them in his saddlebag. When he had done it, he had told himself it was a shame for her to lose such fine clothes and that, if he saw a way to do it, he'd send them on to her in Santa Fe. Under all his good intentions, however, Gideon grudgingly admitted he just couldn't quite part with them yet. After he'd put the little windflower on the train, those clothes were all he had to remind him of her. Lucky for her he was little better than a moonstruck kid. Not so lucky for him, though. He needed this particular distraction about as much as he needed a hole in the middle of his head.

He stopped at sundown. By the time it was dark he had gathered enough wood to see him through a cool night, had watered his horse in a trickle of a creek, then rubbed the animal down. He had even managed a half bath himself and had hung his shirt to dry over the branches of a low-growing juniper.

Gideon settled down by the campfire, waiting. She was out there. Probably shivering now in that scrap of a dress. Probably hungry. But, damn her, Edwina Cassidy probably wasn't afraid. Too stupid to know when she ought to be afraid. No, she wasn't stupid by a long shot. Stubborn, though. He let a quiet curse ripple across his lips. He'd never met a more stubborn woman.

What the hell was he going to do with her? He wished it were just a couple of days ago, and he was reaching for that money bag again, more cautiously this time, anticipating her quick little hands and the click of the cuff. He worried that five years in prison had slowed and blunted him. He couldn't afford any dullness now, in mind or body, considering the task that lay ahead of him. Not only that, but now he was again responsible for the little bank teller.

Gideon narrowed his gaze on an outcropping of rock about twenty yards from his blazing little fire. "You're gonna freeze out there, bright eyes," he called. "Come on in."

It took her nearly half an hour. Probably arguing with herself, Gideon figured. Or trying to hog-tie her own stubborn disposition. He was prepared to give her another thirty minutes before he dragged her, kicking and screaming, to the warmth of the fire.

She emerged from behind the rocks and came slowly toward him. The flames lit up the red satin of her dress and glinted in her hair. For a moment Gideon thought he was dreaming—a lonely man by a campfire who had conjured up a vision in shimmering satin and flame-glossed hair.

She stopped just short of the campfire's circle of light, chewing her lower lip, toeing the ground like a bashful child.

"Come on," Gideon coaxed.

Her only movement then was the stubborn lift of her chin. "How did you know I was out there?"

He smiled. "Just a guess." He rose then, taking the blanket that was draped over his shoulders and placing it around hers before leading her to the fire. "Did you bed your horse down?" he asked.

She shook her head, adding a sidelong, apologetic glance.

Without a word, Gideon disappeared in the direction from which Honey had come.

She stretched out her hands to the snapping fire, feeling the warmth replace the chill that had begun to settle deep in her bones. She didn't think it was possible to be so tired. Too tired even to worry that there was no sign of either money sack—not the one from Santa Fe or the one he had taken this morning in Cerrillos. Right now she didn't want to worry about the money. She just wanted to rest.

His soft footfall drew her gaze to the edge of the circle of light, to the hard musculature of his chest, the long ropy muscles of his arms. He carried her father's big Mexican saddle against one hip as if it weighed nothing at all. For the very first time Honey noticed that Gideon's skin wasn't deeply tanned like most men in New Mexico. It occurred to her he probably hadn't been outside in a long time. Years, perhaps. She found it nearly impossible to imagine Gideon Summerfield in a prison cell, cooped up like a wild animal in a cage. For that was what he appeared to be now—a wild, half-naked, very male animal. Beautiful. Pale. Like a wolf in wintertime.

He dropped the saddle onto the ground behind her, then walked to the juniper where his shirt was draped. He chuckled softly as he shoved his arms through the sleeves. "Well, you've done something I never did in all my years of outlawing, Ed," he said.

Honey tilted her head toward him. "What's that?"

"Stole a man's horse. That'll get you a rope necklace in some counties."

She dismissed the crime with a wave of her hand. Jonquil wasn't stolen, after all. Honey had merely borrowed her. And anyway, even though Gideon wasn't aware of it, she knew her father would never press charges against her. Not publicly at least. Privately, eventually, he'd skin her alive. Unless, of course, she handed him a fat sack of stolen cash.

Gideon searched through his saddlebag, then handed her a biscuit and a small square of beef jerky. "Not exactly a feast," he said, folding his legs to sit beside her. "But you know what they say about beggars not being choosers. Horse thieves, too, I reckon."

Honey's curt reply was garbled by the food she had immediately stuffed in her mouth.

He stared into the fire, then picked up a few loose stones and tossed them into the flames. "You should've stayed with Logan, Ed. You would've been safe."

She swallowed. "Not without the money. He's furious."

Gideon laughed. "So you went and stole his horse just to placate him, huh?" He shook his head in disbelief. "You think he's blaming you because I robbed his bank?"

"I know he's blaming me."

"It wasn't your fault."

Her turquoise eyes flashed in the firelight. "Of course it was my fault. I should have stopped you."

He lifted her wrist, measuring it with his fingers, marveling at the delicacy of her bones, the softness of the flesh that covered them. She seemed so fragile, as breakable as a little porcelain figurine.

And she was, dammit. With a flick of his own wrist, he could have snapped hers. But her iron will and her stubborn heart were ignorant of her body's vulnerability. She needed to be aware of that. He grasped her wrist more tightly in his frustration, and when he spoke, his tone was as rough as his touch. "Do you really believe you could have stopped me, Ed? From robbing the bank? Or now?" His gaze heated intentionally. "From doing anything I want?"

And although her reply was an immediate and sharp yes, Gideon saw the spark of fear in her eyes. Fear of him. God, he hated that. But somebody had to teach her fear for her own protection.

He slipped his fingers from her wrist. "Well, you tried, bright eyes. Now stop trying, will you? It's done."

"Not till I get the money back."

Gideon shook his head. "You're not going to find that sack, and you can be damn sure I'm not going to lead you to it."

She licked a biscuit crumb from the corner of her mouth, and Gideon found himself watching her mouth more than listening to her words. Those lips had such a fetching, downright kissable curve that he had to force himself to look away while she told him, "You'll have to pick it up sometime, you know. It can't be much fun having a sack full of money you can't spend. I'll bet there was ten thousand dollars in there. Did you count it?"

"Yup."

"Well?"

He gave her a sidelong glance. "Well, what?"

"How much was it? Ten thousand? Twelve?"

"Enough," Gideon said, returning his gaze to the fire.

"Enough for what? What are you planning to do with all that loot, Gideon? Buy fast horses? Fancy clothes? Fancy women?"

He grinned, then reached to adjust the blanket that had slipped down on her bare shoulders. "Looks like I've already got me one of those," he said, letting his hand rest on her upper arm.

With a snort, she brushed his hand away. "I doubt if you'd know the difference between a lady and a tart."

"Maybe not," he agreed, "but I know a horse thief when I see one." Saying that, he leaned back against his saddle, crossed his arms over his chest and closed his eyes. "Finish your supper and then get some sleep, bright eyes. We've got a long way to ride tomorrow."

"Back to Cerrillos?" A dull dread filled her. Her father might be waiting there, and he was the last person Honey wanted to see right now. Empty-handed, anyway.

"Nope. We're going south."

"Oh." Honey wasn't sure if what she felt was relief or an even deeper dread. "What's south?"

Gideon dug his shoulders into the curve of his saddle and raised a forearm to cover his eyes. "A big fat bank," he said. "Now be quiet and get some sleep."

A cloud cut across the three-quarter moon. The stars rolled across the sky like diamonds slung out on a black velvet cloth. It had taken five years in prison to make Gideon Summerfield appreciate the warmth of the stars. Before he was forced to stare up at a cold blank ceiling, the night sky had always seemed cold and forbidding to him. Now it seemed warm as a dark wool blanket, rich as spangled black satin.

Nor had he ever appreciated the simple physical nearness of another human being—until he had been denied it so long. He shifted his arm now, careful not to wake the woman who had curled in to him in her sleep like a trusting child. He angled his head in order to rest his cheek against her dark, silky hair. What he felt right now wasn't sexual desire—though that was always there, like a bass chord in a song—but rather a deep pleasure in just being close to another living, breathing soul.

Dear Lord, they had denied him everything that made a man a civilized creature, kept him in solitary so often and so long that he thought sometimes he'd go mad listening to the sound of his own breath.

Now he tuned his ears to the sweet rhythm of Edwina Cassidy's breath. She'd been so tired she hadn't even been able to find the strength to argue with him or to protest when he'd told her they would be heading south to rob another bank. She had just curled up in the blanket, closed her sea green, sky blue eyes and instantly fallen asleep. Only a child, he thought, or an innocent could fall asleep that fast.

And what did that say about him? Gideon wondered as he lay there wide-awake and staring at the sky. He wondered if he had ever been innocent. He knew for certain, though, that he hadn't been a child since '63 when General Ewing had given the order to depopulate Bates and Cass and Jackson Counties. Depopulate! The militia turned better than twenty thousand citizens out of their homes and then burned most of the buildings to the ground.

He had been ten years old, no bigger than a cornstalk in July, when the bluebellies had ridden into their front yard and started ripping the shutters off the house and then hacking at the railing of the front porch. He had run out with a rifle that was bigger than he was, and somebody had grabbed it out of his hands while somebody else pushed him down and wound him tight with rope.

He never saw who threw the torch into the house. In fact, he never even saw the fire because one of the soldiers tugged a feed sack over his head and tied it around his neck. But he heard his mother's screams from one of the upstairs windows as they tossed him on a horse and galloped away. And he heard his own screams. After a while that was all he could hear. And then, for a long time, he couldn't hear anything at all. Or feel anything.

In prison he had once again tutored himself in numbness, learned how to shut down inside his head, not to feel anything.

What he felt now was the sleeping warmth of a woman in his arms. This was what life was supposed to be, Gideon thought as he gazed up at the dark heavens. What it might have been.

He took in a deep breath, choosing to ignore the wet catch in his throat and the way the stars blurred in his vision. The past was the past, dammit. It was over and done with. And there wasn't a whole hell of a lot he could do about his future except to make damn sure he didn't wind up back in prison.

He glanced down at Edwina's face—dark lashes against soft skin, her mouth relaxed in sleep, a tiny bead of moisture cornered there. She'd probably never been kissed much, he thought, judging from her initial startled reaction when they were standing on the train. But judging from the way she had melted then and from the way her soft mouth had yielded beneath his, Gideon suspected it wouldn't take her very long to acquire the habit or to be downright good at it.

"Hell," he muttered. That was fine to think about, but all he planned to do was keep the little bank teller out of trouble for the next few days and see that she got back home in one piece. One *intact* piece. That, he thought, was about the greatest gift a man like him could give to a young lady like her.

Chapter Seven

The sun had been up just long enough to take the chill out of the morning air and had climbed just high enough to light the campsite where Honey stood now, trying to shake the wrinkles out of the dress that Gideon had handed her. Well, not handed so much as shoved into her arms with a gruff "Here" before he had stalked away toward the creek.

She had awakened thoroughly rested, almost cheerful. He, on the other hand, had been as prickly as the whiskers on his face from the minute he had opened his eyes. When she had thanked him for the dress, he'd merely grunted over his shoulder as he continued walking away.

Honey shrugged and continued working on the rumpled fabric of her skirt. His foul mood wasn't her problem, after all. Her immediate concern was seven or eight yards of linen that had been wadded up in a saddlebag so long the wrinkles would probably never smooth out. Wonderful as it was to be wearing a proper dress again as opposed to the red-and-black dance hall delight, Honey had to shake her head in dismay.

"I look like something the cat dragged in," she muttered.

"Smart cat."

Whirling toward the sound of the deep voice, Honey found herself the focus of Gideon's intense, appreciative gaze. The rough stubble on his cheeks and chin, while darkening his face, made his eyes appear nearly silver in contrast. They glinted now, like sunlight on the blade of a knife, as he came slowly toward her.

Her heart vaulted into her throat as he reached for the top button of her bodice, but oddly enough her hands failed to rise in defense. Her arms suddenly felt leaden.

"You forgot one," Gideon said softly as he worked the button through the buttonhole.

He was so close Honey could feel the heat radiating from his body and smell the faint tang of creek water on his damp hair. His breath riffled the hair at the crown of her head, sending a cascade of shivers down her spine.

"Thank you for looking after my dress for me," she said. "It was very thoughtful of you."

"No problem." He was done buttoning now but his hands remained, tracing a shoulder seam. "I figured on a bank clerk's wages you probably didn't have dresses to spare."

Honey thought of the three trunks she had brought home with her from school. Suddenly she wished she were standing before this man in her white satin ball gown, the one that had won her so many compliments from the young men back east. She wished, instead of hanging in bedraggled locks, her hair were swept atop her head and anchored with her pearl-studded tortoiseshell combs. She was accustomed to the appreciative stares of men. Well, boys. Still, even in this woebegone linen and with her hair a jumble of knots, there was something in Gideon Summerfield's voice and in his pewter gaze that made her feel utterly and unaccountably beautiful.

She made herself shake off the feeling. Silly, she thought. She didn't want to feel beautiful, but smart and responsible. And, anyway, it wasn't Gideon Summerfield she was interested in. It was the money. Besides, even if she were attracted to him, he was a bank robber. A married one, at that. The latter fact probably accounted for his proficiency with tiny mother-of-pearl buttons.

Taking a step back, Honey said stiffly, "You're right. I don't have clothes to spare. Or money. I work hard for my wages." She paused, looking around the campsite, trying to locate the canvas sack she'd seen the night before. "Speaking of money, what the devil have you done with it?"

He grinned. "Why, Miss Edwina! Most gals aren't so obvious about where their interests lie with a fella. They at least let the poor fool believe it's true love until they get him down the aisle."

She gave her long, tumbled hair a toss. "Well, you'd know about that, I'm sure, having already taken that little walk down the aisle yourself."

Gideon's smile evaporated instantly. "The money's in a safe place," he growled. "And your stolen horse is saddled. Let's go."

He turned on his heel and walked away, leaving Honey wondering just what he had done with the second sack of money and when he was coming back for it. He couldn't just plant money sacks all over the countryside, could he, in the hope to retrieve them all later? How in the world would he ever get away when the authorities came after him? And when, she wondered, would that be?

She was still wondering about the lack of pursuit when they rode into the little town of Golden a few hours later. It seemed to her that a man planning to rob a bank would have slunk into town like the proverbial thief in the night—shoulders hunched, keeping against walls and looking over his shoulder. But Gideon sat tall and handsome in the saddle as he guided his horse right down the middle of the dusty little street, looking for all the world as if he was an honest man on an honest mission.

After he tethered his roan gelding to the rail in front of the saloon, he lifted his hands to help Honey down. His fingers splayed out over her rib cage, and they remained there—warm and protective—once she was on her feet.

"Thank you," she said.

He just stood there, staring down, still holding her. The dun mare whinnied and sidestepped, jarring them both. Gideon's grip tightened on Honey's midriff.

"I've got my balance," Honey said.

"What?"

"I said I've got my balance. My feet are firmly on the ground. You can let me go now."

His hands jerked away. Damned if he even realized he was holding her, Gideon thought. He'd best gather his wits together or the next thing he knew he'd be walking into a church instead of a bank. Best get away from this warm, sweet-smelling, ocean-eyed distraction before his brain stiffened up like the rest of him.

"I need a drink," he grumbled, reaching into his saddlebag and coming up with a wad of bank notes, which he thrust into her hand. "Here. Why don't you walk down to the mercantile and get us some supplies?"

She blinked. "Supplies?"

"Food. Coffee. Whatever you want," he said curtly. "I'll be about fifteen minutes." Saying that, he started toward the door of the saloon.

"Gideon?"

He took a deep breath and turned back to her. Still standing in the street, tiny between the two horses, clutching the bills in her hand, she reminded him of a little country girl just come to town in her best bedraggled dress. "What?" he asked quietly.

"Be careful," she said.

Gideon felt his heart jam, like logs caught in a swift river. Nobody had said that to him since he was ten years old. Nobody. Not Cora, for sure, and not any of his cutthroat cousins. But he didn't need to hear that now. He couldn't afford what it cost his soul to have anybody care. Not her anyway. Not now.

"I'm always careful, bright eyes," he said, then turned his back on her and walked into the saloon.

* * *

The little mercantile reminded Honey so much of her mother's long-ago, decrepit store in Loma Parda. It had been nearly seventeen years since Honey had last seen Cassidy's Mercantile, the grim little place where she'd spent the first three years of her life, but the minute she walked in the door, memories came flooding back.

The rough-hewn shelves were crammed with dusty bottles and tins. The floor was stacked with wooden crates, and overhead, the ceiling almost seemed to sway with its coils of ropes and chains, its shovels and ax handles and brooms.

"Howdy." The dark-haired young shopkeeper leaned across the counter, smiling a little crookedly as she drawled, "What can I do for you?"

Honey blinked. The scene and the girl were so familiar it was as if she were looking at a version of herself. As if she had been transported through time to a real, remembered place that was inhabited now by someone who had never had a chance to exist. Herself. Not Honey Logan, though. She was staring at Edwina Cassidy.

Suddenly she felt dizzy and a bit off center. The ceiling, with its loops of rope and chain, seemed to shift, and the floor felt as if it were sliding away from under her feet. "I need a few things," she told the apparition on the opposite side of the counter, then proceeded to rattle off the first items that came into her head.

Edwina Cassidy! That was who Honey had been for her first three years. That was who she'd be this minute if her father hadn't come back from the war to claim both her and her mother, to whisk them away from the little store in Loma Parda, to take them to Santa Fe where he'd kept them both in glass boxes, high on pedestals, safe and secure.

Safe, secure and utterly useless. Honey watched her other self move with grace and brisk efficiency behind the counter. The girl hiked up her calico skirt and climbed two steps up a rickety ladder to reach for a jar on a high shelf, then backed down to the floor with the jar tucked under her chin.

"That was strawberry jam you wanted, right?" she asked Honey, who nodded, despite the fact that she had barely comprehended the question.

If Race Logan had never come back, she was thinking, it would be Edwina Cassidy hiking up her skirt and taking the rungs of a ladder in stride. If Race Logan hadn't turned her into a pampered and useless female—a house pet, practically—with his money and his overbearing love, she'd be a competent young woman today. She wouldn't have to battle for every shred of the responsibility she craved.

For a minute, Honey wished her father hadn't come back. For a split second, she found herself wishing Race Logan had died with all the other prisoners at Andersonville so that she might have lived a different kind of life as Edwina Cassidy.

She shook her head to clear her brain of such disturbing, disloyal, even downright evil thoughts. She couldn't, though. The vision of the Edwina Cassidy who might have been kept haunting her, and by the time the dark-haired girl had wrapped and tied her purchases, Honey could barely breathe for the terrible guilt she was feeling. She swept the packages from the counter and raced outside to gulp a great, cleansing draft of air, only to find herself rushing right into the arms of Gideon Summerfield.

Those arms tightened around her. "Whoa! Slow down, Ed. You look like you just saw a ghost."

"I . . . I did," she answered without even thinking. Then, as she realized exactly where she was, Honey corrected herself. "No, I didn't. It was nothing."

Gideon tipped her chin up. "Doesn't sound like nothing. Doesn't look like nothing either. Are you all right?"

She nodded.

The palms of his hands flattened on her neck as his thumbs held her face tilted upward for his inspection. He flicked his gaze toward the mercantile's door. "Did somebody bother you in there? Somebody do something?—"

"No, Gideon," she said, cutting him off. "For heaven's sake. I told you nothing happened. Nobody did anything. I just . . . I just wanted to get out in the fresh air." She took a step back, out of the circle of his arms. "You're crushing these packages," she snapped.

He gave her one last, inquisitive look before letting her go. "If you're sure . . ."

"I'm sure," she said quickly. Standing away from him now, Honey was able to see the canvas sack in the dust by his boots. He must have dropped it, she thought, in order to hold her, but he picked it up now and held it against his leg.

"I guess you're all done with your, um, business."
Honey gestured toward the sack on whose canvas side
was stenciled The Bank of Golden, New Mexico Territory.

"All done."

His reply was as casual as it was amazing. The man
had just robbed a bank, for heaven's sake. Either he
was the most brazen thief in the world or he didn't
have enough sense to hightail it out of town.

Honey stared up at his calm face. "Shouldn't we
escape?" she asked, a thread of panic in her voice.

"You still look a little pale, bright eyes. You sure
you're ready to ride?"

Her gaze flicked anxiously toward the bank. Maybe
Gideon had bound and gagged the people inside, she
thought. Maybe that's why there were no shouts or
shots. She remembered how he had tied her to the
door of the train. But she had gotten loose, hadn't
she? And so could the bank personnel.

"I think we should get out of here. Fast." Clutching her purchases to her bosom with one hand and
hiking up her skirt with the other, Honey began
sprinting toward their horses. "Gideon," she called
frantically over her shoulder, "Come on. Don't just
stand there grinning like the village idiot. Dammit!
Aren't you the least bit worried about getting
caught?"

He shook his head and began walking toward the
horses. "Seems to me you're doing enough worrying
for the both of us."

After Honey had stuffed her parcels into the saddlebag, she jammed her foot in the stirrup and pulled

herself up. Beside her, Gideon leisurely swung up on his horse. He just sat there then, looking at her, a little smile twitching the corners of his mouth.

Panic clutched at her insides as Honey imagined the people in the bank struggling with knotted ropes, and those knots beginning to loosen just as hers had, then the ropes slithering away.

"Gideon Summerfield," she snapped, "it's no wonder you got caught five years ago. You must be the world's stupidest bank robber. You don't rob a place and then just hang around outside it all day."

He settled his hat more firmly on his head. "Is that right?" Though the brim shaded him, his widening grin fairly lit up his face. "Some of the finer points of this business always did escape me."

Honey snorted. "Well, if you're going to do something, you ought to at least try to do it properly." Saying that, she punched her heels into the mare's sides and set the surprised animal off at a furious pace.

Gideon had ridden behind Honey for three hours, watching her, wondering about her. Something had gotten under her skin back in Golden. She had run out of that dry goods store like the devil himself was on her tail, and then she had refused to talk about it. In fact she had hardly spoken at all as they had made their way south through the shrub-dotted hills.

When they finally stopped at an abandoned mine, the little bank teller gazed at the rugged terrain and proclaimed soberly, "This looks like as good a place as any to hole up."

"Hole up?" Gideon laughed out loud as he stretched his saddle-weary muscles. "Who do you think you are, Ed? Belle Starr?"

She merely glared at him before announcing she was going to take advantage of the last hour of sunlight to wash up in the nearby creek.

"Don't get your clothes all wet," he cautioned her. "I don't have time to play nursemaid if you take a chill."

After she had flounced off toward the creek, Gideon gathered enough deadwood to get a decent fire started, unsaddled the horses and then lingered at the mouth of the mine, wondering if she'd had enough time to take care of her private needs. He wouldn't mind a bath himself, he thought. Lord, he hated being dirty. Once this was all over with he was going to spend the rest of his life chin deep in hot, soapy water.

Of course, the rest of his life wasn't scheduled to begin till he located Dwight Samuel, or was located by him. That blessed event should have taken place by now. He'd put out the word in Santa Fe and Cerrillos both. Today in Golden he'd made his identity known in the saloon. It wasn't as if nobody knew him. Hell, half the tavern's clientele today had started whispering right away while the other half had plunked down their drinks and skedaddled.

He was doing his damnedest to stick to the banker's plan, but Gideon had thought from the beginning that it was too cautious. These safe, silent robberies were like taking peppermints from kids, and they didn't seem to be stirring up much interest. God knew they hadn't brought his marauding cousin out of the woodwork yet.

A sudden, blood-chilling scream sliced through Gideon's thoughts. His mind emptied of everything but Edwina Cassidy's safety as he ran toward the creek.

She screamed again, but this time at him as he half ran, half slid down the steep, rock-strewn wall of the gully.

"Don't you dare come any closer," she shrieked from the middle of the shallow creek. "You just stop right there. Turn around. Close your eyes."

The second he had realized she wasn't in mortal danger, Gideon had halted by the trunk of the cottonwood, where her clothes were folded in a neat pile. All of her clothes. Every damn stitch. The little bank teller was naked as a newborn babe out there in the ankle-deep water. Except for the long wet strands of hair that streamed over her breasts, she was all pale smooth skin and luscious, lustrous curves.

"Turn around," she yelled at him now.

He did, leaning back against the rough tree trunk, crossing his arms over his chest. His heart was pounding and he didn't know if it was from his sprint from the mine, or the sleek sight of her nude body, or a combination of both. He could hardly breathe for the tightness in his throat and the quickening in his groin. "Hell, woman. Why'd you scream if you didn't want me to come running?"

"I wasn't screaming for you, Gideon. I was screaming at the damn snake."

"What snake?"

"The one that was crawling into my clothes. It's still in there, I think. I didn't see it crawl out."

Gideon glanced down at the pile of linen and lace near his foot. "What kind of snake?"

"How the hell do I know what kind it was? It was a snake. A snake is a snake."

He poked the toe of his boot into the cloth and watched as a harmless garter snake streaked away toward a clump of scrub. Poor creature was scared to death of them, he thought. Then Gideon felt a slow smile work its way across his mouth and a mischievous glint begin to sparkle in his eyes. It wasn't every day a man was gifted with a naked beauty who was afraid to get into her clothes. And this particular beauty—this overeager bank teller turned Belle Starr—deserved a little twitting for scaring him half to death with her scream.

"He's still all coiled up in there," he called to her over his shoulder.

"Well, get him out!"

"Scared to. Don't have much acquaintance with these western vipers." He bit down on a grin, then added, "Critter might be poisonous."

"Can't you get a stick or something?"

He waited a moment before replying, looking skyward as he said, "I don't see any around here. Leastways, not any that're long enough to do the job."

"Do something," she hissed. "Anything."

Again, Gideon let a minute tick off before replying. "I guess if you can't get in your own clothes, you could make do with my shirt."

She sighed with a certain amount of disgust. "That will have to do, I suppose, at least as a temporary measure. You can just toss it out here."

Gideon shifted lazily, side to side, scratching his back against the tree. "Nope."

"What do you mean 'nope'?"

"I mean if you want the shirt off my back so bad, Ed, you'll just have to come up here and get it." He could almost hear the water around her beginning to boil.

"I'm not walking up there buck naked," she screeched.

He didn't answer.

"I said I'm not walking up there without a stitch of clothes on," she called.

"Fine. That snake'll probably decide to crawl out once it gets dark." He twisted his head, slanting her a grin.

"Don't look at me," she snapped, moving her arms to cover herself as much as possible.

"Aren't you forgetting something?" he asked.

"What?"

"I've already seen just about all there is of you, bright eyes. Who do you think got you out of your wet clothes a few nights ago?"

She sniffed. "You're no gentleman to remind me of that."

"Never claimed to be one."

That was true, Honey thought. And she knew plenty of so-called gentlemen who would be standing on the edge of the creek right now ogling her if they were in Gideon Summerfield's boots. Without a doubt, the outlaw was being horrid to her, but the fact remained that the whole time he was aggravating her he *was* keeping his eyes averted. For the most part.

And he had, after all, undressed her that night in Cerrillos. The thought brought a lick of flame to the pit of her stomach. Had he stared at her? she wondered now. Had he touched her? Surely she would have known if he had touched her. She couldn't imagine that she wouldn't have been aware of those hands on her even in her sleep. Lord knew when she was awake, his touch sent her bloodstream swirling like a wild river.

The thought crossed Honey's mind that perhaps he had looked at her that night and had found her so unappealing without her clothes that there wasn't the least inclination now to peek. Not that she wanted him to, but... Well, she was a woman, wasn't she? She had all the right womanly parts. And he was a man. He ought to want to look, oughtn't he?

All she could see of him was one long leg, a crook of elbow and a wedge of husky shoulder. He was leaning against the cottonwood—casual, unconcerned, uninterested. Damn you, Gideon Summerfield, she thought. What's wrong with me that you'd rather stare off into the sunset than look at me?

"All right," she called as she took a kick at the water. "You win. Take your shirt off. I'm coming to get it."

Chapter Eight

Damnation! Gideon heard her stomping toward him through the shallow water. He'd only been teasing her, for Lord's sake. He had never intended for her to take his ultimatum...well...seriously.

"Now wait just a blasted minute," he shouted.

"I'm freezing, and I'm not waiting one more blasted second. I hope you've got your shirt unbuttoned, mister."

Already his skin prickled with sweat. He couldn't just take off and run, he thought, although that was what he wanted to do—just hightail it away from her tempting flesh and tantalizing curves. Then, not knowing what else to do, Gideon stepped out from behind the tree trunk and turned to confront the oncoming rampage of naked female. He was ready to yell at her, but when he opened his mouth there were no words. She was the finest, the sleekest, the most damned beautiful woman he had ever seen in his life. His knees felt like butter left out in the noonday sun.

Honey halted in midstride, seeing the look on his face, the way his eyes seemed to drink her in, to swallow her whole. No one had ever looked at her that way before. It wasn't admiration. Not even praise. What she saw was a hunger so real, so elemental, so raw that it made her heart stop still.

A moment earlier the outlaw's apparent indifference had irked her. Now his obvious desire quickened something inside Honey, and his gray eyes drew her like a magnet. She had halted, transfixed beneath his metallic gaze, and now it pulled her forward.

He didn't move as she came to him, water whisking at her ankles, then dry leaves whispering beneath her bare feet. He didn't speak when she stopped mere inches away. Then his hand reached out—shaking—to cover the flare of her hip. It remained there a moment, motionless, before moving slowly upward, his palm just grazing her skin.

Gideon's gaze lowered as his hand rose, then both—warm hand, molten gaze—touched her breast. His thumb brushed over her nipple, which came alive to his touch.

"Ah, God," he breathed raggedly.

Honey closed her eyes, feeling the heat that rushed through her body. Her heart had plummeted at the first touch of his hand on her hip, and now it beat crazily in her stomach.

He kissed her then, claimed her mouth with a fierce need as he pulled her against him. His hands, suddenly hard and insistent, clutched at her bottom while his lean hips ground against her. His belt buckles were hot against her naked flesh, his whiskers rough against her face.

When he lowered his head and laid claim to her breast with the same ferocity, Honey felt a surge of liquid warmth, so sweet, so sudden and surprising, it brought a small cry of pleasure from her lips.

Gideon sagged to his knees then, slowly, as if they would no longer support him, and he pressed his face into the slight give of Honey's belly as her fingers threaded through his hair.

He was shaking like a fifteen-year-old boy, Gideon thought. On his knees. Not sure if he was going to cry or pray. He only knew one thing for certain. He was dangerously close to losing control, and if he looked at this woman again, if he touched her, or—God forbid—if she said anything remotely close to yes right now, he was going to explode like a piece of field artillery that hadn't been used in years. She was too innocent to know how quickly, how savagely this little game of hers could get out of hand. She didn't have a clue what she was doing to him or how desperately he wanted her or how damn hard he was fighting for control.

With his eyes nearly closed, he heaved himself to his feet. "Get dressed," he said gruffly.

"What?" Honey's mental fog cleared just enough to remind her why she was naked in the first place. "But the snake..."

Gideon snatched her clothes from the ground and thrust them into her arms, but she dropped them immediately and took a panicky step away.

He raked his fingers through his hair. "There's no goddamn snake, Ed. It's gone. Now get the hell dressed."

Muttering a succession of curses, he picked up the dress again and flung it at her. "I'm trying," he said hoarsely, hands clamped in fists at his sides, "to treat you like a lady." He turned from her and stalked away.

After she was dressed, Honey stumbled up the rocky hill toward the mine entrance. Halfway up, she collapsed in a rumpled heap of damp linen, muttering, cursing Gideon Summerfield up one side and down the other. Cursing herself, too. Mad as she was at Gideon, she was even more angry with herself.

What had possessed her? She had walked buck naked into a man's arms as casually as if she had been wearing her finest satin ball gown and had just accepted a waltz. She had behaved like a bold, brazen tart. Worse. Brazen tarts at least wore little skimpy dresses or feathers in discreet places. She had been wearing creek water—period.

She'd lost her temper and then she'd just plain lost her senses. When Gideon had looked at her with that ravenous, wolflike expression, her mind had emptied of everything. Everything except him. Good Lord! She'd been attracted to men before but nobody had ever turned her brain to mush and the rest of her to a quivering bowl of pudding.

A fool! That was what she had been. A senseless and brazen fool. And Gideon was a man, so of course he had responded to her enticement. But, as a gentleman, he had admirably restrained himself and refused to take advantage of her foolishness.

Honey bunched up her skirt in her fists, and clambered to her feet. She wished she could just turn and walk in the other direction—walk away and never have to face him again. What must he be thinking now? After all the terrible things she had said to him—all the awful names she had called him, from varmint to unprincipled brute—he had behaved like a gentleman and had treated her like a lady even when she had acted little better than a witless tart.

Maybe her father was right, she thought disgustedly. Maybe she was irresponsible to the core and never to be trusted with anything more than ribbons and baubles. Maybe she didn't have the inherent good sense she always had claimed. Nobody with a grain of sense at all would have done what she had just done.

"You're damn lucky he didn't take you right then and there," she muttered aloud. But somewhere down deep inside, Honey didn't feel lucky at all.

When she reached the crest of the hill and saw Gideon sitting in front of the mine, swigging from a whiskey bottle, Honey castigated herself anew. First she'd tempted him to the brink of gentlemanly endurance. Now she'd driven him to drink! She wanted to sit right down and cry. But instead she forced herself to continue toward the mine.

Gideon rested the bottle on his thigh as he watched her coming, her bedraggled skirt swinging with her stride, the sunset giving her long hair a russet sheen and touching her face with a rose-colored glow.

He wondered if his fingers were still shaking like leaves in a stiff north wind. He was clutching the whiskey bottle so hard now he couldn't tell. Thank God, he thought, he'd bought it this morning in Golden. It hadn't been his intention when buying it, but now he planned to get so damn drunk he couldn't even see the little bank teller, much less respond to her. Anything so he wouldn't continue the torment he was going through right now. They'd have supper and then they'd sleep, or she would sleep and he'd drink himself into a safe stupor, and then tomorrow he'd take her into the closest town and...

She strode right up to where he was sitting, so close her skirt brushed over his boot. "I'd rather not even discuss what happened down there by the creek," she said briskly. "It's over, and it's not going to happen again, so there's no use flogging a dead horse."

Gideon's brain had been floundering, trying to come up with a way to explain, if not excuse, his coarse behavior and to tell her he was sorry. He was grateful now that he didn't have to look like an even worse fool, tripping over his tongue. If she didn't want to discuss it, that was just fine with him. "Right," he said flatly. "Let's just have some grub and get some sleep."

He reached into her saddlebag for the parcels she had bought earlier that day. A good meal would be a good distraction, he was thinking as he opened the brown paper of one of the packages.

"Shortbread?" He looked up.

She shrugged.

Gideon tore the paper off another package. "Strawberry jam? You bought tea cakes and jelly for our supper?"

"Coffee, too," she said brightly. "Open the other package."

He did, then stared up at her incredulously. "Did you ask them to grind it, or was the grinder broken?"

"Well, I . . ."

Now he wasn't even going to get a decent meal to take his mind off her firm, sweet breasts. Lord Almighty! How much could a man take? "Didn't your mama teach you a damn thing about homemaking?" he shouted. "Or didn't you bother to listen?"

Honey bristled. Her mother, in fact, never had told her anything about homemaking. Nor had Honey ever inquired. Their servants did the shopping and the preparing of meals. She had never paid any attention to what was going on in the kitchen—only what came out of it. Again, she felt foolish and irresponsible. Why hadn't she ever learned any of those skills? she wondered. What good was she if she could only dance and embroider?

She grabbed the package out of Gideon's hand now. "I can make coffee," she snarled. "Where's the damn pot?"

He angled his head toward the campfire and the small metal saucepan beside it.

Pot in fist, Honey trudged back to the creek, filled it and returned, losing only half the water. She tossed in a handful of coffee beans, then set the pot on a flat rock centered among the coals.

"There." She stood there then, glaring into the liquid as if willing it to boil.

Gideon watched her as he took a bite of one of the dry, sweet biscuits she had bought. It was strange, he thought, that a young woman who had to work for her living didn't seem to know the first thing about cooking or providing decent food for a meal. But then he figured Miss Edwina Cassidy probably lived with a doting mother who wouldn't let her daughter lift a dainty finger around the house. Either that, or she simply hadn't bothered to acquire domestic skills because she had her cap set on marrying some rich old coot who would provide her with servants. For a young woman as beautiful and shapely as Edwina, that was a good possibility. Santa Fe was probably full of rich old bastards who'd be only too glad to make her a wife or a mistress. For all he knew that was precisely why the banker, Logan, had come in such hot and swift pursuit of his little teller.

The biscuit grew even drier in Gideon's mouth as he watched Edwina and contemplated her future. The thought that that future wouldn't include him set a dull ache in his heart. For such a hard case, he thought morosely, he was sure acting like a moony kid. Of course her future wouldn't include him. How could it? He was going to Mexico just as soon as he took care of a couple matters here.

Damn. He had no business thinking about Ed in that way anyway. For all he knew he was still legally married to Cora. And even if he weren't, he was in no position to be asking a woman to share his future. Hell, he didn't even know what that future was going to be, other than on the run.

"Your pan's not heating up right," she called to him now.

He was looking right at her, Gideon suddenly realized, yet he hadn't really been aware of her other than in his imagination. He blinked. "What?"

"I said something's wrong with your pan. This water's not anywhere near boiling." She was squatting down now, peering into the saucepan. "Maybe I should move it farther into the fire."

"Ed! Don't," he shouted. But it was too late. She had already grasped the metal handle and then, whisking her burned hand back, had dumped the water onto the fire and the hem of her skirt. White smoke was curling up from the sodden ashes and she was swearing a blue streak when Gideon got to her side.

He grasped the hand she was shaking furiously, opened it and was relieved to see the burn wasn't as bad as he feared. Her palm was streaked an angry red.

"Why can't I do anything right?" she wailed. "Useless. That's all I am. Just plain useless."

"Shh." Gideon pressed his lips to the inflamed skin. His gut tightened to see her hurt, and he thought he would have gladly put his own hand in the fire if it would have spared her this pain. "Sssh," he whispered again. "You're not useless, bright eyes. You're just tired. It's been a long day. A long couple of days."

Her response was a wet snuffle as Gideon wrapped his arms around her and drew her close against his chest. "Tell you what," he said against her ear. "I'll teach you how to fix coffee, and then you'll never feel useless again."

"Didn't I do it right?" she mumbled into his shirt.

"Almost," he said. "You missed a few of the finer points, sugar, but we'll fix that. How's that hand feeling now?" He took a step back, holding her away from him, searching her face for twinges of pain.

"It's better," she said, cautiously opening and closing her fist.

"Okay. You wrap the hem of your skirt around your hand, pick up that pan again, and fill it to the brim with water. I'm going to get the fire going, and then I'm going to show you how to make one damn fine pot of coffee."

When Honey got back with the refilled pan, it was nearly dark. The fire was bright and crackling, though, and Gideon was sitting beside it crushing coffee beans between two good-size rocks. The whiskey bottle was leaning against his leg.

He smiled up at her. "First lesson, bright eyes. Grind up the beans."

As he continued to tutor her in low and gentle tones, Honey found herself mesmerized, and instead of attending to his instructive words, she was listening to the bass pitch and the rich music of his voice.

"There you go," he said finally, brushing the ground coffee from his hands. "That'll boil in ten or fifteen minutes and you'll have yourself some first-class brew. It'd help if we had some eggshells to settle the grounds." He rubbed his hand across his flat midriff. "A plate of eggs doesn't sound half-bad right now, does it?"

Honey smiled into his warm, firelit eyes. "Who taught you all this? Your mama? Or maybe it was Cora who..."

"Neither." He stood up abruptly and turned away. "I've been on my own since I was ten. Making coffee was just one of the things I picked up along the way."

Honey remained by the fire and watched the warming water a while, then walked to where Gideon was leaning back against his saddle. He said nothing when she sat beside him and busied herself with the wrinkles in her skirt.

"How's your hand?" he asked between swigs from the whiskey bottle.

Honey gave her palm a quick, dismissive glance. "Fine." She tilted her head and spoke softly. "What happened when you were ten?"

He sighed with rough forbearance, clearly indicating it wasn't a subject he wanted to discuss. "Our house burned down. My mother didn't get out."

"I'm sorry."

"Don't be. It was a long time ago."

Gideon took up the bottle again and a silence lengthened between them, broken only by the sloshing of whiskey and an occasional popping of dry twigs in the fire.

"My papa died the day I was born," Honey said finally, a faraway note in her voice. "It doesn't matter how long ago, Gideon, or how young you were. It still hurts."

He studied her face a moment, opened his mouth to speak, then swigged from the bottle instead. A full five minutes passed before he asked, "So you lived alone with your mama after your father died?"

"She married again," Honey said, glancing away toward the fire. It was true enough that Ned Cassidy had perished the day she was born, but she felt dishonest now not telling Gideon about her father—her true father, Race Logan. Still, she held her tongue.

Bankers and bank robbers, after all, weren't exactly a good combination. And after her shocking behavior earlier down by the creek, Honey wasn't all that eager to have Gideon know about her mother's questionable past.

"Who took care of you after your mother died?" she asked now, trying to turn the conversation back to his past.

"Nobody. Well, my cousins."

"You lived with them?"

Gideon shook his head. "I rode with them." He laughed a little drunkenly. "Barely big enough to get my feet in the stirrups. I had a hell of a time keeping up with them, but I did."

"But who did you live with?"

"I told you. Nobody. I hardly saw the inside of a house till Cora and I..." His voice trailed off. "It was during the war," he said then. "My cousins were guerrillas. They kept on the move pretty much."

"Guerrillas," she murmured. "You mean like Jesse James?"

"No, sugar. Not *like* Jesse. It was Jesse."

Honey swallowed hard. She had just arrived in St. Louis in '82 when the legendary bank and train robber had been murdered. The papers had been full of the bloody crime for weeks. She and her classmates had even sung the song about the dirty little coward who shot poor Mr. Howard and laid poor Jesse in his grave. Her eyes felt huge as saucers now. She gulped. "Jesse James was your cousin?"

"Second cousin. On my mama's side."

"Good Lord," Honey breathed.

"That makes me a real bad customer, doesn't it?" he said, a note of amusement in his voice and a glint in his eyes.

She could only stare at him. It did, in fact, make him seem like a very dangerous character. More dangerous than she'd dared to believe. Yet in her heart she knew this full-fledged desperado was a decent and honorable man. She had seen it time and time again.

"I think you're a gentleman," she murmured softly. "Through and through."

His first instinct was to laugh, but Gideon didn't. Rather he looked into this beautiful girl's eyes and felt his heart clench at what he saw there. Trust. Affection. Perhaps even a glimmering of love. He stroked her cheek—so soft and smooth—with his thumb.

"I appreciate that, bright eyes." He cleared his throat and forced a smile, cocking his head toward the campfire. "Maybe you should check on that coffee, huh?"

He watched her—a vision of grace in a wrinkled, raggedy frock out in the middle of nowhere, as beautiful as any lady in any high-toned parlor—move to and from the fire. His heart about melted when she returned, sat back down beside him and sadly confessed, "It boiled over."

"We didn't have any cups anyway," Gideon said. He held the whiskey bottle out to her. "Here. Take a sip. It'll help you sleep."

She swallowed, shivered, then handed the bottle back. He put it aside in order to shake out his blanket.

"Lie back, bright eyes, and I'll tuck you in real good."

Honey did. She closed her eyes, feeling warm and sleepy and oddly safe. "Are we robbing another bank tomorrow?" she asked.

"We?"

"Well, you know what I mean." She yawned wearily then.

After adjusting the rough blanket under her chin, Gideon kissed her forehead. "Go to sleep, Ed. Dream of sweet things. Not about robbing banks. You hear me?"

She nodded. "What will you do for a blanket?"

Gideon picked up the whiskey bottle. "This will keep me warm."

He leaned back and stretched out his legs. After one more long pull from the bottle, he set it aside. Somebody had to watch over the sleeping beauty. He wouldn't be any good if he were falling-down drunk. He smiled as he watched her tuck up her knees and curl a fist beneath her cheek. Gently, he reached out to lift an errant strand of hair from her forehead.

A gentleman! Gideon closed his eyes and sighed roughly. Hell, he was as far from a gentleman as a man could get. But Edwina Cassidy seemed to believe it. That mattered to him. It mattered more than he could ever let her know.

Chapter Nine

Kate stood in the doorway of Isaac's room looking at the two men who were as dear to her as life itself. Sometimes, she thought, it was hard remembering she'd had any kind of life at all before Race Logan and Isaac Goodman had happened into Leavenworth, Kansas, all those years ago, and had changed her life forever.

"Thank God," she murmured now, pulling the sash of her wrapper a little tighter about her waist as she stepped into the room. The lamp was low, and it cast a soft glow across the bed where Isaac lay quiet and still, as he had for two days now ever since collapsing in the kitchen. On the far side of the room, Race slept in a chair with his long legs angled out across the polished wooden floor and his head sagging onto his chest.

Kate touched her husband's shoulder gently. "Come to bed, love. You're only going to wear yourself out this way."

Race rubbed his neck, blinking as he looked at the motionless figure in the bed. "No change, I guess."

"Not that I can see," she said. "You go on to bed. I'll sit with Isaac a while."

When he levered out of the chair, Kate heard the muffled grunt of pain Race did his best to conceal as he worked his sleep-stiffened muscles and joints. He wasn't getting any younger—though he was still the handsomest devil on the face of the earth—and the past two nights, sleeping slumped in a chair if he slept at all, had taken a toll on his fifty-four-year-old body.

He reached out now and pulled her into his arms, then nuzzled his warm, whiskery face into her neck. "This is wearing you down, too, love. Watching over Isaac and worrying about Honey."

"They're both going to be fine. I know that, Race. I feel it in my heart."

He sighed. "I hope you're right, Katie. Lord, I hope you're right."

She stepped back and guided him toward the door. "I'm right," she said firmly. "Now go. Get some sleep. I'll wake you if there's any change."

After Race was gone, Kate pulled a chair close to Isaac's bed. There was enough light, from the low-burning lamp and from the moonlight that washed through the open window, to see the ebony dips and ridges in the old man's face. Kate studied the stubby lashes against his grizzled cheeks and the little puffs his lips made as he breathed. She leaned close.

"Now you listen to me, old man," she whispered. "I'm on to your little scheme. It took me a while, I'll admit, but I finally figured it out. First there was Doc Cullen, who's always been able to say what was wrong with somebody even if he hadn't the least notion, and who's always more than willing to treat people, even if it's only with a poultice. But he just threw up his hands over you and hasn't even bothered coming back. I've been asking myself why. Then, this morning I accused the boys of eating all the fried chicken in the cellar. I didn't believe them when they denied it. But, then, when I was changing your linens I found this."

Kate slid her hand under the mattress now and held up a chicken bone.

"Then," she continued, her eyes fixed on Isaac's face, "this afternoon I happened to be standing outside your window looking at my flower bed, when all of a sudden I got to wondering why those flowers would look wet when it hasn't rained in two weeks. I knew I hadn't watered them. So I squatted down to look a little closer. And then I knew. You've been pissing out the window, you old coot!"

Isaac opened one eye and his mouth slid into a cockeyed grin. "You done found me out, Miz Kate. Doc Cullen said you prob'ly would."

"I don't know whether to strangle you or hug you," she exclaimed. Instead, she leaned forward and kissed his wrinkled forehead, then sat back with her arms crossed. "Now, if you don't mind my asking, Isaac, why are you putting us through this misery? Race is almost sick with worry and from lack of sleep, as I'm sure you know."

"He's why I done it. I couldn't figure out any other way of keeping Horace here."

Kate merely lifted an eyebrow. She had learned long ago to trust the former slave's instincts. Isaac was rarely wrong—about people, about danger.

He continued without being prompted. "When he came home all red-faced and furious 'cause Miz Honey had stolen his horse, I knew something was wrong. Terrible wrong."

"What, Isaac?" Kate leaned closer. "What do you mean?"

"If that little girl stole her daddy's mare to ride off after that Summerfield man, Miz Kate, it's more than money she's chasing," he said. "She's chasing her heart."

Kate fingered the edge of her sash. The thought had occurred to her, too, but she had dismissed it—out of fear.

"You don't know that, Isaac," she insisted.

He raised a gnarled hand to scratch his bristly chin. "No. But I know you. And I know Horace. And I know that little apple of yours didn't fall too far from the tree. Miz Honey's just like her mama and her daddy." He gazed at Kate solemnly. "Tell me something."

"What?"

"What's the onliest thing in the world would prompt you to steal a horse?"

Kate sighed and let her hands drop helplessly. "To chase after Race Logan," she admitted.

"Yup," he said. He nodded his head thoughtfully a moment. "And why do you s'pose that bank robber ain't sent Miz Honey packing back to Santa Fe?

You s'pose he done fallen for those big turquoise eyes of hers and her *sweet, quiet* disposition?''

Kate nodded with reluctant agreement. It was what she had suspected, but hadn't wanted to consider. If the thief Race had hired had stolen his daughter's heart in addition to his bank's money, Race would explode. He'd never stand for it. On the other hand, Honey was as hot-tempered and headstrong as her father. "Nothing good can come of this, Isaac," she said softly. "You were smart to do what you did, keeping Race here."

"I just feel it in my bones." The old man rocked his head back and forth on the pillow. "If Horace tangles with that robber, Miz Honey's gonna be right in the middle. We just can't have that."

"No, we can't," Kate agreed.

Isaac covered her hand with his big, black paw. "Then, if you don't mind, Miz Kate, I'll just keep on ailin' for a while. Won't help Miz Honey much, but at least it'll keep Horace close to home."

"I don't know what else to do," she said, giving his hand a squeeze. "You keep on ailing, Isaac. At least till we figure out something else." Kate sighed. "But please promise me something, will you?"

"What's that?"

She summoned up a tiny laugh. "Promise me you'll stop watering my petunias."

Trouble, Honey thought. Gideon was asking for it, begging for it, as surely as he was breathing. They had ridden down through the rugged hills that morning until they came to the little coal-mining town of Madrid. Once more, she was bewildered by the casualness with which her companion entered the town. Then her mouth dropped open in astonishment when Gideon drew his roan gelding to a halt in front of the bank, got down and tied the horse to the hitching rail.

"We're not leaving the horses right here, are we?" she asked as he helped her to the ground.

"Why not?"

"Well, why not just wear a sign saying Bank Robber, Gideon? Or stand in the middle of the street and announce to the whole town just what it is we intend to do?"

He looked down into her exasperated face. "*We* aren't intending to do anything. *You* are going to walk over to that emporium and buy us something a little more substantial than shortbread and jam." He stuffed a few bills into her hand and turned her by the shoulders. "Go on now."

Honey balked. "I want to come with you."

"Absolutely not."

"Gideon."

His expression hardened. "You're not coming in the bank with me, Ed, and that's final." He aimed her toward the emporium again, and this time gave her a shove. "Go on."

The last thing she wanted to do, she thought as she crossed the dusty street, was go in another small-town emporium. The little store in Golden yesterday had stirred up enough anxieties to last her the rest of her life. Over her shoulder, Honey glimpsed Gideon just as he sauntered through the door of the bank. His gun wasn't even drawn, for heaven's sake. Now how in blazes was he going to rob a bank without using his gun?

Honey shook her head. Sometimes—now, for instance—she didn't think that man had all the sense he'd been born with. Assuming he'd been born with any at all.

Muttering under her breath, she proceeded along the quiet street and into the emporium. To all appearances, it seemed just like the one she had visited in Golden. With one exception, however. One very large exception, who was leaning an elbow on the counter and who wore a very bright, very large tin star pinned to his vest.

As Honey stood motionless just inside the door, the sheriff straightened up to his full six feet, then tipped the brim of his hat in her direction.

"Morning, ma'am," he drawled.

From behind him a voice called cheerily, "Don't let this big fella scare you off, missy. You just come right on in. We don't see too many strangers around here. 'Specially ones as pretty as you."

"Tibbs is right about that," the sheriff said with a slow smile aimed toward Honey. "The pretty part, I mean." He took off his hat. "I'm Will Cummings, ma'am, and I'm right pleased to meet you."

Honey looked from the badge on his chest to the big Colt Peacemaker on the lawman's hip and felt the color drain from her face. If she wobbled she wasn't aware of it, but suddenly Cummings had one arm around her waist and was leading her to a chair beside the potbellied stove. Then Tibbs, the elderly little storekeeper, rushed over to fan her with a newspaper.

Honey kept seeing its dark headline—Third Territorial Bank Robbed—rising and falling in front of her face.

Four banks now, she thought bleakly. Gideon was just across the street. And the sheriff was here, patting her hand, wearing a concerned expression and that enormous gun. What in the world was she going to do?

She said the first words that tumbled into her brain. "I was attacked, Sheriff. Just outside of town. There was this man, and he—" Her voice broke as tears—real ones, she marveled—spilled from her eyes.

Cummings straightened up and planted his hat back on his head. "Where'd this happen, ma'am?"

Honey pointed a trembling hand south.

"What'd he look like?"

Oh, Lord. She could hardly think at all, much less come up with a believable description of a nonexistent assailant. All she wanted to do was get the sheriff out of town so Gideon could get away.

"Was he tall, ma'am?" the lawman pressed.

Honey nodded. "Yes, um, tall. Unusually tall. Six foot three or four, I'd guess."

"Big man?"

"What?" She blinked up at him.

"Was he a big man? Stout?"

She shook her head, as she cast about inside it for details. "No. He was thin, actually. Almost gaunt."

"Anything else about him, ma'am? Was this character bearded? Clean-shaven?"

"He had a beard," Honey said, lifting her hand to her face. "Just along his chin. Right here."

Lord Almighty, she thought. She was describing Abraham Lincoln. The poor man had been dead more than twenty years and here she was resurrecting him and accusing him of attempted rape.

"You just rest easy, pretty lady," Will Cummings said. "I'll ride south of town and have a look around. If he's still around, I'll find him, and when I do, you can bet that varmint will be wishing he'd never laid eyes on you, ma'am, much less his heathen hands."

"Thank you, Sheriff," Honey breathed weakly as he strode out of the emporium. "I'm better now," she told the storekeeper, who was still levering the newspaper up and down in front of her face. "I believe I'll just step outside for a bit of fresh air."

Despite the little man's protests, Honey proceeded out onto the street. She shaded her eyes in order to see the sheriff heading south as fast as his horse would carry him. All she had to do now, she thought, was get Gideon out of the bank and headed north. Fast.

The towheaded boy behind the counter was nervous. Too nervous as far as Gideon was concerned. All the other robberies since Santa Fe had gone like clockwork. The tellers had been informed he'd be coming. The canvas bags had been stuffed and ready to go. He'd barely had to say a word to the teller in Cerrillos or the one in Golden. But here in Madrid this pale, thin-lipped boy was definitely giving Gideon cause to worry. When he had walked into the bank and announced the holdup, the first thing the boy did was ask for identification.

"Gideon Summerfield," Gideon had replied, slowly, distinctly.

The boy had rolled his watery blue eyes. "You *say* you're Summerfield. How'm I supposed to know?"

"Were you expecting me?" Gideon had growled.

"Yeah."

"Well, I'm here."

The towhead, dammit, had crossed his skinny arms and had poked out his pale chin. "Prove it."

He didn't have a paper on him telling who he was, Gideon thought. Not one little scrap. Now he was faced with a seventeen-year-old who was bucking for a medal or a reward from the Bankers' Association. He didn't need this. Didn't need it at all, especially when he saw the boy's hands move out of sight below the counter, no doubt fingering a loaded .45 stashed there.

It was too late to reach for his own gun, Gideon reckoned. If he moved more than a hair now this incipient hero would do something they'd both regret for the rest of their lives. And the rest of the boy's life would be about two seconds.

"Don't be a hero, kid," he told him. "Just hand over the money."

What happened next was Gideon's worst nightmare come true as the door flew open behind him and Edwina Cassidy rushed in, face flushed, hair flying, eyes as big as headlamps on a train.

"Hurry," she urged. "The sheriff's prowling around."

Gideon tried to keep one eye on the youth behind the counter as he responded to Ed. "Get out of here.

Now." He moved his body a few inches to the left, putting himself directly between her and the nervous, perhaps trigger-happy kid in the teller's cage.

"Hurry," she insisted. Stabbing a finger at a canvas sack leaning against the wall, she hurried toward it. "Is this it? Is this the money?" Then she grabbed the sack by the handles and said, "Let's get out of here. We—"

The boy's victorious cry cut her off. "I knew it! Gideon Summerfield was supposed to be alone. You've got a partner, Mr. Whoever-You-Are. And neither you or your partner is gonna rob this bank today."

"Get out," Gideon yelled at Edwina, shouldering her right out the door just as the kid lifted the barrel of the hidden gun and took aim.

The explosion of the .45 reverberated off the walls of the tiny bank and the recoil ripped the pistol from the boy's hand and it thudded on the floor.

Now Gideon's gun cleared leather. "You let that weapon stay right where it is, you hear?" he snarled, his Colt aimed at the teller's heart as he slowly backed toward the door.

The boy went even paler and his Adam's apple jerked in his throat. "Yes, sir."

Outside, Ed was already on the dun mare. She had untied Gideon's horse and now she tossed him the reins. "Hurry," she repeated as he mounted.

Gideon swore under his breath, clamped his left arm hard as he could against his side and slammed his heels into the horse.

* * *

They rode so hard and the footing was so treacherous as they headed back up into the hills that Honey could do nothing but hang on to her saddle horn and hope she didn't pitch off Jonquil's back. By the time they were several miles outside of Madrid, though, Gideon slowed down. Grateful as she was, Honey railed at him anyway as they rode side by side.

"I can't for the life of me figure out how you made a career out of robbing banks," she said, shaking her head. "You just strolled right in there, carefree as a summer breeze and blind as a damn bat. Did it ever occur to you to look around for the sheriff first?"

When Gideon didn't answer, she blithely continued giving him chapter and verse about what, in her opinion, he had done wrong that morning.

"And for heaven's sake, if you're going to wear a gun you might as well use it. I don't mean shooting people, mind you, but that boy would never have reached for a weapon if you had held him at gunpoint. You ought to be thanking your lucky stars, Gideon Summerfield, that he didn't blow your head off."

"Yeah," he grunted.

"And as for the sheriff . . ."

"Toss me that money bag, Ed."

She sat up taller in the saddle. "I will not."

Gideon reached across the narrow space between their horses and ripped it out of her hand, then jammed the bag against his left side and held it in place with his elbow.

Honey simmered in silence for the next mile as he continued to ignore her. Then, finally, when they had reached the entrance to the mine they had left only hours before, Gideon slid down from his horse.

She waited a moment for him to help her down, as was his custom, and when he didn't, Honey slung her leg out behind her, thumped to the ground, then advanced on her sullen companion like a wraith.

"Give me back that sack," she demanded, tugging at the handle and wrenching it out of his grasp.

"Ed..."

Her jaw loosened as she stared at the blood-soaked bag in her hands. "Gideon?" Her voice was barely more than breath, and her lashes fluttered up to his face, to the gray eyes now dull and glazed with pain.

"You're hurt," she murmured incredulously.

"Listen to me now," he said, taking her chin in his right hand while holding his left arm tightly against his side. "Don't go getting panicky. It's not as bad as it looks, Ed, but I've lost a lot of blood and I'm starting to get... to get a mite hazy."

No sooner were the words out of his mouth than his knees buckled and Gideon sagged to the ground.

Chapter Ten

All the while she had struggled up the rough terrain toward the mine entrance with Gideon's solid weight, Honey's lips had moved in silent prayer. He had to be all right. Dear God, he had to be all right. She had fit her arms under his, and inch by inch, pulling for all she was worth, had lugged him up the rest of the hill.

By the time she reached the mine, her dress was ripped where she'd been stepping on the hem, and the seam at her waist had pulled out on one side. She was exhausted. Her face was streaked with tears now as she sat beside Gideon's motionless body. She didn't know what to do. She just plain didn't know what to do. Her mind was empty—a complete, forlorn blank.

"Useless," she said out loud. Even if she had known *what* to do, she didn't know *how* to do it. A person couldn't be more useless than that. She had come back home from school fully determined to show her father and the world in general that Honey Logan was a capable and responsible young woman, but so far, she'd failed every test. And now she was being tested again, only this time it wasn't money that was at stake, or making a pot of coffee. This time it was somebody's life. Gideon's life.

Honey looked down at his pale, damp face, at his side where his shirt was soggy with blood. Her hands fell open helplessly in her lap, exposing the red mark where the hot pot handle had seared her palm. Gideon had known just what to do last night when that had happened. He had rushed at her, then taken her hand and kissed the hurt away. He had been there— caring and competent—when she needed him. Now his life was pouring out of him while she was just sitting here weeping and wailing.

"You're not going to die, Gideon Summerfield," she told him. "I absolutely refuse to let you die." She got up on her knees and hovered over him. "I may not know what to do," she muttered, "but I know I'm not going to let you bleed to death."

She unbuttoned his shirt and gently tugged it from his belt, exposing the torn flesh at his side. The wound was just above his belt so she unfastened that, then unbuttoned his trousers and eased them down a few inches. For a moment her eyes lingered on the corrugated musculature of his abdomen and the soft brown hair that covered it. She touched him gently and those firm muscles twitched beneath her fingers.

As near as Honey could tell, the bullet had plowed across his side, leaving a deep and jagged furrow. The sight of the bright, sticky blood seemed to clear her head some as it stiffened her resolve. Quickly then, she ripped at the side seam of her hem and tore against the grain of the fabric until she had a foot-wide strip of material. It wasn't all that clean, she noted dismally, but it would just have to do.

Gideon groaned and tried to push her hand away as she dabbed the folded linen at the wound. His eyelids flickered.

"I must have passed out," he murmured, running his tongue over his dry lips. Then he raised his head to look around. "We made it back to the mine," he said in surprise. "How'd I get up here?"

"You flew," Honey said with all the briskness a competent nurse might have mustered. "I don't think you should waste your strength or your breath talking right now, Gideon."

He shifted on the ground, levering up slightly in order to peer down at his blood-soaked side. A low curse riffled from his lips. "Do me a favor, bright eyes. Go get the bottle of whiskey from my saddlebag, will you?"

"I really don't think you ought to be drinking...."

Gideon's mouth tightened in pain and frustration. "Just get it," he said, then sagged back and closed his eyes. "Please. Just get it."

As she trudged back down the hill, Honey noticed the trail of blood they'd left behind. Maybe she had hurt him worse by dragging him, but she hadn't known what else to do. She did know, though, that she was lucky the horses were well trained and had remained right where she and Gideon had dismounted.

Saddlebag in hand, Honey spied the bloodstained canvas sack lying on the ground. She sighed. To her way of thinking a bag of money was hardly worth risking a life for. Not Gideon's anyway. She snatched up the sack and carted that up the hill, too.

His eyes opened woozily when she knelt beside him. "Did you get the bottle?"

Honey nodded. "It's in the saddlebag. Your getting drunk might help ease the pain, Gideon, but it isn't going to do me much good in keeping you alive."

"Just keep doing what I tell you." He angled his head toward the cloth she had torn from her dress. "Soak that rag, Ed, but don't use all the liquor. Save some for me." He tried to laugh. "Save most of it."

Honey realized now how fiercely her hands were trembling, and as she tried to pour the brown liquid onto the rag, a good portion of it dripped onto her skirt. "Damn," she muttered, biting her lower lip.

"Take it easy," Gideon said.

"Easy! You want me to be all calm and collected while I sit here like a useless fool watching you bleed to death?" She shot him a look of desperation as tears welled in her eyes. "Tell me you're not going to die, Gideon. Please. And... and tell me what to do. I... I feel so helpless."

He levered up on an elbow. "I'm too mean to die," he said, taking the bottle from her hand. "And you're doing fine, Ed, honey. Just don't spill any more of this rotgut, all right?" He took a long swig and closed his eyes as he swallowed it.

She touched her thumb to the trickle of liquid on his chin. "What can I do, Gideon? Are you in terrible pain?" Her eyes searched his for an answer.

"What you can do right now is hand me that rag," he said, pulling his shirt open farther and grimacing at the bloody wound. "I want to clean this up some and stop the bleeding."

"Does it... does it hurt?" she asked, pressing the cloth into his hand, at the same time that she castigated herself for asking the question. "I'm sorry. Of course, it hurts."

"Not as much as it's about to." Gideon's breath whistled in through his teeth as he touched the whiskey-soaked rag to the wound. He swore mightily.

Honey turned away, unable to bear the sight of his face, even paler now, and the tautness of his mouth, which was nearly white at the corners.

When she turned back, he had sagged onto the ground. His eyes were closed tight and he was taking deep, rough breaths. She clasped his hand and closed her eyes, too.

After a few minutes, Gideon said, "Think you can unsaddle the horses?"

She nodded.

"We're going to need a fire, too, Ed. And some water." He squeezed her hand. "I don't think I'm going to be in any shape to do much but sleep for a few hours."

Honey scuttled up on her knees, preparing to rise. "Don't even think about it. I'll get everything done in two shakes." She pushed her sleeves up. "One shake," she corrected. "You just rest now."

Gideon caught her hand as she rose, pulling her back down. His grasp was weak, however, and Honey noticed the clamminess of his palm. "It might be a rough night, bright eyes," he said, "but I'm going to be all right. Trust me about that. I swear to you I'm not going to die and leave you out here all on your own." His pain-clouded gray eyes searched her face. "Do you believe me?"

Again, she nodded. She wanted to believe that more than anything in the world right now.

Gideon, too, nodded grimly. "Just keep me warm, if you can. That'll help. And if I get out of my head, don't pay any mind to anything I say."

"Well, that all depends, doesn't it?" she answered, forcing a smile. "Maybe you'll rave about what a wonderful, awe-inspiring person I am and how I ought to be the toast of the territory."

"I hope I do, darlin'." He sighed, closing his eyes. "I hope to hell I do."

He didn't though. In the rough bed that Honey had fashioned for him of horse blankets and his saddle, Gideon slept fitfully while Honey built a fire and warmed a pot of water to tend his wound again. This time she remembered to use a fold of her dress to shield her hand from the hot handle, smiling to herself as she recalled Gideon's patience and tender instructions about how to make coffee, how not to get burned cooking over a campfire. She wasn't totally useless now, she thought, thanks to him, and she found herself wishing he were awake to appreciate her small success, to be pleased with her and perhaps a bit proud.

But that was silly, she reminded herself. In the first place, Gideon wasn't concerned with her right now but with his own survival. And in the second place, what difference did it make if he was proud of her or not?

She was a burden to him, nothing more, and he planned to ship her back to Santa Fe at the very first opportunity.

When darkness fell, he seemed to enter a deep, peaceful slumber, for which a bone-tired Honey was grateful. She wasn't aware that she had fallen asleep until a string of curses woke her. The campfire had burned down to glowing coals, but in the moonlight she could see that Gideon had tossed his blanket aside. He lay there now, bathed in sweat and shivering so hard he was almost levitating off the ground.

He pushed her away roughly when she attempted to cover him again.

"Oh, no, you don't," Honey snapped as she tucked the edges of the blanket beneath his hips. "You told me to keep you warm and I'm damned well going to do it. Now hold still."

Gideon clamped his fingers around her wrist. His eyes were feverish and bright in the moonlight. "Goddamn you, Cora," he rasped.

Honey winced and tried to pull out of his iron grasp. "I'm not Cora," she cried. She wasn't sure Gideon heard her, much less comprehended her words. Those steely eyes of his were glittering now and his white teeth flashed dangerously.

"Damn you for shedding tears at my trial and knowing the whole time you were going to run off with Dwight. Damn you for sitting there just waiting, praying maybe, for them to put me away."

"Gideon, I'm not . . ."

Even in his weakened condition, his grip was crushing Honey's wrist.

"You were my wife! You were carrying my child, for God's sake. And it meant nothing to you. Nothing. I could kill you for that." He wrenched her closer. "For that alone, I could kill you, Cora."

"Gideon!" Honey shrieked now as much from her own fear as to shock him out of his blind rage. He was staring right at her, but he didn't know her. "Gideon, stop it. I'm not Cora. It's me. Look at me. Truly look."

His eyes closed for a moment, and when they opened again the fierce gleam was gone, replaced by a dull glaze. "Ed," he whispered as his fingers loosened on her wrist. "I thought... I don't know what I thought." He drew in a rough breath. "I'm sorry. Did I hurt you?"

She smoothed his damp hair from his forehead. "No, you didn't hurt me. You... you frightened me. Here." Honey tucked the blanket more tightly beneath him. "You need to keep warm, Gideon. You told me to keep you warm."

"I'm burning up."

Honey pressed a torn cloth to his sweat-bathed neck. "Your fever's probably breaking," she said softly, hoping it was true as she tried to keep her voice level and soothing. "It'll be morning soon and you'll be better. You'll see."

His teeth began to chatter and he didn't seem to be able to keep his eyes open. His head tossed fitfully. "Just get me through the night, Cora. Please. Just see me through this, darlin'."

Pressing her lips to his fiery forehead, Honey whispered, "I will. I promise you I will."

* * *

Honey watched the sun rise, a hot orange ball pushing its way through violet banners of clouds. Her arms were still wrapped tightly around the man who was finally, deeply, even peacefully asleep.

She yawned now, easing one arm away from Gideon in order to rub her gritty eyes. She knew she should feel exhausted, but she didn't. Instead she felt strong and almost victorious, for she had indeed seen Gideon Summerfield through a long, terrible night. He had fought her and cursed her. He had called her Cora and damned her to hell and worse. Then, toward the end, he had surrendered to his fever, his pain, his tears and to her comforting hands, and had slipped into a deep, deep sleep.

Honey had spent the rest of the night awake, holding Gideon close, wondering if half of what he'd said was true or if it was just the fever talking. Had his wife been carrying a baby when she'd left him? Had Cora sat in the courtroom, hoping they would find her husband guilty, praying they would send him away? How could that be true? Honey wondered. How could any woman turn her back on a man like Gideon Summerfield, no matter what he had done?

This man, she kept thinking, was good and kind and patient. And each time her mind created a list of his virtues, a single thought kept appearing. This man was married. And his rage at Cora probably meant only one thing. He still loved her. She was, after all, still his wife. Through the long, dark hours of the night, Honey found herself wishing Cora Summerfield had never existed, hoping the woman who had walked out on Gideon had gone so far as to vanish from the face of the earth, and once—Lord forgive her—Honey even wished the woman dead.

As the sun climbed higher, she suspected the worst was over. Gideon's brow felt cool now. His color had improved. Remembering her brothers' occasional fevers, she imagined Gideon would wake with a ravenous appetite. He would need a good meal to get his strength back. And all they had left was half a jar of strawberry jam, she thought dolefully. She had rushed out of the emporium in such a panic yesterday she hadn't gotten any supplies.

She'd have to go back. It would take her a few hours to return to Madrid, she guessed. Riding fast, she could make the round-trip in about four or five hours. Judging from his deep, even breathing at the moment, Gideon would most likely sleep several more hours. Maybe she could even be back before he woke. It would certainly make him feel better to wake to the smell of coffee and maybe even bacon sizzling on the fire.

The mere idea of food brought a twitch to her stomach along with a smile to her lips, but the smile quickly faded. What if she ran into the sheriff in Madrid? How was she going to explain her behavior yesterday? She had, after all, participated in a bank robbery. And even if she could avoid the sheriff, how was she going to pay for this feast she was imagining?

Her eyes lighted on the money bag then and her smile returned. Well, of course. She'd use some of the stolen money to pay for supplies and then she'd turn the rest over to the sheriff. Having found the perfect solution to both problems, Honey eased away from Gideon. After she straightened the blanket over his sleeping form and smoothed his hair back, she kissed him softly, then rose and walked to the bloodstained canvas sack. She opened it and promptly thrust in her hand.

All she could do was stare at the stack of paper in her grasp. She reached in and came up with another fistful, then reached back for a third. Her legs folded beneath her and she sat, dazed.

"Newspaper!" Honey opened her hands and watched as a breeze riffled through the bill-sized scraps and began to blow them away. Tears burned her eyes and a lump hot as a coal formed in her throat. "They shot him for a damn bag of newsprint!"

All nine members of the Bankers' Association had gathered in the office of Logan Savings and Loan in Santa Fe. Eight of them sat fidgeting with their watch fobs, or picking lint from their pant legs, or clearing their throats. The ninth man, Race Logan, sat behind his desk like a monolith. Stern. Immobile. His black eyebrows hovered like storm clouds above his turquoise eyes.

"I'm waiting, gentlemen," he said, his fingers beginning a slow drumming on the desk top. A drumming slow and weighty as a dirge.

There was another round of throat-clearing and lint-picking, but no one replied until Amos Tarkington stood, tugged at his waistcoat and said, "We were wrong, Race. I think everybody can see that now."

The others nodded vigorously, continuing to avoid the piercing gaze of the man who sat behind the desk.

Race crossed his arms now. The springs of his swivel chair groaned as he leaned his massive shoulders back. "You're all mighty quiet for a bunch who had so damn many suggestions the last time we met."

Tarkington sat, and John Firestone leaned forward to speak. "It never occurred to anybody that your daughter would get involved in this, Race. Believe me, if—"

"My daughter is not *involved,* John," Race interrupted. "She was *abducted* the day this bank was robbed. Whatever she's done, it's been under duress."

"Not the way my clerk tells it," Firestone said. "The lad said she was acting as lookout yesterday. Said your Honey was the one who actually carried the bag out of the bank. He said—"

Race slammed his fist on the desk top. "I don't give a damn what that trigger-happy idiot said. My daughter does not rob banks." He met each pair of eyes. "Is that clear, gentlemen?"

"Absolutely."

"Clear. Yes, that's clear."

One by one, grudgingly or otherwise, all the bankers agreed.

Then Amos Tarkington rose once more. "What do you propose we do, Race? Do you want to hire some men or organize some sort of posse?"

Race shook his head and replied, "We'll stick to the original plan. From all I can tell, that's what Summerfield appears to be doing. So we'll wait."

Eight heads bobbed in agreement.

"We'll wait," Race said again in a voice that carried throughout the room and sounded less like a banker making a proclamation than a preacher promising hellfire.

Chapter Eleven

Honey had ridden into Madrid the way Gideon should have the day before—slowly, warily, keeping out of sight as much as possible. She had left Jonquil in back of the emporium, then peered through a rear window to make sure the elderly storekeeper was alone. She had walked into the store quietly, and since there was no good way to explain her tattered and bloodstained dress or her wind-tangled hair, Honey had merely pointed Gideon's big Colt at the old gentleman and told him precisely what she wanted.

"Ain't got no bacon," he replied calmly. "Got that ham hanging up over there."

"That will have to do," Honey said, trying to sound equally calm and not to let the man see how badly her hand was shaking from fear as well as the weight of the heavy gun.

He shuffled around behind the counter, taking tins down from shelves, addressing her over one stooped shoulder. "You're that young gal sent Sheriff Cummings off on that wild-goose chase yesterday, ain't you, then helped with robbing the bank?"

She remained silent. Admitting her guilt didn't strike her as such a good idea. And she was guilty. There was no denying it. She was the one who had grabbed up the money sack, after all. Of course, if she had known it was stuffed with newspaper she wouldn't have bothered.

Taking the ham down by its strings, the storekeeper said, "You and that Summerfield caused quite a stir. Yes, sir. Word's gotten around right quick, too. There was a fellow in here just this morning asking about the two of you."

"What fellow?" Honey asked him, dreading the answer. It had to be her father. She glanced quickly over her shoulder as if she expected to see Race Logan himself towering in the doorway while sending her a killing look. Now her voice shook as well as her hands. "Who was asking about us? What did he look like?"

He stuffed the ham in a burlap bag. "Well, now. He didn't say and I didn't ask. Mean-looking character, I'll tell you. Had a beard blacker than night and a nasty scar running from here to here." The old man traced his thumb across his cheek.

Honey let out a small sigh of relief. It hadn't been her father, after all. She decided she had more things to worry about than a black-bearded stranger.

"I believe that's everything you wanted." The man pushed the bag across the counter toward her. "Don't you get twitchy on that trigger, Missy. I ain't going to shout for the sheriff. You look about half-starved to me so I don't begrudge you a few vittles."

"Thanks." Honey pulled the heavy bag from the counter and turned to the door.

The shopkeeper told her goodbye, then added, "Say, Missy, next time you're in need of a meal, I'd sure appreciate it if you'd rob old Hiram Quill over in Golden."

In spite of the crime she had just committed, Honey rode out of town laughing. She had every intention of reimbursing that sweet old codger once she got her hands on some money. Heaven only knew when that would be, though. But at least she had plenty of substantial food now. She was going to fix Gideon the best meal of his life. Not that she knew how to cook any better than a day ago, but determination had to count for something, she figured, even where food was concerned.

As she traveled back up into the hills, Honey kept looking over her shoulder, wondering about the black-bearded man who had been making inquiries earlier in the day. Only now did it occur to her that he might be someone working for her father. Someone hired to find her and to drag her back to Santa Fe.

She touched the gun she carried on her lap. Just let him try. She wouldn't go back. Not now anyway. She hadn't recovered the money yet. And she wouldn't leave Gideon. Not while he was hurt. Not while he needed her. Maybe later...

Jonquil snorted and tossed her head as Honey tugged back on the reins and brought the mare up short. It wasn't the money anymore that was keeping her with him. The thought nearly took her breath away. It wasn't the money at all. The thought of leav-

ing Gideon Summerfield—ever—made her heart feel
as if somebody had just squeezed some of the life out
of it. She'd never see the warm glint in his gray eyes
again. Never hear his patient, reassuring voice. Never
kiss him again or touch him or feel his hands making
her own flesh come alive. If she lived to be a hundred, she thought, there might never be anyone else
who could cause those peculiar knots in the pit of her
stomach with just a glance. It was for certain no one
had ever done it before.

Damnation. Honey shifted in the saddle now,
hooking a knee over the horn. She kept forgetting he
was married. It was as if she couldn't truly believe he
belonged to somebody else, when... When he ought
to belong to her? That was absurd. The man was a
bank robber. A criminal. He'd lived on the wrong side
of the law since he was ten years old. But then who
wouldn't have turned out that way when he was raised
by road agents and thugs?

Jonquil snorted and stamped a hoof, as if to inquire when they would be moving on, but Honey ignored her.

Of course, it might not be too late to change him,
she thought. Gideon was, after all, a gentleman in his
heart. If she could convince him to turn all the money
back in and to stop robbing banks, maybe there was a
chance for him to live a different kind of life. A respectable, responsible life.

"Right," she said out loud, slinging her leg back
down and finding the stirrup. "And he'd be bound to
live that respectable, responsible life with his wife."

She gave Jonquil a kick and continued on up into the hills, trying to empty her head of thoughts about Gideon. Don't even think about him, she told herself. Anyway, it might all be a waste of time. What if he'd taken a turn for the worse after she'd left him this morning? What if he'd bled to death? What if he were calling for her right now and she wasn't there?

Before Honey was even aware of it, she had the mare running flat out, fast as she could. "Faster, Jonquil," she urged. Suddenly nothing mattered, not the missing money—not her father's hot pursuit, not Cora or the black-bearded man—but getting back to Gideon.

Gideon woke with a curse. The sun was like a knife in his slitted eyes, and when he lifted his arm to shade his face, pain shot through his midsection like another bullet.

He hurt like hell, he thought, but at least he was alive. For what that was worth. Lifting his head gingerly, he noted the surroundings. The fire was dead. His horse was still here, bridled, standing over by a clump of broomweed and swishing his tail at flies. Miss Edwina Cassidy, however, was nowhere in sight.

With a sigh, Gideon lowered his head and closed his eyes again. Right then he didn't have the strength or the energy to worry about her. Maybe she was down by the creek. He imagined her with her skirt all tucked up, exposing pretty white knees and those shapely legs. He groaned out loud as his body tightened from the mere thought of her. Wasn't he already in enough pain? he wondered morosely.

For a while he drifted in and out of shallow sleep, vaguely worrying about the little bank teller, vaguely dreaming of kissing her mouth, touching her, losing himself deep within her feminine warmth. On the shoals of the dream, Gideon told himself it was all right. He was only dreaming, after all. He could allow himself those pleasures in his dreams because they would never be his in reality.

He had tried to send her back to Santa Fe, and he meant to do it again just as soon as he could. He couldn't keep her. And then, dreamily, he wondered why not. Why not? She wasn't exactly chomping at the bit to get back home. And it no longer seemed to be the stolen money that was keeping her by his side. She looked at him differently from the way she had in the beginning. At first her big, blue-green eyes had been hard as jade, hot and full of accusations. But of late those eyes had become softer, mistier, replete with warmth. For him.

She was young, untried and probably too innocent to know what she truly wanted. But she seemed to want him. She worried about him, that he knew. He remembered the way she'd called out to him to be careful, and how she'd come flying into that bank just yesterday without any thought for her own safety. And last night—as much as he could remember of it anyway—she had held him and cooled him and warmed him and even kissed him, sweetly, a time or two.

Gideon sighed, still adrift somewhere between sleeping and wakefulness. He could ask her, he thought. No harm in just asking. Wrap her in his arms and whisper in her ear, "Come to Mexico with me. Be with me. Let me love you."

Love! He nearly laughed. Now there was a word that hadn't crossed his mind since he'd been a boy. It had fallen out of his vocabulary as surely as the possibility of it had fallen out of his life. He *liked* the little bank teller. God knew he wanted her. But love? That didn't exist for the likes of Gideon Summerfield. It probably never would.

So, he'd ask her. Maybe. Taking off for Mexico as soon as his side healed didn't seem like a bad idea. The hell with Logan and his plans. The banker would never be able to find him once he crossed the border into Mexico. And the hell with Dwight Samuel and Cora. Let somebody else put his black-bearded cousin in prison or six feet under. And as for Cora...well, let her rot in hell, for she'd never wind up anyplace else.

Gideon drifted. Ed could teach him to speak Spanish. It wouldn't take him all that long to learn. Didn't he already know a word or two? He knew, for instance, that *huevos* wasn't rattlesnake. He smiled in his sleep. Oh, but what he planned to teach pretty Miss Edwina Cassidy would take endless nights, thousands of long lazy afternoons behind drawn shutters, hundreds of bright hot mornings. It might even take forever. He just might make it take forever.

He slept dreamlessly with the blanket pulled over his face to block out the harsh rays of the sun, then awakened with a jolt when the blanket was whipped away. Gideon jerked to his elbows in a haze of sleep and pain to find himself looking along the barrel of a pistol into a pair of eyes as cold as a snake's and a black beard as tangled as a weed patch. The beard split suddenly in a great, jagged grin.

"Well, I'll be damned. I didn't believe 'em when they said it was you. How the hell are you, cousin?"

"I'd be a helluva lot better if you'd get that pistol out of my face, Dwight," Gideon said.

Dwight Samuel glanced at the gun as if he had forgotten it was there, then he laughed and sank the weapon into his holster.

"I 'bout blew your head off, Gid. Didn't recognize you till you opened your eyes." The bearded man sat back on his heels, shaking his head in amazement. "Lord, you take after Aunt Carrie. Got them same wintry eyes. I'd clean forgotten that."

Gideon had no memory of his mother's eyes, but staring into his cousin's now, he clearly remembered those. No matter how much Dwight Samuel laughed, his eyes always remained hard and cold. Wintry eyes. Maybe it ran in the family, Gideon mused. They were a hardscrabble lot who'd left Kentucky only to find worse trials awaiting them in Missouri. The women had learned to be thin-lipped and sullen. The men—Jesse, Frank, Dwight, himself—had acquired the ability to kill without batting one of those wintry eyes.

"It's good to see you, Dwight," Gideon said now, and somewhere deep in his heart he meant it. Despite his anger at his cousin's betrayal and his wish for revenge, the tug of family was strong.

"You, too, cousin. You, too." Dwight's gaze went to the wad of fabric at Gideon's side. "Seems like the last time I saw you you was shot up similar. You mendin' all right?"

"It's coming along," Gideon said, ignoring the pain in his side now that there were other pains and other dangers to consider.

Dwight nodded. He tugged his dirty plaid shirt out of his pants to expose his own hair-covered belly. "Hell, I bet I can match you scar for scar." He touched a ragged, dirt-edged fingernail to a puckered inch of scar tissue. "This here's from that run-in we had with the bluebellies over in Cass County. You remember that?"

He didn't, but Gideon nodded anyway.

"You were just a little cuss then as I recall. Hell, I was nineteen. What were you, Gid? Twelve?"

"Ten," Gideon said quietly.

His cousin shook his head. "Ten. Is that all? Lordy. You were a mean little son of a bitch. Jesse always said you were probably the worst of us." Dwight's mouth twitched. "Hell of a thing about Jesse, wasn't it? By God, I had a mind to track that Bob Ford down and make him eat my gun, but..." His voice trailed off.

Gideon had been in prison in '82 when his cousin— poor, unsuspecting Jesse—had been shot in the back of the head by a member of his own gang. And, at the time, Gideon had had the same notion as Dwight and had spent long hours in solitary plotting Jesse's revenge on that miserable coward, Ford. The thought now that he had so much in common with his vicious, black-bearded cousin was a painful one.

He levered up on one elbow and gazed over the man's shoulder, off into the mountainous distance. "We've probably done enough killing, Dwight, for one family."

The bearded man stuffed his shirttails back under his belt, glowering, muttering under his breath.

"How's Cora?" Gideon kept his voice low and level as his eyes fastened on his cousin's face.

Dwight looked away. "Aw, hell, Gid. She was a faithless whore. You were better off without her, let me tell you. She done me worse than she ever done you."

Gideon didn't reply immediately. When his cousin's gaze finally flicked back to him, Gideon asked, "Did she have the kid?"

"Hell, yes, she had him. Cute little bugger, too. But all she did after that was complain. That woman had a tongue like a braided bullwhip."

Gideon's heart was pounding hard now. His muscles were tensing and his palms were beginning to sweat, but he kept his voice as cool and unconcerned as he could manage. "Had a boy, did she?"

Dwight looked him full in the eye now. "Yours, I expect. She named him Gideon anyway."

"Where is she? Where's the boy?"

"Dead." Dwight shrugged slightly and shifted his stance. "Both of 'em. We were in West Texas. The boy took sick. Cora went about a day after he did. I buried 'em real nice. Bought 'em a marker, too."

The knot in Gideon's throat threatened to choke him as he lowered his shoulders onto the saddle behind him. Good riddance, he told himself. Except for the boy. Christ Almighty! A son! He'd had a son. Just the knowing shouldn't hurt so much.

Dwight reached out a hand to nudge him on the leg then. "Where you got the girl stashed, Gid?"

"What?"

"That girl you kidnapped. Where'd you stash her? How much are you asking for her? Hell, I told the boys I bet Race Logan would cough up plenty, ten or twenty thousand maybe, to get his daughter back."

"She's not Logan's daughter. She's a teller in his bank. And I didn't kidnap her." Gideon felt a grin testing one edge of his mouth despite his grim mood. "The lady just kind of latched on to me."

"Just latched on to you." Dwight chuckled while he dug his fingers deep in his beard to scratch his chin. "Ain't that something? You always were one lucky son of a bitch where females were concerned. But stupid, too. Damn lucky and damn stupid."

"Is that right?" Gideon growled.

"Hell, Gid, you're sitting on a gold mine and you don't even know it." He hooted and slapped Gideon's leg. "You walked out of that Santa Fe bank cuffed to the owner's daughter. His only daughter. Honey's her name. Ain't you one lucky son of a bitch. Damn!" The black-bearded man craned his neck over his shoulder, peering around the mine entrance. "So where is she?"

Oblivious to the pain in his side, Gideon sat up. "Where'd you get that information, Dwight?" Obviously his cousin had been misinformed, he thought. The daughter of the bank president didn't work behind the counter.

"Don't you think I know what's what?" Dwight answered. "I been in the territory better than a year now. I guess I know what's what and who's who around here. And I guess I know who's about the richest man in New Mexico with a daughter who looks right like him.''

Jesus! She did! Why hadn't that ever occurred to him? Gideon wondered now. He'd only seen Race Logan once, that day the banker met him at the train, but the man had memorable looks. Those turquoise eyes, in particular. Just like Ed's. You'd have to be blind not to notice it. Or blinded by your own foolish yearnings.

And those foolish yearnings had led him right up to the threshold of asking her to go to Mexico with him, to share his life. He had thought . . . Hell, what difference did it make what he'd thought? The idea of Race Logan's daughter even looking at the likes of him was laughable. The notion of her going away with him was a joke. A cruel joke. Right now Gideon wasn't sure who had played him for a worse fool—Ed or Gideon himself.

Dwight leaned toward him and nudged his arm. "Now that I've helped you discover that rich little mine, Gid, how 'bout I help you dig out some gold?'' His jagged grin widened.

Gideon didn't answer. His eyes were focused on the dun mare that was rapidly approaching from the south.

Honey's heavy heart lightened and took wing the second she spied Gideon—standing—standing tall— and her face broke out in a happy, relieved grin. He was alive. He was all right. He was standing. She would have known that stance anywhere, she thought, and those broad shoulders, those lean hips and long legs. The fact that he wasn't standing there alone didn't seem to register on her until she had pulled Jonquil to a stop in front of the mine.

The fact that that man had a full black beard and an ugly scar high on his cheek was dawning on her just as Gideon reached up and hauled her off Jonquil's back.

Honey shrieked and struggled.

"Hold still," Gideon snarled.

"That man," she cried. "He's come to take me back to Santa Fe, hasn't he?"

He wrestled both of her arms behind her back and pulled her close against him.

His voice was harsh and low, and his breath rushed hot at her ear. "That man is Dwight Samuel, and he'd just as soon rape you as look at you, Miss Honey Logan. Now, for God's sake, just hold still."

Chapter Twelve

Honey went still within his arms. Her breath ceased and she was sure her heart had stopped beating.

"That's better," Gideon whispered. "Now you listen to me. If you want to stay alive, bright eyes, you do exactly what I tell you to." He clasped his arms more tightly around her, at the same time widening his stance so his legs, too, seemed to surround her. "You hear me?"

"I . . . I hear you."

"Good. Now kiss me."

Her face jerked up to encounter his fierce, implacable gaze. "What?"

"I said kiss me. And make it good, so my cousin over there believes he'd have to walk over my dead body to lay even so much as a finger on you."

He had barely finished speaking before his mouth settled over Honey's with an urgency that rocked her to the soles of her feet. Her attempt at protest only served to make it easier for his hot tongue to invade her while one of his hands splayed over her breast.

When he lifted his head, Honey drew in a ragged breath. She was dizzy. Gideon steadied her with his arm.

"That should do it for a while," he said coldly.

That had done it, all right, Honey thought. Her stomach had dropped someplace impossibly low in her body and her heart had catapulted into her throat. Her brain was in utter confusion and she couldn't quite focus on Gideon. All she saw was the white slash of his smile.

"Why, Miss Logan," he taunted, "don't tell me your rich, fancy boyfriends don't kiss you that way."

She forced her wet, trembling lips to form words. "They... they wouldn't dare."

Dwight Samuel's shadow fell across them. "Lookee what I found in her gear," he said, letting Gideon's gun dangle from his index finger. "This yours, cousin?"

Gideon's wintry eyes held Honey's as he reached for the gun. "It's mine." He jammed the weapon into his belt, adding, "She wouldn't know how to use it anyway."

"All I know how to do is go to tea parties and fancy balls," Honey muttered. "Isn't that right, Mr. Summerfield?"

The dark-bearded bandit looked from the glaring woman to the scowling man. He scratched his chin for a minute, then shrugged. "I found this here ham and some other vittles, too. I believe I'll just give my boys a holler. They're plenty hungry." He handed the burlap sack to Honey. "Let's see what you can do about fixing us some hot grub, little lady."

Gideon laughed. "You'd be better off eating dirt," he said, as he took the sack from Honey's hand and shoved it back at Dwight. "Have one of your boys see to this."

The bandit smirked. "She pretty useless, is she?"

Honey's mouth opened in protest, but rather than speech her breath chuffed out of her when Gideon grabbed her around the waist and moved her uphill toward the mine entrance, calling over his shoulder. "Useless, yeah. But she sure is pretty, cousin. We're going to just have ourselves a little lie-down."

She had no choice but to move forward in his iron grip. "I take back every nice thing I said about you," Honey snarled as she stomped beside him. "You're not a gentleman at all. You're nothing but a goat."

When he didn't answer, Honey continued her verbal attack as much to berate him as to vent her own anger. "How dare you paw me! And in front of a man like that. And how dare you give him the impression that we're coming up here to... to..."

"Act like a couple of goats?" Gideon stopped in his tracks and pulled her into his arms. "That's exactly what I want him to think. And I want him to damn well believe I'm the king of the goats. Now just shut up and help me up this goddamn hill before I fall right back down."

Honey took a step backward the moment his arms loosened. "Gideon! You're bleeding again." The bandage on his side had turned a deep and frightening crimson. It seemed to darken as she watched.

"Only a bucket or two," he said through clenched teeth. "I've got to lie down, bright eyes, before I fall down. Let me lean on you, will you?"

She slipped her arm around his waist, edged her shoulder under his arm and led him to the makeshift saddle and horse blanket bed she had made for him the day before. Once there, Gideon lowered himself with a sigh.

"Lie back," Honey said. "I got some fresh linens in town. Some laudanum, too. They're in my saddle-bag."

He clamped his fingers around her wrist as she got up to leave. "Stay here."

"But, Gideon..."

"Do what I say. Just wait till Dwight's gone. I don't want you anywhere near him."

"All right," she said grudgingly.

"And do me a favor. Get the gun belt you took off me. Put it back on me." He pulled the pistol from his belt. "See that this gets in it, too. Now let me just close my eyes for a minute."

No sooner had he closed his eyes than he seemed to relax into some faraway place inside his head. He stirred only slightly, lifting his hips an inch or so as Honey struggled to put the gun belt on him. When she buckled it, his lips moved just a bit, first in a dreamy smile, and then to murmur, "That's it, Ed, honey. Hold my hand now, will you? Yeah. How'd you get such tiny hands?"

Honey gazed at their joined hands. She wanted to say that hers weren't tiny at all. Only in comparison with his. But Gideon was fast asleep before she could speak.

The campfire cast its wavering orange glow on the faces of the men who were gathered around it. Six men. Twelve eyes that kept straying in her direction. Honey scooted a little closer to Gideon, whose two-hour sleep seemed to have restored much of his strength, to say nothing of his determination to remain king of the goats.

Goats indeed. Dwight Samuel had come back with the rest of his gang of misfits and outlaws. There were two Mexicans, Valez and Cordera, who sat shoulder to shoulder in the firelight and whispered to each other in Spanish. There was a half-breed named Charlie Buck—his black braids falling from the brim of a dusty bowler hat—who barely spoke at all. And there was a boy they all called Shooter, who had wild, curly hair and feverish eyes and hands that couldn't keep still. He spit whenever he talked and his voice was high and whiny. He reminded Honey of a rabid dog she had seen when she was a little girl in Loma Parda. That wild-eyed animal had frightened her, but not one whit more than Shooter frightened her now.

A jug of mescal was making its way around the circle, and the outlaws were slowly and very deliberately getting drunk. All but Gideon, Honey noticed. She watched each time he tipped the jug. He never swallowed. Not once. The drunker and louder the others became, the more silent and sober Gideon seemed to be, although no one seemed to notice but Honey.

Shooter swigged now, wiped his sleeve across his mouth, then passed the jug to Honey. When she grasped it, the boy didn't let go immediately, but spread his thin fingers over hers and made a wet, clicking sound with his tongue.

Jerking the stoneware crock away, she used what remained of the hem of her skirt to wipe the lip and took a long, burning swallow of the mescal she had previously declined. Maybe, she thought, it would help her endure this horrible night.

"Careful." Gideon's voice was low, threaded with amusement. He grinned as he took the jug from her hands. "This isn't like your fancy sherry, bright eyes. It packs a little kick."

She was well aware of that. Her throat felt scorched and her eyes were watering fiercely. "Thank you," she rasped indignantly. "I believe I know what I'm doing."

Dwight Samuel leered at her from across the campfire. "That goes down real smooth, don't it, Miss Logan?"

Honey nodded. The bearded outlaw on the opposite side of the campfire was little more than a blur for the tears in her eyes.

"Give her another little taste," Shooter said, leaning across Honey toward Gideon, reaching for the jug unsuccessfully, then letting his empty hand fall in Honey's lap.

Gideon passed the crock to Charlie Buck on his right, then turned slowly back. His eyes were dark as the night sky, glittering with anger rather than stars.

"If you want to keep that hand, boy, you get it off my woman. Now."

Shooter glanced down at his errant hand, surprised, as if it had landed in Honey's lap all by itself. He giggled nervously, lifting it from the folds of her skirt and wiping the palm along his pant leg. The boy drawled a long curse, then he rose unsteadily to his feet and made his way to the opposite side of the fire where he folded his legs and clamped his wayward hands under his armpits.

It seemed to Honey that she could almost hear an audible sigh of relief rise from the two Mexicans and the half-breed. Her own subsequent sigh was more of a chuff because just then Gideon leaned back against a rock and hauled her roughly onto his lap.

"What are you—"

"Be still," he hissed at her ear as his arms clamped even more tightly around her.

From across the campfire, Shooter glared at them and muttered a string of spit-drenched curses until Dwight shot his elbow into the boy's ribs. "Stealing from banks is one thing, boy," the bearded outlaw said, "but you gotta learn right quick not to trespass in matters of the heart else you're gonna find yourself with a fist in your face or a bullet in your brain." His dark eyes met Gideon's. "Ain't that right, Gid?"

A pine log popped in the fire, sending a shower of sparks high against the dark sky. Honey could feel every muscle in Gideon's body grow taut and then slowly release before he replied.

"That's real sound advice, cousin. I hope your young friend there decides to take it."

No one spoke. Not even Shooter. The men all stared into the flames uneasily. The tension was wire-tight until Dwight leaned back on one elbow, took a long swig from the jug, then slapped his knee and hooted.

"Damn but you always had you a way with women, Gid. Hell, I remember that time when Frank and I took you to that fancy house in Fort Smith. What were you then? Fourteen? Fifteen?"

From her perch on his lap, Honey felt Gideon shift his seat on the ground.

"I don't think that's such a good story, Dwight," he said, "considering the company."

Considering her virgin ears, Honey thought. Too useless to do anything and now too innocent to hear anything. Her curiosity and the mescal she'd swallowed combined to get the better of her. "The company doesn't mind," she said. "Tell us what happened in Fort Smith, Dwight."

At her back she heard Gideon utter something between a growl and a sigh of resignation as Dwight leaned forward to begin his tale.

"Well, now, me and my cousin Frank decided it was high time Gideon got acquainted with the fairer sex." Dwight raised a black eyebrow in Honey's direction. "I 'spect you catch my drift, Miss Logan."

"Indeed I do." But in spite of her reply, Honey was already regretting having given her permission to proceed with the story. Not only was the topic unseemly, but she found suddenly she didn't want to hear stories about Gideon with other women. It was difficult enough to tolerate the idea that he had a wife someplace without having to listen to tales of his exploits with other women. The ones, as his cousin had so aptly put it, Gideon "had a way with."

"Frank and me, we pretty near had to hog-tie Gid to get him through the front door of Miss Lizzy Dolan's fancy house. The boy was shaking like a willow in a windstorm." Dwight laughed. "You remember that, Gid?"

The reply was a terse and guttural "yup."

"Well, we slapped a five-dollar gold piece in his quivering young hand and told him to choose a sweet young thing and take her on up the stairs, but before he had a chance, Miss Lizzy herself took young Gideon by the hand and led him up the staircase."

The bearded outlaw paused to let out a long sigh. "That Lizzy. She was a redhead with the milkiest, whitest skin I ever did see. Woman had a body that would drive a preacher right out of his pulpit." He lifted his hands to his chest, curving them. "She had these..."

Shooter's eyes had widened perceptibly and the boy's mouth gaped as he listened. Honey thought perhaps her own expression mirrored his.

"They get the picture, Dwight," Gideon said, angling his head toward Honey to remind the outlaw of her presence.

Dwight snorted. "Yeah. Okay. Where was I? Well, there they went upstairs, redheaded Lizzy and shaky-kneed Gid. Frank and me, we sat downstairs and waited. And we waited. We sat there with our hats on our knees half the damn night till Frank finally sent one of the girls upstairs to inquire. Miss Lizzy sent her right back, saying young Gideon would be along in a day or so. Said we oughta just make ourselves right comfortable till then.'' He snorted again and chuckled. ''Hell, we got so comfortable, Frank and me, we robbed two trains and a savings and loan while we waited for Lizzy to let that boy come on back downstairs.''

The two Mexicans laughed quietly, whispered to each other in Spanish and nodded approvingly in Gideon's direction.

Shooter glowered. ''Hell, I don't know why anybody'd want to spend his time with a damn whore when he could be out robbing a train. Don't make no sense to me.''

It made complete sense to Honey, even though she had only the most vague and hazy notions of what might have been taking place upstairs in that fancy house in Fort Smith. The whole time Dwight had been speaking, Gideon's fingers had been drifting up and down her arm, a feathering touch that stood her nerves on end.

She had tipped her head back onto his shoulder, angling her gaze in the hope of seeing one of his slow smiles, only to witness a faraway look in Gideon's eyes as he listened to his cousin. It was that distant expression, Honey thought, that bothered her more than anything. Because he was touching *her,* here and now, and all the while his fingertips were bringing all of her senses to life, he was apparently reveling in the memory of some alabaster-skinned, redheaded madam in Fort Smith.

Shooter continued to scowl and to spit his protest. "I'd sure as hell rather be sticking up a train than sticking—"

"Shut up, kid," the half-breed, Charlie Buck, warned him abruptly.

Suddenly Honey became aware of the eyes that had stopped staring into the flames and were staring now at her. Dwight Samuel's eyes glittered above the dark mat of his beard, and the scar that sliced across his cheek glowed menacingly in the firelight. The Mexicans were staring at her, too, while they exchanged low, sibilant whispers.

In addition, Honey became intensely aware of the rise and fall of Gideon's chest against her back, the hard tension in his thighs, the coiled power in his arms. She counted his heartbeats through her shoulder blade, his warm, even breaths on the side of her neck. And, even though she couldn't see it, Honey could feel the chill of his gaze as it connected with each pair of eyes around the campfire.

Then Gideon's hand moved—slowly—sinuously— sliding from her arm to her rib cage, then up, coming to rest just underneath one breast.

From the other side of the fire, Shooter's eyes opened wide and burned hot as they followed the progress of Gideon's slow hand. The other men's gazes were dark and shuttered. Dwight Samuel's mouth twitched in the black depths of his beard.

"Don't s'pose you're willing to share, are you, cousin?" the outlaw asked.

Honey, already barely breathing, held what wisps remained of her breath as Gideon slowly moved his hand higher. His warm fingers splayed out, one at a time it seemed to Honey and in slow, slow motion, until he engulfed her. Then, while the five men stared, Gideon grazed his thumb blatantly back and forth across her nipple. "Nope," he said. The word was a low rumble in his throat.

The campfire crackled and shot sparks toward the night sky. For a long moment—one of the longest in Honey's whole life—no one said a word. No one blinked. The entire world, it seemed, and all of the eyes in it, focused on Gideon's hand as it laid public claim to Honey's breast.

At last Dwight coughed, slapping his hand on his knee. "Can't blame a man for askin'" he said with a shrug, then he tipped the jug of mescal and took a long drink before he passed the liquor to Shooter. "Here, boy. You drink enough of this and pretty soon you won't even know what a woman is, much less what one is for."

The highly charged atmosphere around the campfire seemed to dissipate following Dwight's remark. Valez and Cordera leaned back on their elbows, extending their boots to the fire. Shooter dug his head into his shoulder, ignoring everything but the jug of mescal. The night air itself seemed to grow cooler then, and Honey shivered beneath Gideon's hand. He slid both hands around her waist, then lifted her to her feet.

"We're going up the hill now," he said, unwinding his long legs and rising. His gaze circled the campfire, pausing briefly on each man. He touched his gun briefly before he rubbed the flat of his hand over his belly. "See you gents in the morning."

As Honey climbed the hill, away from the firelight and into the darkness, she was bewildered by her behavior. It wasn't like her to keep silent when threatened, and yet she hadn't said a word when those outlaws had ravaged her with their eyes, had regarded her with the same hungry intensity as five coyotes coming upon a defenseless doe. She had sat there—on Gideon's lap, in the warm curl of his arms—and allowed him to be her savior, her protector. And she had allowed it, not simply because it was the sensible thing to do under the circumstances, but because she wanted his protection. Despite the danger of the situation, in Gideon's arms Honey had felt more secure than ever before in her life.

His display had been a ruse, of course, meant to warn the outlaws to keep away from her. Yet Honey found herself wishing it were real. Ruse or not, his touch had set up a tingling in her nerves and had warmed her blood to the boiling point. If Gideon had only touched her to proclaim himself undisputed king of the goats, she decided, then she wanted to be queen.

His hand was warm on the small of her back now as he guided her up the hill, and when they reached the entrance to the mine there was only moonlight.

Gideon kept his hand on her back as he said, "You'll be safe tonight. Nobody will bother you, bright eyes."

Honey lifted her face to his. In the moonlight Gideon's eyes were silver. Silver and soft and beguiling.

"Nobody?" she whispered.

Chapter Thirteen

Gideon couldn't resist. He didn't know how any man with any blood at all in his veins could have, though he damned himself anyway as he lowered his mouth to Miss Honey Logan's inviting lips. She was soft and warm, sweet as her name. "Honey," he breathed against her lips. She melted beneath his kiss, and a tiny, breathless moan escaped her. And when he circled her with his arms she felt boneless as a rag doll. But warm. So warm.

His head was swirling with the faint taste of mescal on her tongue and the fragrance of her hair. He'd spent the last few gut-chilling moments at the campfire proclaiming his right to this woman in order to keep Dwight and his randy cutthroats at bay. The woman had been his, all his, for all of them to see. And for a brief moment back there, as he was touching her, Gideon had believed it, too.

But she wasn't his. Even as he drank from her sweet, deep mouth, he knew she wasn't his. Maybe if she were still Edwina Cassidy, still just a simple bank teller. Maybe if her prospects were slim, if life were going to offer her nothing beyond hard work. If she were still his Ed. But she was Honey Logan, the daughter of one of the richest men in the territory. That meant her life held promises that Gideon Summerfield couldn't keep.

He dragged his lips from hers, breathing hard as he held her soft, yielding body against his. If he had been a religious man, he would have been praying. For strength. For oblivion. For an end to his torture.

Honey was breathing hard as well. Her arms clung tightly around his waist, then tighter still until Gideon winced. Suddenly remembering his wound, Honey let go and took a small step back.

"I'm so sorry, Gideon. Did I hurt you?"

He drew in a slow breath, let it out even more slowly. "You didn't. I'm fine."

"Good," she said, not totally convinced as she studied his face in the moonlight. If it wasn't pain she saw in his expression, then what was it? Disappointment, perhaps? Or guilt? Married men, after all, weren't supposed to be going around kissing other women. And she had invited his kiss just then. There was no doubt about that.

"It was my fault," she said. "I shouldn't have—"

"Ed," he snapped, interrupting her, "it was nobody's damn fault. It was a kiss."

"Yes, but I shouldn't have..."

Gideon lowered himself to the blanket, pulling her along with him. "You didn't do anything you have to be ashamed of. And we're not going to do it again, so just stop talking about it. All right?" He dragged his fingers through his hair. "Hell," he said gruffly, "it didn't mean anything anyway."

"It meant something to me," she said softly. "You mean something to me, Gideon."

He stared up at the bright disk of the moon, so bright it diminished the stars.

Honey continued, her voice very low, hardly more than a whisper as she watched Gideon's stern profile, edged by the soft light of the moon. "I know it's wrong. I know I shouldn't have feelings for a married man." Her voice wavered. "But I do. Lord help me, I do."

Gideon didn't answer immediately. Lord help *me,* he thought as he gazed on high. "I'm not married," he said at last.

"But Cora—"

"Is dead," he said, cutting her off. "She took a fever a while back. In Texas. Dwight buried her. He buried my son, too."

Honey rested her cheek against his shoulder. "Oh, Gideon, I'm so sorry."

"Don't be. Don't waste your sympathy on a whore who ran out on her man."

"I wasn't," she said. "It's you I'm sorry for, Gideon Summerfield. Sorry that you've had to lose so much. You deserve better. More."

"You think so, bright eyes?" he murmured, unable to look into those bright, sea-colored orbs right now. They'd be shimmering like moonlight on a midnight sea. They'd make him forget who he was and what he had to do.

"I know so," she answered softly.

It should have been so easy, he thought. This, after all, was what every man wanted—a woman, a mate who believed in him, in whose warm and misty eyes he could see himself as good and strong and even deserving of life's best. It would have been so easy to turn then, to fit his arms around her fragile shoulders and tilt her head just so for his kiss, to adjust her body beneath his for his need. So easy. And so damn wrong.

For if Honey Logan believed he deserved more, he believed the same about her. She deserved more than he could ever offer her. His desires for her happiness and well-being far outweighed the physical desire he was feeling now. Bleakly, Gideon wondered if that was love. If it was, he thought, it was a fine joke on him. Having spent all his adult years believing the emotion was beyond him, to feel it now for a woman he couldn't have was the darkest, grimmest joke he could imagine.

"Go to sleep, Honey," he said, a bit more gruffly than he had intended.

"But I..."

The strain in his voice was evident now. "Just go to sleep."

Honey curled up beside him on the blanket. Judging from his voice, she thought his side was probably bothering him more than he wanted to let on. She was tired, too, and wrung out from the tense situation around the campfire. But tired as she was, her mind couldn't let go of what Gideon had just told her. Cora was dead. He wasn't married anymore. He was free. Well, in a manner of speaking.

He was still a bank robber on the run. So, in fact, was she. But there had to be a way to solve that problem. Honey drifted into sleep, trying to figure it out.

"I just don't understand him, Mama," Zack Logan grumbled as he sat at the dining room table finishing his breakfast. "Or maybe I do. Maybe all those stories about Papa are nothing more than a lot of hot air."

With two of her three youngest sons fed and dressed and sent off to school, Kate reclaimed her seat at the foot of the table. "Pass me the butter, please, Zack," she said briskly. "And quit dawdling. You're already late for school." And don't press this subject, she was thinking. Please.

The boy slid the covered dish in her direction. "My sister's run off somewhere in the company of a thief. God only knows what's happening to her, and Daddy's acting like everything's right and dandy with the world."

Kate buttered her toast with deliberation. "Your daddy's first concern right now is Isaac," she said. She lifted her gaze to meet her son's. "You might express a little more concern for the man whose name you bear, Zack. Seems to me you've hardly been in to see Uncle Isaac more than two or three times since he took ill."

The boy slumped in his chair, fidgeting with his spoon. "I can't stand seeing him that way. And anyway, Uncle Isaac doesn't even know whether I've been in to see him once or two hundred times."

"You don't know that for certain," Kate said, glad that she was still the only one who had guessed the true nature of the wily old man's condition. "At any rate, your father believes his place is here with Isaac now." She sighed before adding, "And I agree."

"My father," Zack snarled, "ought to be out hunting down that outlaw and getting Honey back, instead of wringing his hands and keeping watch in a sickroom like...like some old woman."

Kate's knife met the edge of her plate with a resounding clack. "And you, young man, ought to watch your tongue. I won't stand for it."

"But, Mama, he's—"

"That's enough, Zack. Leave the table now, please. If you'd like to stop in to say good-morning to your Uncle Isaac before you leave for school, I'd appreciate it and I'm sure he would, too. Otherwise, just go on."

"Yes, ma'am." Unable to meet his mother's fierce gaze, Zack slid out of his chair and stomped out of the dining room.

He moved like Race, Kate thought as she watched her son walk out the door. He was already nearly as tall as Race. She marveled at how broad he was becoming in the shoulders. His face was showing the first shadows of whiskers, and it wouldn't be long before his daddy or his Uncle Isaac would be showing the boy how to lather up and shave.

She sighed as she picked up her methodically buttered wedge of toast. Through the years, she had always been able to cool her son's hot temper and make him listen to reason, but it wouldn't be long before

Zack stopped listening to her. The boy had grown up not only to look just like his father, she thought, but to act like him as well. Stubborn. Convinced of his own opinions. Determined to do what he wanted to do.

But it was different somehow with Race, who had been his own boss since the day his father was killed by Indians out on the Santa Fe Trail. He had been three years younger than Zack back then. But Race had had responsibilities he'd had to shoulder. His stubbornness and determination had been channeled into his business, and those qualities had served him well. Plus, Race had always had Isaac Goodman by his side like a dark guardian angel.

Kate smiled, biting off a corner of the toast. Isaac was still looking out for Race, playing sick to keep him home, to keep him from killing Gideon Summerfield. Zack, on the other hand, if he went off half-cocked as she was afraid he might, had nobody to restrain him. He had his father's oxlike strength and his mulish streak, all right, but he lacked his father's skills, the ones Race had learned so early and so well in order to stay alive.

Kate reached for a second piece of toast. Of course, Race and Zack weren't the only mules in the family. There was stubborn Honey. Even Kate had been accused of that trait a time or two, though when it came to herself she preferred thinking of it as determination and strength of will.

If only Honey would come home, she thought. "Daughter, daughter, what are you doing out there?"

Kate murmured as her gaze drifted to the window. "What's keeping you away?"

She didn't have to wonder who. Race had described Gideon Summerfield in a single word—wolf. A cold, cautious creature who lived on the fringe of the civilized world. It occurred to her then that perhaps she—rather than Race or Zack—should be the one to go looking for Honey and to bring her back. Certainly a worried and unarmed mother was no threat to Summerfield, to the wolf. If it were Kate who went after Honey, there would be no danger of anybody's getting killed. She might not be successful in her quest, but she wouldn't leave a trail of blood in her wake.

Kate frowned. Except Race would never let her go. If he knew.

She chewed thoughtfully and stared out the window. Race wouldn't have to know.

"Wake up, bright eyes."

Honey struggled to open her sleep-ridden eyes. For a second she didn't know where she was. Only that the sun was shining down on her. The sun and Gideon's warm, gray eyes.

He slipped an arm beneath her shoulders and sat her up. "Come on, Miss Stay-Abed. We're riding out."

She simply sat there, still half-asleep, trying to fit her dazed thoughts together like some kind of jigsaw puzzle.

Gideon's fingers began to comb through her hair. "As soon as we get to Cerrillos," he said softly, "we'll get you a hairbrush. A new dress wouldn't hurt, either.''

Honey looked down at the stained and tattered rags she'd been wearing for days. Her father had never spared any expense in clothing her, and she had always believed she needed elegant dresses to achieve true beauty. But when she raised her eyes to Gideon's, Honey—in her rags and ratty hair—felt more beautiful than she'd ever felt in her life.

And then Gideon's words fit together like puzzle parts in her brain. "Cerrillos?"

"Uh-huh," he said, still running his slow fingers through her long hair. "I'm taking you back there and then, since I can't trust you to stay on the train, I'm going to telegraph somebody in your family to come get you."

Somebody, Honey thought gloomily. That somebody would undoubtedly be her father, ready to skin her alive for the robbery at his bank, as well as for taking his horse.

"I'd rather stay with you," she said. "Couldn't we just..."

"No." Gideon's fingers withdrew from her tresses, then he lunged to his feet. "Come on. Let's go. I've already got your mare saddled. The sooner we get away from here the better."

Grudgingly, still stiff with sleep, Honey stood. Well, she had to admit she wasn't looking forward to spending any more time than she had to with Dwight Samuel and his greasy, leering gang. She followed Gideon down the hill, where it appeared only the dark-bearded outlaw was awake. The rest of the men were still sprawled under their blankets.

Dwight Samuel touched his hat brim. "Mornin', Miss Logan."

"Good morning, Mr. Samuel," she said, trying to sound prim as a schoolmarm as she glimpsed the little leer the man's dark beard couldn't disguise. Honey felt the color rise in her cheeks. The outlaw's thoughts were obvious. And why not, after the way she and Gideon had left the campfire the night before? It galled her to feel embarrassed for something she hadn't even done, to be hung for a sheep rather than a wolf. Or a goat.

Gideon led the dun mare toward her. "Let's go," he said.

"Don't you forget that telegram now, cousin," Dwight Samuel said. "We'll be waiting right here. How long you think it'll take?"

As he gave Honey a boost onto the mare's back, Gideon said, "Two or three days."

The bearded outlaw laughed. "Hell, I've been in the wrong business all these years, Gid. If I'd known how easy—"

"I hear you, cousin." Gideon scowled as he jerked on Honey's stirrup, fitting its length to her leg. "How's that?" he asked her.

"Fine," she said.

Gideon swung up on his horse then.

Dwight Samuel swept his stained hat off his head and pressed it over his heart. "It's been a real pleasure knowing you, Miss Logan. Do give your daddy my regards. And," the outlaw said with a chuckle, "tell him Dwight Samuel said 'thank you kindly.'"

While the man stood there laughing, Gideon gave Jonquil a slap on the rump that sent both Honey and the mare off at a furious pace. It was only after several minutes, when they had ridden well out of earshot, that Honey was able to ask, "What did he mean by that? About thanking my father?"

Gideon shrugged. "Probably just Dwight's roundabout way of saying he appreciates your looks, bright eyes." He gave her a slow wink. "Ignorant as my cousin is, he still recognizes a fine woman when he sees one."

Honey gave a tiny snort. Gideon was lying to her, she knew, but she didn't feel like confronting him just then. It was a beautiful morning and she was awake enough now to appreciate it. The sun washed her face with warmth while a gentle breeze played through her hair. Even Jonquil seemed to respond to the loveliness of the day as she trotted along smoothly. There would be time later, Honey decided, to quiz Gideon about his cousin's odd remark.

Anyway, there was something else she wanted to discuss with him. He was riding a few paces in front of her, relaxed in the saddle, apparently enjoying the beautiful morning as much as she was.

"Gideon, I was just wondering," she began, her voice light and as free of guile as she could manage, "what would happen if you gave all the money back?"

He laughed as he glanced back over his shoulder at her. "Why, I suppose half a dozen bankers would rush to shake my hand and to tell me what a superior fellow I turned out to be."

Honey scowled. He wasn't supposed to be so cavalier about this. "I'm serious," she insisted. "What would happen? If you gave the money back, I mean. Would you still be sent to prison?"

"No." He angled around in the saddle, facing her. He wasn't laughing anymore. His expression was as dark and serious as she had ever witnessed. "I'm never going back to prison, Ed."

"But what if..."

"Never."

Gideon kicked his horse, bolting away from her, and Honey had to make Jonquil pick up her pace in order to keep up with him. She watched his back, no longer relaxed, but tense. Each taut muscle pressed distinctly against the fabric of his shirt. She longed to smooth her hands over that wide expanse, to soothe the tension there. She thought perhaps if he talked about his experiences in prison, if he brought those ghosts out into the sunlight, then they wouldn't be able to haunt him so.

After he slowed down, she said, "Tell me about it. I've never even seen a one-cell jail."

His tone was terse, low. "I hope to hell you never do, bright eyes. Prisons are about as ugly as you'd expect them to be. They tend to make the men inside them ugly, too."

She raised a curious eyebrow. "Then you weren't treated well?"

Gideon laughed harshly. "Maybe for a dog! The warden and I didn't exactly see eye to eye. He was a

Union officer during the war, and even though he'd traded in his blue uniform he still had a battle or two to get out of his system. Plus with every lick he took at me, he figured he was getting one in on my cousins."

"How cruel. How unfair," she said.

"Maybe. But that's the way it was. The thinking in the prison system is that a man's spirit has to be broken before it can be healed."

Honey sniffed. "Well, obviously they couldn't break yours."

"No," he said, then added softly, "but they sure as hell tried. I really don't want to think about it anymore, Ed, honey, much less talk about it."

"Please," she urged. "I'd like to know you better, Gideon. I want to know everything about you."

"Everything!" He laughed. "I'm not that interesting, believe me. Just another border state ruffian who got pushed every which way by the war. Without that damn war, my life would have been a lot different."

She cocked her head. "What would you be doing today if there hadn't been a war?"

Gideon shifted in the saddle, turning toward Honey, and felt his heart quicken at the sweet expression on her face. It wasn't an idle question. This woman truly seemed to care about his yesterdays. And the light in her eyes told him she cared about his tomorrows, too. Nobody had ever expressed such interest or wide-eyed concern. Gideon felt his throat thicken.

Swallowing hard, he tried to clear his head, to clear his heart so full now with childish longings and adult desires. He'd never known a woman like Honey Logan, but he told himself that he'd never known a female of quality, a daughter of wealth and promise. Maybe they were different. Maybe at fancy schools they taught these females how to dazzle men with personal questions and fake concern, how to reel in the unsuspecting fools with their big, quizzical eyes and sweet, false-hearted tones. That had to be it. She was merely playing the role she'd been taught. And here he was falling for it like a two-ton elephant. Like an ignorant slip of a kid.

He pulled back on the reins at the same time that he snagged the mare's bridle, halting her.

"What do you want from me?" he snarled.

Honey's eyes widened now, not from curiosity but from fright. She had seen Gideon's face look fierce before, but never quite like this. His eyes were dark, diamond hard. His knuckles were white where he gripped the mare's bridle, preventing Honey's escape. She had no idea what she had said to set him off this way, to make him this furious with her.

"I d-don't know what you're t-talking about," she stammered now.

"The hell you don't, bright eyes," he said as he swept her off Jonquil's back and hauled her onto his lap.

"Stop it," she shrieked. "Gideon, what's gotten into you?"

His arms tightened around her, holding her hard against him. His words were a hot rush against her ear. "You. You've gotten into me with your big eyes and your well-schooled sympathies. Bankers' daughters don't care about thieves, Ed, honey. They don't give a damn about their yesterdays and they care even less about their tomorrows.''

"But I . . .''

He caught her chin with a viselike grip, turning her face for the full brunt of his gaze. "Maybe you can play your rich boyfriends like fancy violins. Maybe they like it. But I'm not one of your elegant, well-raised boys, Honey. I'm not used to ladies like you who say one thing when they mean another. I'm not some damn yo-yo on a long string that you can just twirl around your little finger.''

"I didn't—''

"What do you want from me?'' he shouted. "What do you want from a man who can't give you anything? From a man who can barely see straight from looking at you or barely walk anymore from tripping over his own confounded heartstrings?''

"I don't . . . I mean . . . Oh, Gideon, are you? Are you truly tripping over your heartstrings?'' She threw her arms around his neck and whispered against his ear. "Oh, I hope you are because I love you so.''

He closed his eyes, feeling her heart beating against his, breathing in her sweet flowery fragrance, savoring her words and, at the same time, hating himself for his own.

"Honey,'' he whispered, letting his lips touch her soft hair. There was nothing else he could say. And, sadly, there was nothing he could do. Not now. Not ever. Only send Miss Honey Logan back to her father, back to a man who could care for her properly, the way she deserved.

Chapter Fourteen

Cerrillos was quiet when Honey and Gideon rode up to the hotel where they had stayed just days before. They didn't see anyone on the street. Only a few scrawny hounds and a pig, which was rooting through a pile of garbage.

"Siesta time," said Honey when Gideon lifted her down from Jonquil's back.

He smiled. "That doesn't sound half-bad."

His lazy drawl, coupled with the idea of curling up in the warmth of his arms, sent a quick little shiver the length of Honey's spine. She raised her eyes to his, but only to witness that warm smile fading to cool purpose. He turned away from her then, removed their gear from the horses and, with one saddlebag draped over each shoulder, ushered Honey inside the small lobby.

The gangly young clerk at the desk snapped to attention immediately. "Howdy, Mr. Summerfield. Ma'am." He lifted a key from a hook on the wall behind him. "I got your same room all clean and made up. That the one you want?"

"That'll do fine," Gideon said as he signed the clerk's register. "The lady will be wanting a nice hot bath."

"Yes, sir."

Honey, who was leaning wearily against the wooden counter, let out a long sigh. "A bath! Lord, I'd almost forgotten there were such things."

The first thing she did once they were upstairs in their room was to sit on the bed and bounce. "A bed and a bath!" she exclaimed. "I do believe I've died and gone to heaven."

Gideon slung the saddlebags onto a chair, then just stood there grinning at her. Her sheer joy over such simple pleasures almost made him forget the luxuries she must have been accustomed to. It pleased him to please her, to bring that happy light to her eyes and such a bright smile to her pretty mouth. Even if it was only a lumpy bed in a cheap hotel and the promise of a bath.

He tamped down on the urge to join her on the bed. Sighing, he walked to the door. "They should be up with the tub and the water soon. Don't open this to anybody else, Ed."

"Where are you going?"

"Telegraph office."

Her smile evaporated. "Oh."

His hand was on the doorknob now. "Be sure you lock this after I'm gone, all right? Ed, honey? All right?"

"Yes. I heard you," she grumbled.

He had almost closed the door when she called to him. "Watch out for those heartstrings, Gideon. I wouldn't want you tripping down the stairs."

His muffled curse coincided with the click of the door.

The telegraph office was in the squat frame building that also served as the train depot. It wasn't far from the hotel, and by the time Gideon arrived he had already framed the message he was going to send to Race Logan in Santa Fe. He wrote it out quickly for the stationmaster, but as he handed him the message, a gun clicked at Gideon's head.

"Tell him to read that out real loud."

When Gideon recognized the voice of the half-breed, Charlie Buck, he shook his head with disgust. He was getting slow-witted, he thought, probably because of Ed. He should have figured Dwight would send somebody after him to ensure that the ransom demand was sent.

"Read it yourself," Gideon said.

"Can't." Charlie Buck aimed his pistol at the stationmaster, whose pale face was now glistening with nervous sweat. "Read it."

The man glanced at Gideon for permission. After Gideon nodded his assent, the stationmaster cleared his throat and read. "To Race Logan, Santa Fe, New Mexico Territory. Your daughter is waiting for you at the hotel in Cerrillos."

"Is that all?" Charlie Buck asked.

Nodding, the man thrust the paper in front of the half-breed's face. "That's it. That's all it says. Ain't even signed. See."

The half-breed didn't even look at the paper. Instead he turned his dark eyes on Gideon. "Do it proper now."

Gideon grabbed the paper from the stationmaster's trembling hand and snatched the pencil from behind the man's ear. He turned the paper over and scribbled furiously. "There," he said, shoving the note across the counter. "Read it to him now."

After clearing his throat again, the man read, "Your daughter is at the hotel in Cerrillos. Bring ten thousand dollars if you want to see her alive."

Buck's mouth widened in a smile. "Send it," he ordered the man.

Once again the stationmaster looked to Gideon for permission, as if it were Gideon who held him at gunpoint rather than the half-breed.

"Go ahead. Send it." Gideon shrugged, turned on his heel and stalked toward the door as the telegraph key began its nervous tapping.

"I'll be watching you, Summerfield," Charlie Buck called to him.

"That's what I figured," Gideon said. He walked out the door and slammed it behind him.

He muttered and cursed himself as he stormed into the hotel lobby, then pushed through the batwing doors into the saloon. The bartender immediately put a bottle of rye on the bar, and Gideon poured himself one quick shot and then another.

Damn! Where had his head been this morning? He could easily have bushwhacked the half-breed, leaving Dwight none the wiser about the ransom note. But, he thought dolefully, his head had been somewhere in the clouds and his eyes had been on Honey Logan's pretty face and his heart had been unraveling like a ball of twine in a litter of kittens.

Gideon cursed again.

The barman leaned forward on his elbows. "That rye's not the best, Mr. Summerfield, but I've got some that's worse."

"It's fine." Gideon poured another glass. After he drank it he slapped a coin on the bar. "I'll just take the bottle," he said, turning and walking back through the saloon doors.

He climbed the stairs slowly, ignoring the half-breed, who was seated in the lobby now with his bowler hat tilted to one side and his rifle across his knees, watching out for Dwight Samuel's greedy interests. Well, hell, Gideon thought. Honey didn't have to know that Charlie Buck had followed them. He'd just keep her in the room till tomorrow.

The ransom demand had been sent. And tomorrow Race Logan would come, but whether it would be with ten thousand dollars or half a dozen hired guns, Gideon had no idea. All he knew was that he couldn't let Logan's daughter out of his sight now, especially with Charlie Buck sour-faced and rigid as a cigar store Indian in the lobby. And Gideon also knew he wasn't looking forward to sharing a small hotel room with Miss Honey Logan for the next twenty-four hours.

Clutching the bottle in one hand, his other gripping the wooden banister, he recalled her words earlier in the day when she had proclaimed that she loved him. Fool that he was, he thought now, his heart had drummed at the sound of the words. He had felt like a pup, wagging his tail, rolling over to get its belly rubbed.

Gideon scowled. Love. That wasn't what she meant. Maybe if she were still Edwina Cassidy, bank teller, working girl, he might have believed her. But Honey Logan was a rich girl in the midst of an adventure. He was probably the first man she'd ever been alone with. Lord knew she'd hardly ever been kissed before. And, healthy female that she was, the situation was stirring up things inside her. Feelings and desires she'd never felt before. What she said and what she meant were two entirely different things. She wanted him, sure, but her breeding and her fine education made her clothe those naked, indelicate desires in the finery of love.

Loved him! Hell, even Cora had never said she loved him, and her subsequent behavior had proved that to be all too true.

At the top of the stairs, Gideon stumbled. The bottle thunked against the wall, and he grasped the banister to keep from pitching backward down the stairs. He told himself it was the three quick shots of rye, that it had nothing to do with heartstrings or the fact that just thinking about Honey Logan made him dizzy with desire and regret.

He paused with his hand on the doorknob. All he had to do was get through the next twenty-four hours.

This would conclude one of two ways—Honey would either be ransomed from him quietly or wrenched away at gunpoint. All he had to do was keep her safe until then. That was the easy part. The hard part would be keeping himself safe from her.

Gideon turned the knob, and when the door gave easily, he charged into the room.

"I told you to keep the goddamn door locked," he bellowed.

Honey grabbed for the bath sheet on the foot of the bed at the same time as she slid down neck-deep in the metal washtub.

Gideon just stood there looking at her. The anger that had blazed in his eyes seemed to alter as she watched. They turned a soft and hazy ash gray, a shade that set the butterflies skittering in her stomach again.

"I'm . . . I'm almost through," she told him. "The water's still warm, Gideon, and I haven't dirtied it up so much that you couldn't have a wash yourself. If . . . if you wanted to, that is."

He blinked and the gray haze dissipated. "I told you to lock the door, Honey," he said gruffly. "You're damn lucky it was me who walked in and not some dirty prospector looking for a good time."

She shifted in the tub, sloshing water over the side. "Well, I don't think I'm so confounded lucky, Gideon, to be walked in on by somebody in such a foul mood. At least some dirty prospector might have a kind word to say to me." She sent a spray of water in his direction.

Gideon released his breath in a low growl as he walked toward the bed. He unbuckled his gun belt, slung it on the bedpost, then slung himself down on the mattress. After sighing roughly he didn't say a word.

Honey arched another spray of bathwater in his direction. "Why are you always so put out with me, Gideon?"

"You didn't do what I told you. You didn't lock the damn door."

"I'm sorry. I forgot. After the boy from downstairs poured all that wonderful, steaming water into the tub, I couldn't think of anything but jumping out of my clothes and into my bath."

Gideon merely grunted in reply, reaching up to punch the pillows beneath his head. Then he crossed his arms over his chest and settled his hat over his face. He could hear her swishing around in the water, and then the distinct sounds of a wet body rising out of a tub and the rustle of dry fabric against damp skin. If anybody had told him back in prison a few weeks ago that he'd be in this situation and not even be tempted to peek, Gideon would have laughed and called the fella six kinds of fool.

But he wasn't tempted now. Just listening to her was enough to start his bloodstream rushing south. He didn't need to ache worse than he already was. The way he was feeling right now, he thought, he'd be lucky if he could even talk much less walk by tomorrow afternoon.

The mattress shifted then and he edged up his hat an inch to see Honey—her pale skin still glistening and damp—sitting quietly beside him. She was clutching the towel around her, but it dipped in back to reveal a length of spine that was as beautiful and as delicate as a rope of pearls.

"Did you send that wire to my father?" she asked. Her voice was quiet, inquisitive, without a trace of anger.

"Yes, ma'am," Gideon said, trying to sound stern and decisive despite the pummeling his heart was giving his rib cage just from her very nearness.

She sighed. "I suppose that means he'll be here sometime tomorrow."

"I expect so."

She turned to him then, crooking one long, bare leg up on the mattress. Her eyes were huge, soft, sad. Her voice was barely a whisper. "Then we don't have much time, do we? To be together, I mean."

Gideon couldn't help himself. He lifted his hand to push a damp strand of hair from her shoulder. Then he traced his finger across her cheek. "It's just as well, bright eyes," he said softly.

"I meant what I said this morning, Gideon. About loving you."

His hand gently cradled her cheek now. The warmth of her skin made his palm tingle. "You've got feelings for me, Ed, honey. Stirrings inside that you've probably never had a chance—"

She cut him off with a snort and a toss of her head. "I'm twenty years old, Gideon. I believe I know the difference between what my heart tells me and what the rest of my body is fairly screaming." She drew in her lower lip then, as if trying to suppress the warm flush that was dappling her cheeks.

"Ed, honey, you shouldn't—"

"Don't you tell me what I should or shouldn't feel," she snapped. "I can love you if I want to, dammit. And I love you, Gideon Summerfield. With all my heart and all my soul. I love you." Her eyes flooded with tears and she took an angry, backhanded swipe at them.

He wanted to run out of the room and get as far away as fast as he could. And he wanted to hold her close, closer than his own hard-pounding heart, and never let her go. Between those two extremes, Gideon was nearly paralyzed.

She lifted a tear-dampened hand to touch his cheek, whispering "It's all right. I don't expect you to love me back."

Gideon could hardly breathe now for emotions churning in him and the unspoken words that were nearly choking him. This was crazy. It wasn't meant to be. Ever. Yet there she was—loving him. Truly loving him. He could see it in her eyes. And here he was, about to blubber like a baby, about to blurt out that he loved her, too.

He reached up and drew her against him, feeling her tears dampening his shoulder. He stroked her hair then. "Don't, Honey. Don't cry. Hell, darlin', I can't give you anything except my love. And that's a worthless commodity if ever there was one."

She sniffed as she lifted her head from his shoulder. "Are you saying you love me?"

He rolled his eyes in exasperation and clenched his teeth, but she persisted.

"Gideon, is that what you're saying?" Turquoise eyes honed in on his now. Her pretty mouth twitched in a taunting grin. "Tell me you don't love me."

"I wish I could," he said somberly.

"You wish you didn't love me?"

"Yeah, bright eyes. I wish I didn't love you."

Nestling into his shoulder again, she breathed, "But I'm so glad you do."

As Gideon held her close, he stared at the ceiling, thinking she wouldn't be so glad or so in love tomorrow when her father showed up with her ransom.

Kate was playing a game of ringtoss with three-year-old Neely when the boy from the telegraph office came through the gate in the adobe wall. She straightened up from gathering one of her son's wild pitches, brushed the hair from her temples and greeted the gray-uniformed messenger.

"I got a wire for Mr. Race Logan," the boy said, looking beyond Kate toward the front door.

"I'll take it," she said. "I'm Mrs. Logan."

"I'm to give it to the mister," he said, moving to step around her.

Though he was nearly as tall as she was, Kate caught him by the collar. "The *mister* is taking a siesta, young man, and if you disturb his sleep, the *missus* is going to make sure this is the last message you ever deliver." She snatched the paper out of his hand.

Grumbling as he straightened his jacket, the boy then stomped back to the gate. He turned, though, before he was out on the street, and he shook his fist at Kate and called, "I guess I know about you, Mrs. Logan. I guess what people say is right. You ain't no real lady. You're..."

Kate launched the hard rope ring toward his head, and the boy ducked through the wall and disappeared. As her son laughed and charged across the courtyard to retrieve the ring, Kate read the telegram.

Her hands trembled as she folded the message from Cerrillos and tucked it into the pocket of her skirt. Then she collared little Neely, deposited him in the kitchen with the cook and proceeded to Isaac's room.

Kate's voice was an urgent whisper. "Isaac, I need your help."

The black man opened a single eye. "Uh-oh."

"Uh-oh is right," Kate mattered, fishing in the depths of her skirt for the telegram, perusing it once more. "That Summerfield man wants ten thousand dollars in exchange for Honey's life."

Elbowing up, Isaac took the message from her. As he read it, his grizzled eyebrows drew together and his forehead furrowed. "Horace know about this?" he asked when he had finished.

Kate shook her head. "No, and he's not going to if I can help it. That's why I need your help."

"You could get in a heap of trouble, Miz Kate, taking this on all by your lonesome. Horace'll go right through the roof."

"I'd rather have him going through the roof alive than lying dead in Cerrillos, Isaac," Kate snapped. "I want my daughter back safe and sound. If handing ten thousand to that...that greedy, thieving varmint will accomplish it, then that's what I intend to do. I'll take the morning train tomorrow. That ought to get me to Honey by noon, at least.''

''Well, that's the getting there. How 'bout what you're taking? You just gonna pull all that money out of the air?''

''I wish I could.'' She sighed. ''I'm going to the bank right now while Race is sleeping, and I'm taking whatever I can find in the safe. There's some currency. I believe there's some gold as well.''

The old man shook his head. ''I figured that criminal wrong, Miz Kate, thinking he was keeping Miz Honey purely out of affection for her.''

''I guess we both figured wrong.'' Kate stood up, once again stuffing the telegram in her pocket. ''I'm depending on you to keep my secret and to do whatever you have to to keep Race here after I'm gone.'' She paused, taking the old man's hand in hers. ''You've never let me down before, Isaac.''

''I ain't about to start now, Miz Kate,'' he said.

Gideon shifted in the washtub, seeking a more comfortable position. It was like trying to take a bath in a thimble, he thought, with his long legs draped over the end of the tub and his elbows either poking him or cracking against the metal rim whenever he moved. A bath had seemed like a good idea earlier, but not only was the washtub smaller than it looked, the water wasn't as cold as Gideon had hoped it would be when he had undressed with his back to Honey a while ago. In fact, the condition he had attempted to hide from her was no better now than it had been before. He was still hard as a smithy's hammer, he thought grimly, and Honey's ravishing, sheet-draped pose on the bed wasn't helping his situation one little bit.

He sighed and squeezed the washrag above his head, letting the cool water run through his hair and trickle over his face.

"Gideon," Honey said from the bed, "you never did answer my question about what you'd be doing if it hadn't been for the war."

There she went again, asking those wide-eyed, curious questions about his yesterdays. But the question hit him differently now that he knew her interest was genuine, prompted by affection rather than guile. For the first time in his life, Gideon found he actually wanted to share his memories.

"I guess I'd be farming," he replied. "More than likely anyway. It's what my father did before he died. I guess it's what I always assumed I'd do. Till I was ten anyway."

She shifted so her head was at the foot of the bed. Lying on her stomach, she propped her chin on her hands. "What did he farm?"

"Hogs mostly. We had a few acres of corn." Gideon tilted his head back onto the rim of the tub and closed his eyes. "Lord, how I loved that corn."

"To eat, you mean?"

He shook his head. "That, too. But I remember I used to stand in the field with cornstalks taller than I was on all sides of me. Just stand there in all that green, feeling the sun on my face and listening to the wind. The wind makes a peculiar sound moving through a cornfield. It sounds almost alive. Like a big green animal twisting and shouldering its way to where it wants to go."

Honey shivered. "Sounds scary."

"No. Not scary. It was..." He paused, his eyes still closed, searching for a word, finding it deep in his heart. "It was holy. Made me feel more religious than any church I was ever in."

"Would you try farming now? I mean, if you could?"

Gideon opened one eye, riveting her with his gaze. "What do you think, bright eyes? Kind of hard to farm when you're on the run, don't you imagine?"

She sat up, crossing her legs and readjusting the bath sheet around her. "So stop running."

Something between a laugh and a curse escaped his lips, then he closed his eyes again.

"I'm serious, Gideon," she insisted, scooting closer to the foot of the bed.

"Ed ..." he growled.

"Listen to me for just one minute, will you? Gideon, I have property back in Kansas that was left to me by my grandparents. A couple hundred acres, I guess. To tell you the truth, I never paid much attention to it before. It's being farmed by tenants now. But there's no reason why you couldn't take on some of it. Or all of it for that matter."

He was silent a moment—deeply touched by her offer. She meant it, by God. This beautiful woman would do that for him. And a part of him yearned to say yes, ached to go back to the life that was wrenched away from him when he was a child. It would be,

Gideon thought, like getting a chance to live his life all over again. This time as it was meant to be.

"Gideon? Did you hear me?"

All he could do was stare into the tepid bathwater and nod. He was afraid to speak. He couldn't bear hearing himself saying no.

Then Honey reached down from the bed and brushed the damp hair from his forehead. "Gideon Summerfield," she whispered, "did you hear me asking you to marry me and take me to Kansas?"

Chapter Fifteen

The late-afternoon sun cut a golden swath across the room, and where Honey's fingers threaded through Gideon's hair, the rich light picked out a few silver strands among the cool, damp locks. Cinnamon, she thought. Delicious cinnamon shot through with sugar. He sat silently, eyes closed and head tilted back, as if mesmerized by her touch.

She remembered once seeing her Uncle Isaac stroking a wounded mountain cat to calm it. The animal's eyes had closed with a strange mixture of fear and pleasure, and it had made a low, guttural sound somewhere between a purr and a hiss as its tawny pelt had rippled beneath Isaac's hands. Gideon was like that now, she thought. A wild thing just gentled for a moment. Not tame. No. Far from tame. But gentled all the same.

Honey had felt vague stirrings earlier when she had watched Gideon undress. Her attention was drawn first to the bruised, torn flesh at his side, but then her eyes roved over the powerful muscles of his shoulders, the hard planes of his backside and the long sleek cords of his legs. Those stirrings had increased when she glimpsed the desire he was making such an effort to conceal. More than mere stirrings now, they seemed to tighten, whirling like a cyclone, a storm centered deep and low inside her.

As they talked, she had watched the water wash over the contours of his chest, intrigued by the way the soft hair flattened then sprang quickly back to life. By the time their conversation had turned to farming, Honey had barely been able to remain on the bed. Her hungry eyes had begun to devour the man in the washtub, and her hands had fairly itched to slide over his glistening muscles.

With her heart nearly bursting with emotion, the proposal of marriage had sprung from her lips without even passing through her brain. It had surprised Honey almost as much as it had Gideon. But she didn't regret it. In fact, she was glad for once her brain had failed to censor her heart.

You didn't even know he was alive a week ago, her brain told her now. How could you love so fast? And marriage! That's forever. Longer. Forever and a day. This is crazy!

But it wasn't, her heart replied. Hadn't her mother loved her father the minute she'd laid eyes on him? And hadn't she given herself to him that very day?

She slid off the end of the bed and curled her arms around Gideon's neck, pressing her lips to the damp hair at his temple. "I can barely breathe for loving you, Gideon," she whispered.

He wasn't breathing at all, he thought. And when Honey's hand slid down his chest and came to rest over his heart, Gideon knew she had to feel the hard hammering there. It would be a pure miracle if it didn't burst right out through his ribs. He kept his eyes closed tight, trying with every ounce of his being to maintain control, to keep from succumbing to her whispers, her warmth, her gentle touch. To keep his mind cool while his body was hot enough to boil the water in the tub.

"Love me, Gideon."

Her breath shivered over his ear, sending a shock of wanting clear through him.

He covered her hand with his. His voice was thick with desire, edged with restraint. "Ed, honey, I . . ."

Her warm tongue tested his ear then and her voice was barely more than moist breath. "Love me, Gideon, please. I want you so."

His restraint—what there was of it—snapped like wire strung too tight between fence posts, and all his defenses collapsed as Gideon reached back and pulled Honey around to the side of the washtub and drew her close. The visions that swirled through his head then were of the two of them, somewhere, Kansas perhaps, lost in the midst of tall green corn with sunshine pouring through the golden tassels and wind singing through the broad curved leaves.

He wanted nothing more in the world that moment than to possess that vision in all its beauty and warmth and innocence. He wanted this woman with a fierceness that he could no longer deny. Drawing his legs beneath him then, in one fluid movement Gideon rose from the water with Honey cradled in his arms. She gave a happy, surprised little cry, lifting her arms to circle his neck as he carried her to the bed.

It was sunset now and the white sheets where he laid her reflected the rich colors of day's end—the warm golds and brilliant pinks. Gideon smelled like soap and sweet, sweet summertime. His skin, still wet from the bath, was cool and smooth beneath Honey's palms.

There was nothing cool or smooth about his kiss though. He held her head between his hands, angling it for the ferocious ravishment of his mouth, the plunder of his tongue. It seemed less kiss than claiming. When Gideon sank his teeth softly into her lower lip, a searing heat went rushing through her like wildfire, and Honey strangled a gasp.

Gideon rose on an elbow, breathing hard, his fingers still tangled in her hair. Honey read the question burning in his eyes as he gazed down at her.

"Yes," she said. "I'm only a little afraid. I've never... Oh, Gideon, I want to do this right, to please you and I...I don't know what to do...or how...or..."

"Ssh." He stilled her with a brief, undemanding kiss, then his lips quirked into a grin. "It's been such a long time since I've done this, sweetheart, it's like my first time, too. I'll take it as slow as I can," he said, dipping his head to nibble at each corner of her trembling mouth. "Lord, you taste good."

Honey sighed as much with pleasure as with relief. "Should I...should I touch you?" she asked, sliding her hand as far as his waist.

Gideon's grin weakened as he drew in a rough breath and captured her wayward hand with his. "Not yet. Let me touch you." He levered up farther on his elbow and slowly peeled the drapery of bath sheet from Honey's shoulders.

"Ah, Ed, honey," he whispered as his warm gaze slid from her collarbone over her breasts and firm, flat belly. "Look at you, darlin'. You're beautiful. You're so damn beautiful."

His fingertips drifted down from her neck to trace a lazy figure eight around her breasts. Eyes blazing as he watched their crests tighten in response to his touch, Gideon lowered his head to take one rosy bud in his mouth. Honey's fingers threaded through his hair as his warm tongue played over her nipple.

"Gideon," she murmured. "You're making me all wild and skittery inside."

He lifted his head only long enough to reply "Good" and then lavished the same attention on her other breast while his hand moved slowly over the flare of her hip and down her legs. When his fingers found the damp heat between Honey's thighs, he caught her little moan of pleasure with his mouth. And now it was Honey whose teeth dragged gently on his lip, whose tongue invited him more deeply, more sweetly inside her.

She whimpered and her hips thrust upward against his hand.

"Slow," Gideon whispered against her ear. His voice was ragged, hoarse, as if even his vocal cords had tightened along with the rest of him in a fierce effort to hold back until he gave her the pleasure she so eagerly sought. The pleasure this beauty deserved her first time, her every time. Maybe he couldn't give her the world, he thought, but he could make it magically explode for her.

He forced himself to turn his thoughts inward, away from her warm sleekness, toward Kansas or wherever it was that the corn grew tall as elephants and the wind stalked like a green beast through the fields. If he could be there someday, with Honey, maybe his life could begin again, could happily end. Maybe. Maybe. The words pounded in his brain like a chant, distracting him from his own increasing need. Maybe. And then Honey was arching against his body, hot as pure sunshine, gasping, sighing his name like a sweet summer wind.

"Gideon."

The whole room seemed to shimmer as Honey opened her eyes. Her whole body was shimmering, from her scalp to the tips of her toes. Then Gideon was kissing her again, urgently now, as his body moved over hers and his knee separated her legs. He whispered something quick, something she couldn't quite comprehend, just before his mouth took away her breath and consumed her little cry of pain and surprise as he thrust into her, filling her, completely, beautifully.

"Slow." The word rumbled deep in his throat as if he were talking to himself. His big hands grasped her hips and held them still for the slow and rhythmic movements that soon set Honey burning again, reigniting the fire that she was sure had burnt itself out only moments before. And when his pace increased she moved with him, her hands roaming restlessly up and down his slick back, her breasts damp with his musky sweat, his name like a song on her lips.

There was a tight coil deep inside her. It tightened until Honey didn't think she could stand it another second, and then it sprang loose and wild at the same moment that Gideon shuddered fiercely and bit down on a groan.

He sank into the crook of her neck, his heart battering against hers, replicating the rhythm of her own. In the silence, as evening fell about them and darkness penetrated the room, Honey was sure she could hear their hearts beating as one, singing the same song. She knew no other heart would ever match hers the way Gideon's did now. Now. Tomorrow. Forever.

She drifted into sleep listening to that precious music.

Something brushed against Gideon's shoulder. He twitched in his sleep, then his hand snapped up and grabbed, twisting and crushing the object in his grasp. At the sound of a small voice crying out, he came fully awake to find a hank of Honey's long, dark hair in his tight fist.

"I'm sorry I woke you," she said softly.

"It's all right." He hadn't meant to sound gruff, but he did. He had been dreaming he was back in prison, in solitary, on the cold stone floor of a cell. When the soft hair brushed his shoulder, he'd immediately taken it for a rat. Some of them were nearly as big as cats in Jefferson City.

Not a rat at all though. Rather a cat, purring now and curling sensuously against him. Gideon shifted his arm to pull Honey closer. He stroked her silky hair.

The room was nearly dark with only wavering light from a torch or two somewhere down below on the street. Noise from the saloon drifted up through their open window. The string band was playing a sprightly tune Gideon didn't recognize. That was what happened when you lost five years of your life in a hellhole like the Missouri State Penitentiary, he thought as he stared at the dark ceiling. The whole world carried on, writing new books, making up new songs, making love—while men moldered in cold, silent cells, alone.

As Honey snuggled against him, Gideon sighed inwardly. He had just made love to a beautiful woman. He had just given and received more passion than ever before in his life. He ought to be lying here glowing like a log on the grate, or up crowing like a rooster. Instead he was cursing himself for his loss of control, for taking Honey's innocence when he had nothing to offer her in return.

Hell, she was so innocent he wasn't even sure she knew the risk she was taking or the consequences of their lovemaking. What if she ended up carrying his child? At the thought, Gideon's heart felt as if it were folding in upon itself. He'd had a son with Cora, a child he'd never even laid eyes on, a boy buried in a little grave somewhere in West Texas. He had Dwight Samuel to thank for that.

Honey moved sinuously, draping one leg over his, pressing her small hand over his heart. "Do you suppose we've made a baby, Gideon?" she murmured, as if she had read his very thoughts.

Christ Almighty! He hoped not. "I doubt it," he said tersely. "It's pretty unlikely the first time."

She was quiet, letting her fingers drift over his chest. Finally she said, "That's how my mother got me. Her first time. One skyrocketing Fourth of July night with my father. She told me she loved him the minute she laid eyes on him."

Gideon chuckled softly as he began to thread his fingers through her hair. "That would explain it then, I guess."

"What?"

"That peculiar light in your eyes. Must have something to do with all those fireworks when you took hold."

Honey sighed. "Maybe. My father went away the very next day and Mama married somebody else to give me a name. That was my papa, Ned."

"Cassidy?" He remembered the name she had told him originally. Still, Gideon had a hard time picturing Race Logan abandoning a pregnant female. He had an even harder time imagining the tall, virile banker allowing his child to be raised by another man. He recalled his own torment when Cora had run off with Dwight. And he felt an even more piercing stab of pain now imagining Honey turning to another man, child or no child.

He smoothed a hand along Honey's arm, and asked as much out of curiosity as a wish to change the subject, "What happened to Cassidy?"

She didn't answer, but moved more closely against him.

"Honey? What happened?" he pressed.

"He died." Her voice was cool, almost indifferent, then it warmed slightly as she continued. "My real father, Race Logan, came back from the war and claimed Mama and me, and we lived happily ever after."

Not all that happily from the sound of it, Gideon thought as his fingers combed idly through her long hair. If anybody deserved to be happy, it was this warm, loving woman. He only wished he would be the one to provide her with that happiness. Given half a chance, he could. He was sure of that. Only problem was nobody was going to give him that chance.

Not Race Logan, that was for sure. Not now. The banker had promised a parole after Gideon upheld his part of their bargain. Once he had lured Dwight Samuel and his gang into the doomed holdup in Santa Fe, he was supposed to return to Jefferson City, pick up his papers and then he'd be a free man. Gideon wasn't sure he'd ever trusted that to happen. Now he knew it never would. If he had figured Logan right, Gideon thought, the banker would just as soon see him rot in hell right now for what he'd done to his daughter.

Fair enough, Gideon thought. He'd feel the same way about any man who hightailed it with his daughter, not to mention taking her to bed. And besides, the parole—whether it happened or not—wasn't why he'd agreed to come to New Mexico in the first place. His purpose had been revenge, pure and simple. He'd come to find his cousin and his runaway wife. He'd never been quite sure, though, what he'd meant to do to Dwight and Cora once he'd found them. Now, with Cora dead, there was only his cousin to be dealt with.

Honey's hair warmed to the touch of his hand, slipped like smooth summer lake water through his fingers. He wondered if her property in Kansas had a lake, and fleetingly imagined the two of them swimming in it, naked and joyous as children. But that was just a dream, one he'd likely keep dreaming now for the rest of his life.

Prison was what was real. Gideon had never truly counted on Logan's ability to get him out. Now he knew the banker would gladly slam the door himself and throw away the key. So his well-made plan was going to have to change some. The fake holdup was going to be a real one, at least for him, and while Dwight and his thugs were being picked off one by one, Gideon was going to arrange his own parole—a quick and permanent trip across the border.

Despite Honey Logan. Or maybe because of her. Despite his feelings for her. Or maybe because of those feelings that were already making his heart ache like a rotten tooth. He loved her. That was a fact. But still he had to leave her. He couldn't go back to prison. Not now. Not again.

Once was enough. He'd been tough enough once. But not twice. And not now. For as surely as Gideon knew he loved Honey Logan, he also knew that with the first crack of the whip, the first boot in his ribs, the first cold touch of the hard stone floor and the first long silence of solitary—without Honey—his mind would snap and he would never be whole again.

Right now his mind snapped back to the present, to Honey's soft hand traveling slowly over his abdomen, moving down.

He stopped her, clasping his fingers gently around her wrist, berating himself for not getting up as soon as he woke, getting dressed, getting away from . . .

"I want to touch you," she said, her breath shivering over his breast, her hair shimmering across his skin. "Don't you want me to, Gideon?"

His sigh was as frayed as each and every one of his nerves. Once, twice? he wondered. How many times could he take her, how many times could he pour his love into her without tempting fate beyond its limits? And how could he say no when this was all he would ever have of her, when a single night would have to provide them both with a lifetime of loving?

"Touch me, darlin'," he whispered hoarsely. "I love your sweet, soft hands."

Chapter Sixteen

Kate Logan tugged off a glove, then used the heel of her hand to rub a patch of dirt from the window of the train southbound from Santa Fe to Cerrillos. When her view was cleared, though, she hardly noticed the passing landscape or the bright incandescence of the morning sky.

Every once in a while she moved her foot to reassure herself that the small leather valise was still safely stowed on the floor beneath the folds of her long gray skirt. Once again she clicked open the filigreed watch pinned to the lapel of her jacket, then tucked in her chin to read it.

Nine o'clock. Race would have been to the bank by now, she thought. If she had done a good enough job rearranging the contents of his safe, he'd never notice the missing cash or the fact that there were only eight gold ingots now rather than a dozen. She didn't believe she could count on that owlish teller keeping his promise not to tell Race she had been in the bank, but if she was lucky, her husband wouldn't realize she was gone until late afternoon, when she was already coming back from Cerrillos on the northbound train. Coming back with their daughter.

Kate dropped her gaze to her lap where her fingers were twisting the gold ring she had worn for so many years. She felt the rhythm of her heartbeat change, making her take in a quick, unsteady breath. Whatever had possessed her to think she could fool Race? Kate wondered. Her husband would know she was gone just from the feel of the air—just as she could detect his absence. The world wasn't right when they were apart. The sun didn't slant properly. Something was always wrong with the air. It felt too thin to sustain a proper breath, too vapid to sustain life.

Staring at the ragged line where the rough hills pushed against the sky, Kate wondered if she'd ever draw a proper breath again. She wasn't sure Race would ever forgive her for what she was doing. In all the years they'd been married, she had never defied his will. Argued with him, yes. Confronted him with her opinions, most definitely. But defied him? Gone behind his back? Never. But, until now, there had never been a reason.

She could have shown him the ransom demand, then argued till she was breathless and blue in the face that he shouldn't go, that it was too dangerous, that his hot temper clouded his judgment especially where Honey was concerned. She could have pleaded that Race, at the age of fifty-four, wasn't a match for the younger, more desperate Summerfield. All to no avail.

Her mouth flattened out into a grim line. She was doing what she had to do—for Honey, for Race. Honey would be indignant about being bailed out of another scrape and would harbor a grudge for being made to feel, once again, useless and irresponsible. But the girl would get over it eventually.

Race, on the other hand, might never forgive Kate for this deception. She knew him so well, and she knew his stubborn pride. The wound she was inflicting now might never heal.

The sagebrush and scrub beside the tracks began to shimmer as Kate's eyes filled with tears. So be it, she said to herself. If it cost her Race's trust and love, she thought, at least she'd still have his life.

With her hand on the door, Honey turned to look at Gideon, still asleep in the rumpled sheets, one arm still outstretched in the warm space she had quietly vacated only moments ago. Heat flickered in the pit of her stomach and for a second she yearned to return to the bed, to feel Gideon's heat and his weight, to be filled by him.

Soon, she thought, quietly opening the door and walking out into the empty hallway. She'd be back in two shakes or less—with warm tortillas and sweet butter for their breakfast, with a ready-made frock to replace the rags she was wearing now.

Despite lack of sleep, Honey felt fresh and strong and competent. She felt complete. It was as if Gideon's loving had filled in all those empty spaces inside her. Her feet were light, almost winged, as she trotted down the stairs and whisked out the hotel door onto the street.

The half-breed, Charlie Buck, was catnapping in a corner of the lobby. His dark head snapped up just as

Honey sailed out the door. "What the hell," he muttered. He made a grab for the rifle beside him then
and, when his elbow hit the oil lamp and sent it crashing to the floor, the startled Indian dropped the remnants of his smoldering cigarette into the little
spreading puddle of kerosene and broken glass at his
feet.

Outside, all Honey saw was a glorious day. The sky
was a fierce blue and the sun glittered in the cotton-
woods that ran along the creek just west of town. A
little breeze played at the ragged edge of Honey's skirt
and lifted her long hair off her shoulders as she pro-
gressed along the sidewalk. She wanted to skip down
the middle of the dusty street, telling the whole world,
or at least all of the inhabitants of Cerrillos, how much
she loved Gideon Summerfield, and how—if she never
did anything else in her life—she'd finally done something absolutely, perfectly, beautifully right.

For the first time in her life she was happy just being herself. She had nothing to prove—to herself or
anybody else, her father in particular. If she recovered the bank's money now, she thought, she'd give it
back for Gideon's sake and not in any effort to impress her father or to garner his praise. No, she corrected herself. Not *if* she recovered the money. *When.*
For she still had every intention of retrieving the stolen cash. Now that she loved Gideon, there was no way
on God's green earth she'd let him go back to jail.

She was concentrating so hard on her plan to rescue both Gideon and the money that when she walked
into the dry goods store it took a moment for the sense
of familiarity to strike her. Like the mercantile in

Golden, this one also bore a haunting resemblance to her mother's place in Loma Parda where Honey had lived as Edwina Cassidy. This time, though, the memories rushed back sweetly, unaccompanied by a sense of loss or might-have-beens. She didn't long for the lost Edwina. She was happy to be Honey—here and now.

"Help you, miss?" The gray-haired matron stood behind the counter, her expression sour and her arms crossed, as Honey plucked a simple calico wash dress from a pile on a table.

Under the woman's disapproving gaze, Honey slipped out of her tattered dress and into the simple frock. The sleeves were much too long and the waistband too loose and the hemline dragged on the ground, but it was clean and whole, and that was all Honey was seeking at the moment. She didn't need fancy clothes to feel beautiful with Gideon.

With delicious memories from the night before still drifting through her head and the taste of Gideon's kisses still on her lips, Honey twirled in the new dress. She felt giddy and glad, and only slightly childish beneath the glare of the matronly storekeeper. But when Honey whirled to a breathless standstill, the sour-faced woman wasn't watching her at all. Instead she was peering out the window.

"Looks like the hotel's on fire," the woman said as she gave a prim little pat to her iron gray hair. "Won't mind one bit if the place burns down to a cinder. It'd serve those whores and drunks right to fry here on earth rather'n wait for their share of hellfire."

By now Honey's gaze had moved to the window, and as she stared she barely heard the woman's starchy voice. Smoke was pouring from the ground-floor windows of the hotel. Flames were licking up the north wall of the wooden structure. Horrible tongues of fire.

Wild eyed now, with a panicky scream rising in her throat, Honey looked around her at the shelves and the stacked dry goods and the oddly familiar wooden crates and lidded jars. The brooms and shovels and pickaxes hooked to the ceiling seemed to sway above her head, and for an instant she wasn't sure where she was—it seemed so much like her mama's store in Loma Parda. Then, when she glanced down at the oversize calico dress, she wondered fleetingly why she was wearing her mother's frock. She wasn't allowed to play dress up in the store. She . . .

"Lookee there," the shopkeeper exclaimed. "See. The roof's caught now. Lord have mercy. I sure hope those sparks don't blow across the street."

Honey looked, staring dazedly at the hotel where she had just left the man she loved, deeply asleep.

"Gideon!" His name tore from her throat as she grabbed up the loose yardage of her skirt and went flying across the street, oblivious of the shouts of the storekeeper behind her.

A hand clamped on Honey's shoulder when she was about to enter the burning lobby and Charlie Buck's stern, chiseled features loomed through the smoke.

"You're not going in there," he told her.

But before he could get a good grip on her, Honey drove the heel of her hand up into his chin, and as the big half-breed reeled back, she ran into the hotel.

Inside, the smoke was dense. Though she could barely see, Honey remembered that the stairs were just ahead and a little to the right, so with the hem of her skirt covering her nose and mouth, she made her way through the heat and the acrid haze.

Her fingers had just touched the banister when there was a *whoosh* at her back. She looked over her shoulder in time to see orange flames rushing up the curtains, more flames crawling across the lobby floor toward the stairs where she stood now as if she had grown roots, long deep roots that wouldn't let her move. Then the fire hissed her name.

It wanted her. Its hot orange eyes were unblinking.

Honey's mouth opened in a voiceless scream. And the flames screamed back.

In his dreams, Gideon wavered between the pleasures of the angels and the tortures of the damned. One moment he'd be with Honey in a field of tall green corn, losing himself in her sea-colored eyes and her feminine warmth, then the next moment the cornstalks surrounding them would darken to iron bars and the woman in his arms would disappear like a wisp of smoke.

One minute he'd be listening to the sweet music of her voice, then the honeyed notes would turn to the harsh rasp of convicts walking in lockstep, dragging their chains along a stone floor. Now, in the confusing welter of his sleep, he heard the clanging of a bell and the high-pitched cries of frantic men that signaled an escape.

Gideon sat up, quick as a switchblade opening, and in less than a heartbeat he realized where he was and exactly what those bells and shouts signified. The hotel was on fire. And in the blink of an eye he realized Honey was gone. But rather than panic at her absence, he felt a sense of relief. All he had to worry about now was getting himself out.

He dressed quickly, all the while watching the fingers of smoke curling up under the door, bending over to avoid the acrid haze that was beginning to collect at the ceiling. He strapped on his gun belt, secured it, then slung a leg over the windowsill and eased himself out onto the rickety porch roof that ran along the front of the building.

A cheer went up from the crowd below and somebody gestured to a hay wagon parked close to the front of the building.

"Jump, mister," a voice called.

"Jump," others chimed in.

Gideon did, landing with a dull thud on the loose bales. He climbed over the side of the wagon, then turned, expecting to see Honey's face—happy, shining with relief—somewhere in the crowd, but instead he found himself staring into the stony countenance of Charlie Buck.

"Where's the woman?" the half-breed growled.

With the clanging of the fire bells and the raucous shouts of the crowd, Gideon could barely hear him. He leaned closer, cupping a hand to his ear. "What?"

The half-breed clamped a hand on Gideon's shoulder. "I said where's that ten-thousand-dollar piece of female? What'd you do, Summerfield? Stash her somewhere out back?''

"She's not out here?'' Too concerned now with Honey's whereabouts to even react to the man's accusation or pay any mind to his grip on his shoulder, Gideon's eyes searched the crowd for a single pretty face, a pair of sea-colored eyes.

"When did you last see her?'' he yelled at the half-breed.

Charlie Buck angled his head toward the hotel's front door. "Couple minutes ago. She ran in there looking for you.''

Gideon cursed as he shook off the half-breed's hand and pushed his way through the crowd to the door. The front of the lobby was already engulfed in flames. There was no way in hell—and that was what the interior looked like to him—he could get through that. Or even if he could, he wouldn't be in any shape to help Honey once he'd gotten through.

Charlie Buck was suddenly beside him now, grimacing in the smoke, swearing viciously about ten thousand in ransom money going up in flames.

Gideon turned and ran back to the hay wagon. He leapt up on the bales. Reaching up, he was able to grasp the edge of the porch roof. Slowly then, his shoulders straining the seams of his shirt and the wound on his side ripping open as he stretched, he pulled himself up far enough to swing one leg onto the roof.

He slid back through the window he had escaped from moments earlier, bending double beneath the room's lowering curtain of smoke as he made his way toward the door.

And, though Gideon Summerfield hadn't prayed since he'd been ten years old, all the while he moved he was praying. Hard.

At the foot of the stairs, Honey stared at the fiery creature slowly making its way toward her. The fire would advance, then snake back upon itself, and then slither forward once again. It flicked its orange tongue at the hem of her skirt.

She lifted her arm to shield her face. The intense heat was drying her tears before they were halfway down her cheeks. She could barely breathe now. She was choking on smoke and on the words she wanted to scream back at the burning beast.

It lunged at her just then, and Honey lashed back with her foot. Her fear gave way to rage.

"No," she screamed. "Not now. You can't take me now. Please. Gideon's upstairs sleeping and I have to get him out. I love him. I love him so. I'd die if anything happened to him."

The fire struck out at her again, rushing, crackling. But it was only fire now, not a fearful, flame-breathing dragon. Honey recognized it for what it was. Unafraid, able to move her trembling limbs, she turned her back on it, squeezed her eyes shut against the smoke and started up the stairs.

In the middle of the burning staircase, she collided with Gideon.

The hem of her skirt was blazing as he swept Honey into his arms, then took the steps two at a time, returning to their room. He stood her in the tub of cool bathwater, still holding her, afraid to let her go. She was safe. She was alive. The tears that stung his eyes now were only partly from the rising smoke.

"What a fool thing to do, Honey." He wanted to shake her for risking her neck, but he could only hold her tightly against him.

"I had to find you," she said, sighing, resting her head on his shoulder, circling her arms around his waist.

Gideon pressed his lips to her hair. "You found me, darlin'," he whispered. "You found me." In more ways than one, he thought. He'd been so lost so long he'd given up hope of ever being found. His heart had been so cold for so many years he didn't think it was possible to feel the warmth it was pouring through him now. Or the hope that was rising in his soul like something on the wing.

He tipped up her chin, found her big, turquoise eyes through the haze and wanted to tell her he would never let her go. That he'd do whatever he had to do in order to be with her. If that meant going back to prison in Jefferson City until the parole board granted him his freedom, then so be it. She was worth whatever price he had to pay.

There was so much he wanted to tell her, but all Gideon could do just then was whisper her name. "Honey."

"Ask me to marry you, Gideon," she whispered back, a soft urgency in her voice.

Her eyes were shining in spite of the smoke that was building in layer after layer above them, and Gideon thought he could quite happily drown in those ocean-colored orbs, or—more happily—live the rest of his days exploring their blue-green depths. He thought if he were any other man he'd already be on his knees begging her to be his wife. The wish was so strong it nearly choked him.

"If you won't do that," she whispered now, "then kiss me."

That he could do, though it struck him as a half mile past insane. The hotel was going up in flames around them and Honey was standing in the washtub where he'd dumped her to put out her smoldering skirts. For all he knew, theirs was the last unscathed room in the entire building. They ought to be running for their lives. . . .

Which was what it felt like when he lowered his head to kiss her. Breathless and wild and urgent. Because he might never kiss her again. Because he wanted to spend the rest of his life kissing her. The fire raging through the hotel was nothing compared to the one racing through him now—through his body, but his heart and soul as well. He had never wanted anything as badly as he wanted Honey Logan, now and always.

"Marry me, darlin'," he whispered against her lips. "Marry me forever."

"Yes."

Her sigh was lost in the depths of another kiss, and Gideon's head was swimming. He was a crazy man, proposing to a woman he couldn't have while the whole blasted world—or their small part of it—was going up in flames. For a wild, suicidal moment he imagined them dying, locked in this embrace, their flesh and bones melting into a single being and their ashes traveling on a warm wind to a sacred place.

Crazy. Here he was thinking about dying when he'd never wanted so badly to live.

"We're getting out of here. Now." He lifted her out of the washtub, then strode to the open window, only to turn and discover Honey had gone the other way.

"Where the hell do you think you're going?"

"Out," she answered.

Now who was crazy? Gideon glared past Honey at the door. "You can't go that way. It's an inferno out there."

"Well, I can't go *that* way, Gideon." She stabbed a finger at the window and widened her stance stubbornly.

"Why the hell not?" he growled.

"It's too high. I...I just can't." Saying that, Honey reached for the doorknob and promptly jerked back her hand. "It's red-hot."

Gideon resisted saying he had told her so as he watched her stare at the window, her eyes enormous with panic.

"Oh, my God. I can't, Gideon. I can't."

He crossed the room, swearing under his breath, swatting the lowering cloud of smoke out of his path, then he slid one arm around her waist and crooked a finger to lift her stubborn chin. He grinned for all he was worth. "Ain't no such word as can't, darlin'. If your mama never taught you that, you're about to learn."

* * *

The moment she had stepped off the train it had been obvious to Kate that the cloud of smoke hovering like an evil specter over Cerrillos hadn't come from the smokestack of the big black locomotive. Something was definitely on fire. And when she had heard somebody shout that it was the hotel, Kate had clutched the leather valise in one hand, rucked up her long skirt with the other and hurried toward the building where the flames were now shooting through the roof.

In a panic, she scanned the faces in the crowd. Where was Honey? There couldn't be another hotel in this little town, and this was where that Summerfield man's telegram had said she would be.

Kate caught the sleeve of a female bystander. "Please, can you tell me, is there another hotel in town?"

The gray-haired woman shook her head.

"Do you know if everyone inside has gotten out?" Kate asked, her voice tightening with panic and climbing to a higher and sharper register, her fingers digging into the woman's sleeve.

The woman shrugged out of Kate's grasp, then replied sourly, "Well, if they ain't out, they're getting a well-deserved little taste of hellfire right about now, don't you think?" Her gaze returned to the conflagration.

A shout went up from the crowd then and somebody pointed to the porch roof where a man was easing himself out from a window. Once out, he leaned back in and gently guided a woman through the open space. Her hair fell over her shoulders in long, dark tangles. She looked so tiny. Like a bedraggled child who had just walked through a puddle in her mother's calico dress.

Honey! Kate's hand moved to cover her wildly beating heart. She wanted to cry out but her mouth was as dry as ashes, so she simply stood there and watched as the man led her daughter to the edge of the roof. He leapt with the grace of a wildcat onto the hay wagon below, found his balance quickly on the wobbly bales, then turned, smiled up at Honey and held out his arms.

Honey took a hesitant step toward the edge of the little roof, then stopped. Even at that distance Kate could see her daughter's lips quivering with uncertainty. Her face was pale and her eyes were huge and afraid. As huge and afraid as they had been when Honey had been just a tiny girl and Kate had caught her on top of the bureau in her bedroom.

"You get down from there this instant," Kate had commanded her.

"I can't."

"You managed to get up there, Honey Logan. Now you get right back down."

"I can't."

And she couldn't have, Kate remembered. Perhaps not even if her little life had depended on it. Honey was that afraid of heights.

A flaming piece of the front wall came down now, and the crowd surged back.

"Jump, Honey. You can," Kate breathed.

The tall stranger on the hay wagon called up to her. When Honey only stood there unmoving, he dragged his fingers through his hair, then planted his fists on his lean hips. He glared up at the recalcitrant, terrified young woman for a moment, but then his hard expression broke into a wide, gleaming grin.

"If you want to go to Kansas with me, bright eyes, then you'd best take that first step," he shouted above the roar of the flames.

Honey smiled, a smile far brighter than the fire at her back. And then Kate watched her terrified daughter leap—with perfect trust—into the stranger's outstretched arms. He caught her easily, and for a moment it seemed to Kate those two were the only people in the world, holding each other, kissing and laughing with pure joy.

With sparks shooting up from the burning hotel and the shouts of the crowd, for an instant the scene reminded Kate of the Fourth of July so many years ago when her daughter was conceived. The night Kate herself had leapt with such perfect trust into Race Logan's arms.

The tall, lean stranger was Gideon Summerfield. Kate knew that as surely as she knew her own name. And she was no longer afraid for her daughter's life. It was Honey's heart that was in terrible danger now.

Gideon saw the diminutive woman with the red-gold hair before Honey did. In a single glance he took in the purposefulness of the woman's stride, the determined set of her mouth, and the delicacy of a nose that was identical to Honey's. There was green fire in the eyes that locked on his as he lowered that woman's daughter from the hay wagon to the ground.

"Mama!" Honey's exclamation hovered between surprise and happiness. Then, with a tiny squeal of delight, she threw her arms around her mother. "Oh, Mama!"

Gideon jumped down from the wagon, still caught in the Logan woman's hot emerald glare. Well, he deserved a look as hot as she could stoke, he figured. Or worse. He nodded to her. "Ma'am."

But fiercely as her gaze burned, the woman's voice was cool. "Mr. Summerfield, I assume."

Honey stepped back from embracing her mother then, and Gideon held them both in his gaze. The shining daughter. The fiery, protective mother. Beauties, both of them. And both of them in his care now as, out of the corner of his eye, he saw Charlie Buck approaching them, his black eyes on the satchel in Mrs. Logan's grip, one dark hand resting on the butt of his gun.

There wasn't a damn thing he could do, Gideon thought. Still, his mind swirled, reaching for answers, testing the grim alternatives. If the big half-breed didn't get his hands on the ransom Dwight Samuel had sent him for, he wouldn't hesitate to take both women captive and demand twice as much. Even though Gideon was sure he could take Charlie Buck, and even though he was willing to die trying, there was no way he was going to put Honey and her mother at risk.

On top of that, tipping his hand now with this ransom would blow the banker's plan to smithereens. If he did that, Gideon thought bleakly, he might just as well head for Mexico this minute because nothing would convince Dwight to follow him to Santa Fe after that, and nothing remained to prevent Logan from hunting him down and clapping him back in chains.

There was nothing he could do. Nothing, that was, but break Honey's unsuspecting heart, right here, right now, and hope to God he could repair it later.

"Did she bring it?" the half-breed asked now, his dark eyes moving from Gideon to the satchel in Kate's hand.

Gideon's gaze flicked to Honey. Suspicion already clouded the bright warmth in her eyes, and the smile that had been poised on her pretty mouth only a second before was wavering now as her mother raised the leather valise.

"There's your ransom, Mr. Summerfield," Kate Logan said. "Take it. We've lived up to our part of the bargain so I trust you'll allow me to take my daughter home now."

Honey stared at the satchel in her mother's outstretched hand, then raised her eyes to Gideon's—slowly, painfully—as if the sight of him right then were more than she could bear.

"What's in it, Mama? How much? How much was I worth to him?"

Chapter Seventeen

"Ten thousand," Charlie Buck growled as he grabbed the valise from Kate's hand and unbuckled it. "Better all be in here, too." He shot Kate a last hard look before he began pawing through the contents.

Honey wasn't even looking at the half-breed. Her eyes were burning into Gideon's now like sheer blue-green flame searing through gunmetal. "Was I worth it, Gideon? Was I? Did you get your money's worth?"

Gideon's mouth twitched though he said nothing, and when he saw the blow coming, he did nothing to deflect it, allowing Honey's hand to crack across his cheek.

"Bastard," she hissed, then spun on her heel and marched—head high and shoulders stiff with pride—toward the train depot.

He didn't lift a hand to rub his stinging face. Gideon did nothing to ease the pain that Honey Logan had had every right to inflict. Compared to the piercing pain in his heart, however, her slap had felt more like a caress. It was Honey's mother then who touched gentle, cool fingertips to his jawline. Gideon blinked.

"My daughter has her father's blazing temper, Mr. Summerfield, as well as his blistering tongue," Kate said quietly. Her earnest gaze searched Gideon's face. "Unlike me, Honey doesn't understand what's happening here or just who the true villain is." Her head tilted slightly now to indicate the half-breed, who was ignoring them while he continued to search through the leather valise. Her voice lowered another notch. "Thank you for preventing what might have happened."

"I didn't have a choice, ma'am."

Kate smiled. "Yes, you did. But you chose my daughter's safety. And mine, too. I'm grateful to you for that."

His eyes shifted toward Charlie Buck, gauging his distance and the extent of his interest in the satchel. Gideon's voice was little more than a whisper as he leaned down toward Kate. "Tell your husband the plan's still set. For the bank in Santa Fe. As soon as I can make it happen. I'd say two days. Three at the most."

Kate's eyes narrowed on his. "I'll tell him. But you need to be aware that things...well, my husband's attitude has changed. He's a very protective father. He would have come here with a gun instead of a satchel, if he had known about the ransom." She drew in a wavering breath. "I don't know what Race promised you, Mr. Summerfield, in return for your help. But, if I were you, I wouldn't count on it now."

His mouth curved upward in a tight smile while his eyes remained a cool and humorless gray. "I never did, Mrs. Logan." He angled his head toward the rapidly disappearing Honey. "Take care of her for me, will you?"

A small ripple of laughter broke from Kate's throat. "Easier said than done, Mr. Summerfield, as I'm sure you already know." She extended her hand. "I want you to know that I saw my daughter's face when she was flying off that burning roof into your arms. She looked happy as a new angel. Seems to me you're the one responsible for that."

Gideon took Kate's hand. The smile on his face now was more like a wince, as if she, too, had slapped him rather than given him a kind of blessing. "Angels belong in heaven, Mrs. Logan. All I seem to manage is hard times and hell."

Her emerald gaze met his squarely. "Well, Mr. Summerfield, I'd say it's probably high time you had an angel on your side." Kate turned then and followed in her daughter's wake.

Gideon watched her a moment, then turned when he heard the remaining walls of the hotel collapse in upon themselves. The whole building now lay in soggy, smoky ruins. Kind of like his heart, he thought. A lot like his heart. And if he stood here thinking about that even one second longer, he'd be on his knees, crying like a baby.

There'd be plenty of time for that in Mexico, he told himself. All the time in the world.

"Let's get going," he snarled to Charlie Buck.

The train waited at the depot, snorting and shuddering like a big coal-colored beast while it built up a head of steam to carry it north, back to Santa Fe.

Honey sat with her arms crossed, her shoulders dug into the leather-tufted seat, staring at the burned hem of her dress. Her eyes were stinging, just as they had when she had stood in the depths of the burning hotel, but now the fire was raging deep inside her. She was determined not to let her mother see her cry, and she vowed that even if she had to draw blood from the inside of her cheeks, she'd do it to keep the tears from spilling.

Only moments ago Honey had rebuffed another one of her mother's attempts at conversation, snapping, "Not now, Mama. I don't want to talk now. About anything. And I especially don't want to talk about that thief. That lying, conniving, snake-tongued son of a—"

"That *thief*," her mother had interrupted forcefully, "just saved your precious hide two times in the space of about ten minutes, Honey Logan."

Honey had sniffed and crossed her arms more tightly. Her response had been an icy hiss. "Of course he saved it, Mama. You bet he did. My precious hide was worth ten thousand dollars to him."

The locomotive lurched forward, and the last coach, in which they sat, jerked at its couplings then started to sway and creak as it rolled in the wake of the big engine. Honey closed her eyes to blot out the sight of the rugged, piñon-dotted hills where she had ridden with Gideon. She tried to erase him from her head, to erase him from the entire universe and pretend the man didn't even exist. When that tactic proved unsuccessful, Honey willed herself to hate him. Hating Gideon Summerfield, no doubt, would be an easier accomplishment now than forgetting him. Oh, but loving him, she thought dismally, had been the easiest of all.

Honey glanced at her mother, whose face appeared calm despite the fact that she seemed preoccupied with twisting the wedding band on her finger. For the first time in her life, Honey realized, she felt a kinship with her mother that surpassed their natural bond of mother and daughter. Kate Logan—the woman, not the mother—was going home to her man, Honey thought. A man who adored her. A man who would trade his own soul to the devil without a second thought to spare his wife a single moment's pain.

A knot of envy formed in Honey's chest, pulling up tight. It was so easy for her mother. Why, why in the name of the Almighty, did it have to come so hard for *her?* she wondered. Why did she always do things wrong? She squeezed her eyes closed, as much to contain her tears as to make the hurting stop. But she couldn't do either one. Pain sliced through her heart like lightning and tears streamed down her cheeks like rain.

Kate leaned close to her daughter, her head tipped, mingling her red-gold hair with Honey's dark tresses. "I can't stop the way you're hurting, Honey. I can only tell you it will stop. Eventually. One way or another." She sighed. "Do you love him, Honey?"

Honey swiped at one wet eye. "Gideon Summerfield? Right now I hate him."

A smile tipped the edges of Kate's mouth. As she pulled a lace handkerchief from her reticule, she said, "Right now you're hating yourself, Honey Logan, and wondering what it was you did wrong. I've known you longer than you've known yourself, Miss Fix-It, and don't you forget that.''

"Miss Fix-It can't fix anything." Honey accepted the hankie, then sank lower into her seat.

"Sometimes there are things that don't need fixing. They just work out by themselves. The right things do anyway, in my estimation."

Honey's reply was a wet, forlorn sigh, after which Kate tipped her head even closer to her daughter and spoke in a tone that hovered just beneath the resonant chuffing and clacking of the train.

"Honey, I never regretted that first time with your daddy. Even when I realized he wasn't coming back for me, when I thought he'd left me for good and forever. Even then, as forlorn as I felt, I wouldn't have changed what happened between us. Not one sweet kiss. Not one single touch. It was worth it, loving him the way I did. Being loved by him."

When Honey began to protest, Kate held up a silencing hand. "Hear me out now," she said. "I married somebody else, for your safety and for propriety's sake, but I never stopped loving your daddy. Don't you let anybody make you feel that you did wrong if you know in your heart that it wasn't.''

With her eyes closed and her head resting against her mother's, Honey whispered brokenly, "He traded me for a sack of money, Mama."

"He did it to spare your life, child. And it cost him dearly, only you were too blinded by your own hurt to see it." Kate sighed. "My life, too. That big half-breed would have been only too glad to hold the both of us for twice the price."

"That big half-breed is part of Dwight Samuel's gang. So is Gideon. Now." Honey managed a tiny cluck of her tongue. "He's Dwight Samuel's cousin, you know. I guess that old saying's true about blood being thicker than water. And that other saying, too. Once a thief, always a thief."

Kate tipped her head away, studying her daughter's face. "He didn't tell you then?"

"Tell me what?"

"Summerfield's working for your father," Kate said quietly. "He's supposed to link up with the Samuel gang and then lure them into Santa Fe so the Bankers' Association can finally put a stop to all these robberies. Race got him out of prison to help. In return for Summerfield's help, your father is supposed to arrange his release. Only..." Her hands fluttered in her lap. "Only now I don't know what Race is going to do."

That explained it, Honey thought suddenly. All the puzzle pieces that hadn't fit before—the way Gideon went about his robberies without apparent care or caution, his indifference to the spoils of each job, the lack of pursuit.

She bolted upright in her seat. "Why in blue blazes didn't he tell me?"

"Probably for the same reason I almost wasn't going to, Miss Fix-It." Kate's hand came up to touch her daughter's tangled hair. "Honey, if anybody has a plan, they can always count on you to be the little monkey wrench that gets in the middle of it, twisting and turning and trying to make things right. Trying to prove to yourself and the world just how capable you are.''

''What did you mean, Mama, when you said you didn't know what Daddy's going to do now?'' Honey asked urgently. ''If he promised Gideon...''

Kate's emerald eyes flashed at her. ''That was all before his precious daughter inserted herself dead center into the plan. I don't have to tell you how your father feels about you, Honey. Right or wrong, he feels a need to protect you. From everything and everyone.'' A sudden sheen of tears glistened in her eyes. ''I don't know. Maybe it's because he didn't have you those first few years. Or because you were born with Ned Cassidy's name instead of his. Maybe he feels he has to make it up to you somehow. I just don't know.''

But Honey wasn't listening anymore. She was seeing Gideon's gray eyes—gray and steely and cold as the bars of a cell. He wouldn't go back to prison, he had said. Never. And if he still believed her father was going to get him out, then he'd be riding right into a trap. A trap that she'd helped set with her interference.

Snap—like steel claws around the leg of an unsuspecting wolf. She knew what wolves did when they were trapped like that. Desperate to get away, they would chew off their own legs. Gideon would be that desperate. Just like a wolf.

Honey stood up, clambering over her mother's skirt toward the aisle. ''Excuse me, Mama. It's so close in here. I'm just going to step out on the platform for a minute to get a breath of fresh air.''

* * *

Race's grasp on Kate's arm was meant to guide her from the train to the carriage that waited in front of the station. If he knew how hard he was gripping her, Kate thought, his fingers would open immediately, soft and harmless as the petals of a flower. And when he saw the bruise tomorrow, his eyes would cloud and his cheeks would color with shame.

But that was tomorrow. At the moment her husband was mad enough to choke somebody with one bare hand. Knowing him the way she did, she supposed she was glad it was just her arm his fingers were digging into. Better that right now than her throat, or Gideon Summerfield's.

He practically tossed her into the carriage, then hauled himself up beside her. He picked up the reins, dropped them, then dragged his splayed fingers through his dark, silver-shot hair. His voice was harsh with anger, rough with frustration.

"Katie! For chrissake, how could you let her go? Why didn't you make them stop the goddamn train?"

Staring straight ahead, unwilling to hazard the ice in his eyes, Kate said, "I tried, Race."

It was almost true. Right after Kate had gone out to the platform for a breath of fresh air herself, and right after she had seen Honey ballooning in calico off the back of the train then collapsing between the rails, Kate had almost plunged back inside to demand to the conductor that the train be stopped then and there.

But something had stopped her. Kate had stood there a moment longer, fingers white around the metal railing, and had watched Honey—growing smaller moment by moment as the train pulled away—but at the same time growing larger than life itself as she got to her feet, swatted dust and cinders from her skirt, then turned and headed back toward Cerrillos.

Kate had let her daughter go with a whispered blessing. Standing there on the rear platform of the train, she wondered how her own life might have been different if she had taken off after Race all those years ago rather than merely accepting the wretched fact that he was gone. It would have taken her only a day or two to catch up to him out on the plains where he was lying in the back of a wagon with the broken leg that had prevented his return. She never would have married Ned Cassidy then. Race would have been Honey's daddy from the day of her birth.

And, Kate thought now, Race wouldn't be sitting like some granite statue beside her in this carriage, reading her his own unique version of the Riot Act.

"I have more to say to you, Kate Logan, but I'm too damn angry with you right now. Between Isaac being sick and you running off and your eldest son telling me what a goddamn coward I am, I'm hardly fit to do anything right now but wring somebody's neck."

Kate looked at his big, fisted hands before she reached down for the reins he had dropped. She rippled them over the horse's back. "Let's go home, Race. I might be ready to listen by the time you're ready to talk."

It took Honey a good three hours to get back to Cerrillos—three hours of tripping over her hem, stubbing her toes on unexpectedly high cross ties and spikes, stumbling and muttering curses to herself as well as to the hot sun over her head. By the time she traipsed into Cerrillos, the hotel was a heap of charred lumber where an occasional flame spurted up, then flickered out. A few men loitered nearby, scratching their heads and looking dazed, but otherwise the town seemed to have returned to its customary quiet.

In the livery stable, Jonquil nickered as if happy to see her, and Honey looped her arms around the mare's big, warm neck, wetting it with her tears.

"I need to find him, girl," she whispered. "Help me. Please. Help me find him."

It didn't matter, Honey thought, if Gideon didn't love her. It didn't matter if everything he'd said had been a lie. If he had only used the dream of a future together in Kansas to lure her off the burning roof, Honey didn't care. She loved him. That was all that mattered. And she couldn't bear the thought that his going back to prison would be all her fault. Worse, she couldn't rid herself of the image of the wolf in the trap. Gideon, if caught, might very well choose death over a return to prison.

Her mother had jokingly called her Miss Fix-It. Maybe so. But Honey knew that if she failed to fix this, Gideon might very well die. And if Gideon died, so would her heart.

She saddled Jonquil as quickly as she could. Then, once up on the dun mare's back, Honey headed up into the hills again, toward the abandoned mine, toward Gideon Summerfield, she hoped, before it was too late.

Chapter Eighteen

Dwight Samuel lowered the jug of mescal, then used the back of his hand to wipe away the liquor that had drizzled into his dark beard. Above the beard and the black mustache, his eyes gleamed drunkenly in the firelight.

"Damn, Gid. You did right well by us with that ransom. I thank you. I truly do." He passed the jug to his cousin, who was leaning on one elbow, legs slung out and boots pointed to the fire.

"Family," Gideon grunted. He tipped the jug, barely wet his lips with the fiery brew, then passed it on to Charlie Buck.

"We ain't got all that much family left with Jesse gone." Dwight's voice was a rough mix of sorrow and bitterness and mescal. Then he laughed. "And, hell, them that's left won't claim us."

Young Shooter took his turn with the jug, passing his sleeve over his mouth in imitation of Dwight. "You got *us*, Dwight," the boy said, then flashed a lop-sided grin.

"You ain't exactly in Jesse's league," the bearded outlaw muttered.

"Well, I never claimed I was," the boy countered. "Could be, though. I damn well could be."

Charlie Buck nudged his elbow into Shooter's ribs. "Sure you could, kid. Just like I could be governor of the Territory of New Mexico." The Indian jerked his thumb toward the two drunk Mexicans. "Or like Cordera there or Valez could be U.S. marshals."

While Shooter sulked and the Mexicans laughed, Gideon just stared into the fire. Family. The word clanged in his head, off-key as a cracked bell. He flicked his gaze toward Dwight, one of the cousins who had picked up a ten-year-old boy by the scruff of the neck, put him on a horse, then rode him off into a life on the run.

He'd been running—a thief in the night—the devil at his back and the law on his tail—for more than twenty years now. Except for the time he'd tried to settle down with Cora. Except for the years he'd been in the penitentiary. But he'd been running from other devils then. God Almighty, he was tired of running.

At the edge of the campfire a dry branch of juniper ignited, crackling and sending up a quick blue-green, sea-colored flame. Bright eyes! Gideon's mouth tightened as he envisioned the color of Honey Logan's eyes, as he recalled the fierce fire that had raged in them when she'd cracked the flat of her hand across his cheek that morning.

Her mother had probably set her straight on the train back to Santa Fe. Kate Logan didn't strike him as the kind of woman who'd let her daughter live with a lie, so she would have told Honey just what was what—how he was doing this on the right side of the law for Race Logan, how demanding the ransom hadn't been his idea, how he truly cared about her, cared too damn much to ruin her life.

And that, he thought gloomily now, was something he might already have done. What if she were carrying his child? Honey herself had mentioned the possibility—with a certain wistfulness in her voice and happy stars in her young eyes, as he recalled. He never, never should have touched her. Gideon cursed himself for the thousandth time that day, and for the thousandth time reveled in the memory of that touching, that loving. He pictured Honey's dark shawl of hair, slipping over her shoulders, sliding away to reveal the perfect paleness of her skin, the sweet perfection of her breasts.

Hell, that baby, if it existed, would be better off being raised a Logan rather than a Summerfield. Honey's mother would make her see that, too. He hoped.

What was it the Logan woman had said to him? Something about needing an angel on his side? Sweet notion, that, but didn't she know he'd only drag her daughter down? Or did she truly believe, as Honey seemed to believe, that she could raise him up, share her own white, feathery, hopeful wings with him?

Up, Gideon thought bleakly, wasn't where he was headed. And it wasn't Kansas either with its green and wind-touched rows of corn and wheat. And not prison. If he didn't know anything else, Gideon knew that. He wasn't going back. For a while, under Honey's warm spell, he had thought he could go back, put in his time and earn the freedom to be with Honey. Now that she was gone, he was thinking a bit more clearly.

He levered up now and shifted his legs, leaning closer to his black-bearded cousin. "If you liked the taste of that ransom, Dwight, maybe you'd like to hear about a sweet little bank in Santa Fe."

Dwight Samuel's eyes glittered. He inclined his head a notch in Gideon's direction. "I'm listening, cousin. Matter of fact, I'm all ears."

Gideon proceeded to describe, in succulent detail, the rich little savings and loan in Santa Fe—its recent deposits, its ideal location on a quiet side street, its lax-to-nonexistent security. As he laid out his plan, he watched his cousin's eyes. They reminded him of the eyes of a hungry black bear, contemplating a honeycomb just out of reach.

Rage flared in Gideon a moment, when he remembered Cora. But the feeling left as quickly as it arrived. Dwight had probably done him a favor by taking Cora away. Anyway, by Gideon's reckoning, that betrayal canceled any debts he owed his cousin. The wife stealing, and the day Dwight had left him to the mercy of Missouri law. The only debt he owed Dwight now was to pay him back in kind.

"Sounds like easy pickings, cousin," Dwight said when Gideon had concluded. "How you figure to split it?" He angled his head toward the other men around the fire.

Gideon smiled lazily. "Half for the family," he said, "and let your buzzards fight over the rest."

"I like your attitude, cousin." Dwight took in his gang with a dark sweep of his eyes. "That sound all right with you boys?"

As Gideon knew they would, the men nodded silently. It was either that or take a bullet or a blade sometime between now and morning.

"Tomorrow," Gideon said to Dwight.

The outlaw grinned. "Tomorrow."

There you go, Banker, Gideon thought. I've done it. And right on time, too, just like I said, despite the distraction of your delicious child. I'm bringing you my part of the bargain. I'm leading the black sheep to the slaughter.

Then it's done. And I'm gone. I won't even take the cash I'd planned to grab to see me across the border. I'm just going. Provided I don't catch a bullet in the cross fire. But either way I'm gone. Clean and sweet and forever. Because of her. Because of love. Because it's too damn late for angels.

The fire had died down to glowing coals and the outlaws lay where they had passed out. Over the snores and the rough sounds of drunk men sleeping, Gideon heard something. He lifted his head from the blanket, listening. Something. He didn't hear it so much as feel it.

He rose slowly, soundlessly, and moved to the rope line where their horses were picketed. His hand hovered near his hip, a breath away from his gun.

When he saw the dun mare grazing in the moonlight, he bit off a curse. Crazy, headstrong female! What was she doing now, coming back to retrieve her own damn ransom? Instinctively, his hand remained close to his gun. "Honey," he called softly, half-expecting to be answered with the blast of a shotgun.

She rose from behind a tall clump of broomweed. The moon just touched her face with its pale light, glossed her long dark tumble of hair and sparkled like blue diamonds in her big eyes.

"Oh, Gideon. I thought...I wasn't sure it was you." She came rushing then—headlong and hem-tripping and hell-bent—into his arms.

Gideon breathed out a long sigh as he held her. This was so confounded wrong. And so right, the way she fit his embrace as if she had been born to do just that.

His throat was tight and his voice tinged with frustration when he whispered, "What the hell are you doing here, bright eyes?"

"I had to come back to warn you. About the Savings and Loan. My father..."

"Ssh." He pressed her face into his chest, stilling her words on the off chance that Dwight or one of his men had awakened. "We'll go up to the mine. We can talk there. I'll just get the saddle off your horse first."

Honey watched his easy movements as he relieved Jonquil of her tack. Hard muscles rippled beneath his shirt. Moonlight made deep shadows on the planes of his face while it touched his cinnamon hair with a sugary gloss. He spoke softly to the mare, his voice like a lover.

"Gideon," Honey said softly.

He looked at her over the horse's back, arms resting on the loosened saddle, eyes silver as mercury now, their lashes shadowed by moonlight on his cheeks.

"I'm so sorry I slapped you this morning. I thought..."

He raised a finger to his lips, angling his head toward the hill that led to the mine, then he swung the saddle from the mare's back. "Come on."

There was a twinkling light in his eyes as he fit one arm around her, pulled her against his hip and started up the hill.

"I've never seen a woman so crazy about sleeping out under the stars." He chuckled low in his throat. "Hell, Ed, honey, haven't you figured out yet you can do that right in your own backyard?"

"Not with you, I can't." She smiled up at him. "I like sleeping under the stars with you, Gideon Summerfield."

His response was a rough growl.

"In fact," she continued as he propelled her along, "I like sleeping with you just about anywhere. Under the stars. In a little room in Cerrillos. Here."

His steps accelerated until he was practically dragging Honey up toward the mine. Once there, he dropped the saddle and pulled her into his arms. "If you had one lick of sense, Honey Logan, you'd be back in Santa Fe right now in your own clean little bed." His hand curved over the warm richness of her hair. "You'd be dreaming sweet dreams that wouldn't have anything to do with me."

She lifted her face to his. "If you had one lick of sense, Gideon, you'd stop all your grousing and kiss me the way I want you to."

He didn't have any sense. Not anymore. That had fled the second he saw her. And with a little groan of

surrender, Gideon claimed her mouth, losing himself
in its sweet pliant warmth, drowning in the rich fragrance of her hair, in the echoes of the tiny moans his
kiss drew from her.

It was Honey, breathless, who pulled away. "You
take my very breath away, Gideon."

He cupped her face in his hands, thumbs caressing
her cheeks, eyes softly grazing over her. "Do I, bright
eyes? Best not kiss you anymore then. I wouldn't want
to be responsible for your untimely demise."

Her lower lip slid out. "That isn't what I meant, and
you know it. I . . . do I take your breath away, too? Is
it the same for you?"

He laughed softly. "Not quite." Taking her hand,
he pressed it over the savage pounding of his heart.
"That's what you do to me. That and more."

Honey grinned as she slid her hand down his chest,
over the buckle of his belt, then the lower buckle of his
gun belt. "More?"

With a gruff exhalation, Gideon scooped her into
his arms and walked to the entrance of the mine.
There, he lowered himself to the rock-strewn ground
and leaned back against one of the solid wooden
planks that supported the mine's opening. He settled
Honey on his lap, pressing her head against his shoulder. "Tell me why you came back, Miss No-Sense-At-
All. Did you think you could wrestle ten thousand
dollars away from five desperate men?"

"I came back to warn you."

Gideon pressed his chin to the crown of her head.
"About what?"

"My mother told me about my father's plan. About bringing in Dwight and his gang to earn your parole." Her voice rose a notch, tinged with fear. "But Daddy's not going to honor his promise, Gideon. Not after what's happened with me. He's just not reasonable where I'm concerned."

"Well, if I were your daddy, I don't suppose I'd be all that reasonable myself, bright eyes."

She sniffed. "He wants to keep me under his thumb."

"He wants to keep you safe from lowlifes like me," Gideon countered gruffly.

"I don't want to be safe *from* you, Gideon. I want to be safe *with* you. The way I feel right now."

Chin still resting atop her head, Gideon sighed wearily. "You'd have been better off handcuffing yourself to some slick-haired, shiny-faced young banker. Or maybe I should have just cut your hand off at the wrist that day. Might have hurt a lot less in the long run than breaking your heart."

"Then don't break my heart." She shifted in the circle of his arms, leaning back, raising her face to his. "Love me, Gideon. Marry me. Let's go to Kansas and grow corn and blue-eyed babies."

He shook his head, closing his eyes to blot out the impossible dream she kept dangling before him like a mesmerizing charm. She promised him life. But to get that life, first he'd have to go through the gates of hell, make his home in hell until they let him go. Assuming he survived. Assuming Honey would wait.

"I'll go with you," she said, as if reading his thoughts. "Anywhere. Mexico. South America. If Kansas means prison, then let's go the other way."

"I wouldn't do that to you, bright eyes. It's a hell of a life. You deserve better."

Her eyes locked on his, fierce, determined, full of need. "I deserve a life with the man I love. No more. No less."

"That's the problem, darlin'. I can't offer you anything more than less."

"Well, fine." Honey flattened her hands against his chest, pushing away, as her feet struggled to find a purchase on the rocky ground. "Just go ahead and walk away from me, Gideon. I'll find somebody else. Someday. Somebody who won't walk away. Somebody who doesn't think love can't survive if it doesn't come easy." Honey kicked the hem of her skirt out of her way and walked to the opposite side of the mine entrance.

"I'm not made out of spun sugar and lace, for your information," she shouted. "I'm not looking for a bed of roses either."

Dammit, Gideon thought. A bed of roses was the least she deserved from any man. But the thought of any man lying down with her in that bed was almost more than he could bear. She *was* made of spun sugar and lace on top of all that iron and grit. She was as beautiful and innocent and stubborn as God's stubbornest angel. The angel he needed on his side. His, if he was man enough to have her, strong enough to earn the right to have her by his side.

He stood and walked slowly to her, drew her more slowly still into his arms, burying his face in the warm sweet hollow of her neck. "Angel," he whispered brokenly. "You almost make me believe there's a heaven."

Her arms circled his waist. "There is, Gideon. There is a heaven, and you make me feel worthy of it."

She tilted her head, seeking his face, discovering the tremor of his mouth and the glistening moisture in his eyes. Honey rose on tiptoe then, kissing him, tasting the hot brine of the tears that clung to his eyelashes. "Choose heaven, Gideon. Please. Choose me."

He had no choice. No choice but to take her sweet, wet mouth like a man dying of thirst in the desert, to taste his own tears on her cheeks, to drink them like a life-giving elixir. No choice but to lower her gently to the ground and lose himself in the soft heaven of her, find himself in the passionate light in her eyes, give himself to her with tears and whispered words of love, take her, body and soul, unto himself.

"Angel," he murmured almost soundlessly into the drift of her hair. "Please wait for me on the other side of hell."

"Honey. Wait."

It was just after first light when Gideon and Honey were walking down the rocky slope toward the campfire where Dwight Samuel and his four men were sitting, their heads bent over morning coffee.

Gideon's hand tightened on Honey's arm and his voice was low. "We need to give them a good reason why you came back," he said. "I don't want my cousin to be suspicious. Not even for a minute."

Without a word then, and in full view of the men at the bottom of the hill, Honey turned and looped her arms around Gideon's neck, whispering, "Then I guess you'll just have to kiss me the way the king of the goats would kiss a woman who couldn't stay away."

She arched on tiptoe and fit her lips to his before he could reply, and the next thing Gideon knew he was lost again in the deep, warm cavern of her mouth. A groan of pleasure unlocked in his throat and the wish that this kiss could go on forever blossomed in his heart.

But it couldn't. And much as he wanted to stand there with Honey in his arms and hope in his heart, he couldn't. There was too much to do—beginning with keeping this beautiful woman alive long enough to get her back to Santa Fe and the safety of her father's house.

When he broke the kiss, she blinked. "You *are* irresistible," she whispered.

Gideon didn't feel much like grinning, but he did. "Just as long as they believe it, darlin'." He glanced toward the campsite where five pairs of eyes were now trained in their direction. "Can you act like you're crazy in love with me till we get to Santa Fe?"

"Better than that. I can do it till we get to heaven, Gideon Summerfield, and it won't be any act."

They descended to the waiting circle of outlaws, where Dwight Samuel was smiling and shaking his head.

"Well, if that just don't beat all, cousin," the bearded man said. "You got the ransom and you got the girl back, too. You're something purely else, Gid."

Gideon winked. "Guess she thinks so anyway. Don't you, Honey?"

She leaned against him and answered breathlessly, and utterly sincerely, "You *are* something purely else."

Chapter Nineteen

Race Logan swore as he shifted on his haunches, all the while refusing to take his eyes off the street and the front door of Logan Savings and Loan. He felt as if he'd been here, scrunched up by the front window of the apothecary shop, for days rather than hours. To further blacken his mood, the druggist's snub-nosed wife had snatched his last cigar right out from his teeth, tossed it out the front door and told him she didn't care who he was or what, but nobody was going to be fouling the air in her establishment.

About the way Kate had told him earlier in the morning he was spoiling whatever slim hope their daughter had for a happy future.

"She loves him, Race," Kate had said, "I saw a happiness on Honey's face I've never seen before. And it's my firm belief that Summerfield loves her back and has her best interests at heart."

"And I don't?" he had shouted at his wife. "You're telling me some hardened criminal cares more about my daughter than I do? Is that what you think, Kate?

Good God, woman, you've taken leave of your senses."

Kate had just about run him through then with her bladed glare. "You might be better off taking leave of your senses for a few minutes and using your heart instead, Race."

As best he could remember, Race had just told her where she could put her own overwrought and senseless heart before he had stalked out of the house.

Zack had followed quickly on his heels then, calling, "Wait up, Papa. I'm coming with you."

Race had turned, stunned to see his seventeen-year-old son carrying a rifle. Had everyone gone completely crazy in his house? he wondered. He had accosted Zack in the same gruff tone he had used with Kate. "Just what in blazes do you think you're doing?"

"I'm going with you," the boy had said, standing his ground and meeting Race's dark gaze with one of his own. "I have about as much use for that outlaw as you do. I'd like to see him roast for what he did to my sister."

"If there's any roasting to be done," Race had shot back, "I'll be the one to do it. Now back in the house with you. I don't want to see your face or that weapon anywhere near the bank today. Do you understand?"

The boy had held his ground, and his turquoise eyes were so much like Race's own that for a moment Race had been taken aback by their glittering defiance.

"Do you understand?" Race had repeated, his voice a low growl, his hand ready to snatch Zack by the scruff of his neck if the boy said anything other than yes.

His son had blinked and muttered, "Yes, sir."

Sitting in the apothecary shop now, Race wondered if he hadn't been a little disappointed in Zack's capitulation. And as he played the scene over in his mind, he felt his mouth twisting into a lopsided grin. Honey wouldn't have given in to him, by God. She was so much like him it almost frightened him sometimes, and that was probably why they butted heads so much. For all he ranted and raved about her Cassidy inclinations, Race knew his daughter was a Logan through and through.

He squinted out into the sun-bright street. Love! Kate had said Honey loved Summerfield. Race told himself that was impossible. He tried to summon up a mental picture of the man and could only remember his eyes—cold, hard and gray as steel. They had barely talked that day when Race had met him beside the train tracks. What little conversation they had had was about bank locations and timetables. Summerfield had listened for the most part—cool, cautious, self-contained. A wolf, Race remembered thinking. A dangerous man. Surely not a man capable of love and tenderness as Kate claimed.

Race recalled feeling a certain grudging respect for the convict. But not enough to hand his daughter over to him on a damn silver platter the way Kate seemed to expect.

Hell! Was everybody blind except him? People didn't fall in love in a few days. Love took time. It took...

It took him all of a glance to fall in love with Kate, Race thought, shaking his head in bewilderment, finding it nearly impossible to believe that same lightning would strike his daughter and leave an irreparable scar on her heart. Even if the girl thought she was in love now, she'd get over it.

She'd damn well have to get over it, he thought, because Gideon Summerfield—if he didn't meet up with a bullet today—was going to be on his way back to Jefferson City and the penitentiary tomorrow.

The closer they came to Santa Fe the sweeter the air became with wood smoke. It filled Gideon's lungs the way just looking at the woman who rode beside him filled his heart. He wasn't sure he'd make it through the day. He was riding with vicious men, but they weren't stupid and they'd turn on him as soon as they got wind of the trap he was leading them into. That trap, as far as Gideon knew, was set to catch him, too. And why not? If he were Race Logan, he'd do the same thing out of love for this dark-haired beauty who was smiling now, looking as if she were heading toward paradise instead of perdition.

He reached out and clutched the mare's bridle, drawing the horse closer so his leg brushed Honey's voluminous calico skirt. "You're almost home, bright eyes."

She gave him a smile that would have brought the devil himself to his knees, and the brightness in her turquoise eyes wasn't because she was nearing home. It was because she was here, with him. All that light and love was meant for him. All that, and all the generous warmth of her body where he had lost himself so irrevocably the night before, where he longed to lose himself this minute. Gideon's throat tightened with emotion as the rest of him quickened with desire.

Tugging both their horses to a halt, holding the mare's bridle firmly, Honey leaned into the space between them. "Let me taste your pretty mouth, darlin'." One last time, he finished inwardly. One last sweet time.

Her smile remained, only curved to fit his mouth, then parted to receive his tongue. Gideon struggled to keep his head clear, to capture every sensation—the softness of her lips as they cushioned her teeth, the tender warmth, the greedy little intake of her breath that stole his own away. It was so easy to forget there was anything or anyone else in the world. So easy to drown in the ocean color and depth of her eyes, the warm pull of her mouth, the silken streams of her hair.

Too easy. He was going to need his wits about him today as he'd never needed them before in his life. He was a wolf who was about to turn on his pack. And then he'd be alone, his vicious brethren at his back, while the banker stood before him, dangerous and determined, and no longer bound by promises.

He pulled away from Honey's mouth with a rough sigh but kept his eyes on her face, flushed now from his kiss. "The first time I laid eyes on you, Ed, honey, you reminded me of a brand-new spring blossom. You were like a windflower when it first opens, all hungry for sunshine and thirsty for rain. I loved you. Right then. And I'll never stop loving you. I want you to remember that."

It sounded more like a eulogy than a declaration of love, Honey thought, and Gideon's mouth, only a second ago so soft upon her own, had thinned now to a taut line. His eyes seemed to darken, like gray skies working up a storm. Her heart missed a beat.

"Gideon, you promised me you'd stay out of the way during all this. Stay out of the way and then, when it's all over, sit down with my father and tell him how things are with us."

His reply was a lazy drawl. "That's still the plan, bright eyes."

Honey gazed around her at the familiar landscape. Ahead, over the shoulders of Dwight and his men, she made out the shapes of familiar buildings. She could see the territorial flag waving against the bright sky above the governor's palace.

Gideon was lying to her. The knowledge came so suddenly, with such sharp clarity, that Honey felt as if a knife had just slipped between her ribs in the vicinity of her heart. And he was doing it not so much to deceive her as to keep her calm, to keep her in the dark about what was truly about to happen. Of course he couldn't stay on the fringe of the robbery as he had promised to do. In order to draw his cousin and the others into her father's trap, Gideon had to go in first. If he didn't, Dwight Samuel and his gang wouldn't follow. It was that simple.

That simple, and that terrifying. Honey saw clearly what awaited him. The betrayed outlaws, the angry banker and Gideon in the middle. He'd be lucky to get out alive. No wonder he'd sounded more like a preacher delivering a eulogy than a lover declaring himself.

Nearly panicky now, Honey tried to think of a way to keep him safe. And she couldn't. Her brain was numbed by fear for him and anguish for herself.

Gideon reached over once more and caught Jonquil's reins.

"Where's your house from here, Honey? How close?"

She pointed. "Just a few streets from the plaza. Why?"

"Can you get there without going by your father's bank?"

Honey tried to pull the mare's bridle out of his hand. "I can," she said, "but I won't. You're not just going to send me packing, Gideon. I won't go."

Just on the edge of her vision, Honey saw that Dwight Samuel and the others had reined in their mounts. All of them—Dwight, Shooter, the half-breed and the two Mexicans—were watching as Gideon slid off his horse and gripped his hands around Honey's waist, hauling her down and holding her tightly against his chest.

His words were hissed, like a rattlesnake passing close to her ear. "Choose, Honey. Either head this mare back to her warm stable right now or I'll handcuff you to the nearest hitching rail. And don't think I won't. I don't want you anywhere near that bank and if I have to clamp you to a damn post to keep you out of harm's way, then that's just what I'll do."

"I'm afraid for you, Gideon," she whispered in a tone of utter desperation. "You'll be right in the middle...."

"I'll be dead right here with five bullets in me if you don't keep quiet," he snarled. Then his tone softened as well as his tight hold on her, and his lips just grazed her ear as he continued. "I know what I'm doing, darlin', but I can't watch out for you and me both. Please. Please go home. Give me that peace of mind I need to get through this still in one piece and breathing."

Honey dragged in a long breath, assenting by her silence and by the way her body sagged against him.

Gideon cupped her chin with one hand, tilting her face toward his. He wanted to tell her that no matter what happened the love she had already given him made him a better man, a man who might even be deserving of heaven after all. His throat thickened, though, and those words wouldn't come. Only "I love you, bright eyes. I always will."

Always, he thought, watching her guide the dun mare up a narrow side street and then turn out of his sight. Chances were pretty good his always was about to run out and his eternity begin.

Gideon nudged his mount in the ribs, pulling abreast of Dwight. His grin caught the warmth of the noonday sun. "You ready to see a man about some money, cousin?"

In the apothecary shop, Race Logan held his breath as he watched the outlaws converge on Logan Savings and Loan. They came from both directions, three of them coming west from the plaza, three riding east on San Francisco Street. Let them come, he muttered under his breath, hoping he'd adequately impressed his men—the score of men who were flattened on rooftops now and hunkered down behind windows up and down the street—to wait. Let them walk in, get the money, come out. Then. Then.

Race could see Gideon Summerfield clearly. The man moved like a wolf—each step deliberate and wary, as if the street and sidewalk were strewn with invisible traps, steel jaws he couldn't see but sensed all the same. His gray, cautious gaze swept the street, and damned if he didn't seem to spot every window where Race had a man with a weapon hidden. He stared longest at the apothecary's window, as if looking right in Race's face. Then he pivoted, and followed the other five rough customers through the bank's door.

Hearing himself swallow, Race realized his mouth had gone dry as the desert floor. Wait, he told himself. He could see shadows through the bank's plate glass window. Only shadows, yet he imagined poor Kenneth Crane, pale, trembling, six pistols aimed at his heart. All the teller had to do was walk into the office, yank the safe open, stuff all those very real bank notes and gleaming gold bars in sacks. Just as they'd planned.

Sweat trickled down Race's sides. It was going like clockwork, but each second seemed a minute, each minute drew itself out like an hour. Clockwork. So far so good. They'd be coming out shortly, loaded down with their booty, and then twenty men would appear with twenty rifles. Six men would be dead or behind bars by sunset. And tomorrow one of the six would be on the northbound train, in leg irons and wrist cuffs, going back the way he came. Race would personally weld the steel restraints onto the prisoner to prevent any chance of escape.

Sudden movement out on the street sparked Race's attention. Then his whole body, already wire-tight, wound tighter. His son Zack was edging down the bank side of San Francisco Street, a rifle hard against his hip. The boy wove in and out of the shadows made by the noon sun and the buildings, then he edged like smoke down the little alley beside the bank and disappeared.

Race Logan's heart moved into his throat. He stood up and walked to the door of the apothecary shop, estimating his own chances for crossing the street directly in front of the bank without being seen. Deciding it was impossible, fury and fear combined and twisted in a hard knot in the pit of his stomach. If that boy came through this without a scratch—Dear God, please! My son! My son!—Race was going to beat the living daylights out of him.

And then, as if having a son in mortal danger weren't enough, Race caught sight of Honey coming west from the plaza, dark hair flying as she rode Jonquil at a fast clip, then tugged the mare to a halt directly in front of the bank.

Race called to her—a gruff, strangled plea. If she heard it, she ignored it as she stomped up onto the sidewalk, then strode through the front door of the bank.

* * *

At the sight of her, Gideon holstered his gun, then ripped the fingers of both hands through his hair, unleashing a string of curses.

Dwight Samuel was squatting down in front of the safe, shoving bank notes into a canvas sack, but he stopped long enough to frame a grin between his black mustache and beard. "Well, lookee who's back. Gotta hand it to you, Gid. You sure do know how to handle women."

Gideon answered him with a scowl as he grabbed Honey's arm and towed her to a far corner of the office. He cursed again, too angry to form any other words, too fearful for Honey's life to clear the shards of panic from his brain.

"If I'm with you, you'll be safe, Gideon. No one will shoot for fear of hitting me," Honey whispered urgently.

"Be still," he hissed. He was torn, part of him wanting to keep her close beside him where he could protect her, the other part wanting to shove her under the massive desk or even in the safe itself to keep her out of harm's way.

There wasn't much left in the safe now. Dwight was stuffing the last few banded stacks into his bag.

From the front window, Shooter called. "Not a soul in sight out there, Dwight. Looks like we'll have a clean and easy getaway."

The souls who weren't in sight were all on rooftops and hunkered down behind window after window. Gideon had almost smelled their anticipation as he had ridden down the street. He had felt scores of eyes boring into him, had sensed their hearts pounding like drums in a parade. Which one, he remembered thinking, had sweat-damp hands on the weapon with the bullet meant for him? One of them, certainly. Probably Race Logan.

"Gideon, let me help you get out of this."

Honey's whispered plea brought him back to the present.

Then Dwight clamped a hand on his shoulder. "We got it all, Gid. Come on. You want to bring her along as a hostage?"

Gideon shook his head. "She'll only get in the way," he said gruffly. "You go ahead. I'll make sure she stays put."

"Just like you did before, huh, cousin?" Dwight laughed, then turned his dark, glittering eyes on Honey. "I thank you for the contribution to our retirement, missy. I truly do." The outlaw turned to leave the office then.

"Dwight." Gideon's voice brought his cousin to a halt.

"Yeah, Gid?"

Gideon gave a quick shake of his head. It was too late. It had always been too late for Dwight, just as it had been for Jesse and Frank and the others. Death always lurked outside the bank door. They knew every time they walked in with guns drawn that it might be the last bank, the last moment. The only difference was today Gideon knew it for certain. He knew, too, that Dwight wouldn't hesitate taking as many innocent men or women with him as possible.

"Nothing," Gideon said now. "Nothing you don't already know, cousin. I'll catch up as soon as I take care of the woman."

When the outlaw disappeared through the office door, Gideon tightened his grip on Honey's arm. "Where's the back door?"

Her eyes widened, then glowed with comprehension. "Come on. Follow me."

She threw the bolt on the door behind the teller's area. Her hand was on the knob when Gideon stopped her.

"Wait. Take off your underskirt, Ed."

"What?" She laughed and looked down at the limp gathers of the big calico skirt. "I'm not wearing any."

"We need something white. A handkerchief. Anything." He looked around. Maybe he should take off his shirt, he thought. It wasn't white but it might do for a flag of surrender as he preceded her out the door.

"We need to get out of here," Honey said with urgency. "There's only an alley out back. Nobody's there. Come on." She twisted the doorknob.

"Honey!" Gideon reached for her but it was too late, and the door swung open on a boy with a rifle.

The rifle cracked and spit a tongue of fire just as Honey cried out, "Zack! Don't!"

The world had exploded in gunfire and pure hellfire then, in shattering glass and the shouts of frantic men, all while Gideon sat on the floor with Honey's limp and bloody body in his arms. The back door was still wide open and the rifle lay in the dust. The boy, though, was gone. A moment ago, an hour ago— Gideon was numb to the passage of time—the boy had stumbled to the door, staring down, his face a twisted mask of pain. Gideon remembered an instant of recognition—the dark hair, the shape of the face, the fierce, blue-green color of the boy's eyes. Her brother!

When the gunfire faded to a few random shots, Gideon became aware of the ticking of the clock on the wall, aware that he was rocking Honey's body to the rhythm of the passage of time.

"Let go of her."

The command skimmed through Gideon's awareness. It meant nothing. Then a hammer clicked back on a pistol and he felt cold metal touch his temple.

"Let my daughter go, Summerfield."

No. Never. He'd never let her go, Gideon thought. And it took a hard boot in his ribs and the butt of the gun crashing against his skull to make him release his hold on her.

Chapter Twenty

The bull-necked guard prodded Gideon—a quick, practiced jab to the kidney with his rifle stock—guaranteed not to bruise, only to hurt like hell. "Come on, troublemaker. Can't you shuffle any faster than that? There's people waiting."

"Let 'em wait." They could wait till hell froze over for all he cared, Gideon thought. Or maybe it already had. The long corridor was chilly and he was shivering in the thin cotton shirt the guard had given him to replace the stinking shirt he'd worn for weeks. Still no belt, though, or shoelaces. For chrissake, if they wanted him dead so much, why'd they go to such extremes to see he hadn't any means to do it himself?

The leg irons and the loose shoes crimped his gait, and even with wrist cuffs on, he had to keep his elbows close to his sides to keep his beltless pants from sliding right off his hips. Whoever was waiting for this sorry spectacle wasn't going to be disappointed, he thought, as the burly guard prodded him around a corner and down another long, windowless corridor.

"Wait here," the man grunted when they reached a closed door.

Gideon flashed him the grin that usually guaranteed an elbow in his gut and a heavy boot on his instep. "I ain't going nowhere, boss," he drawled.

In return, the guard merely scowled and sucked briefly on a tooth before he opened the door. "I have the prisoner," he announced to whoever was waiting inside.

"Bring him in."

One more quick jab to his kidney sent Gideon into the room, where daylight from tall windows stabbed his eyes, nearly blinding him.

Race Logan shifted abruptly in his chair at the far end of the large table. For a second it seemed he wasn't looking at a prisoner in the Missouri Penitentiary. He wasn't seeing a man at all, but instead was staring at a lean, gray wolf. Every nerve in Race's body took warning at the sight, and his hands curled into tight fists beneath the table.

Slowly, the wolf's gray eyes adjusted to the light. And slowly, they grazed each face at the table until they came to rest on Race. Without surprise. Without hope. Without a trace of warmth. But there was something in them meant for Race alone. Sorrow. And, miraculously, honor.

Almost against his will, Race felt his fisted hands relax. He leaned toward the dour man on his right. "Let's get on with this, Governor."

An hour later, as soon as the door clanged at his back, Gideon felt the raw November wind bite into him. A few months ago it would have elated him, just to feel weather—any kind. Now it only served as a sharp and bitter reminder that life indeed went on outside the penitentiary walls. Why? he wondered now.

He took a few steps forward, briefly enjoying a length of stride uninhibited by chains. When he looked over his shoulder at the hulking, redbrick institution, he knew he should have felt happy or grateful or just plain relieved to be on the outside. But he wasn't. The fact was if they opened the door this minute and said there'd been a mistake, Gideon would have shrugged indifferently and walked right back inside.

Prison only hurt and rankled when a man believed there was something better beyond its walls. There wasn't though. Not for him anyway. Hell was intolerable only because a man yearned for heaven. With his heaven dead, Gideon was indifferent to hell.

"Summerfield."

Race Logan was standing in an arched doorway, the collar of his dark wool overcoat turned up against the wind. The resemblance to Honey turned Gideon inside out once again, just as it had earlier when he'd first seen Logan in the hearing room. She seemed to gaze out at him from her father's turquoise eyes, full of impossible promises and dead dreams that shredded what was left of his soul.

"Banker." He had no other words for the man. Certainly no gratitude to express. If they shared a sorrow, it would have to go unspoken. Gideon shrugged, and turned to walk away.

"She's not dead, Summerfield."

Gideon halted. The sidewalk seemed to be coming up into his face. The red bricks of the prison wall appeared to rearrange themselves right before his eyes.

"She came damn close," Race continued. "When I put you on that train back to Missouri, I didn't think Honey was going to make it another twenty-four hours. But the fact of the matter is I lied when I told you she was dead."

He turned toward the banker slowly, as if moving too quickly would make him disappear or somehow change what the man was saying. All he could do was search Race Logan's face, quizzing him wordlessly, afraid even to speak now.

"I didn't want you ever coming back to look for her," Race said. "I thought she'd be better off without you."

He had to force his lips to shape words. Cautious words. Cool ones. "Probably right."

"No. I was wrong."

"I'm the same man I was four months ago, Logan. Nothing's changed."

"Only one thing, Summerfield. My daughter's carrying your child."

Gideon's heart, which had just begun to feel less than numb, surged now, crowding the air from his lungs. "Where is she?" he rasped.

"Before I tell you that, I want to get a few things straight."

In two long strides, Gideon was directly in front of the taller, heavier man, his hands clamped on Race's lapels. "You get *this* straight, Banker." Drawing back one fist, Gideon unleashed a solid punch at Race's face. "That's for letting me believe the light of my life was dead." He stepped back then, hands at his side. "You're welcome to hit me back if you want, but know that short of killing me, there's nothing you can do to keep me away from Honey or from claiming what's mine."

Race's blue-green eyes burned for a moment like the deep heart of a flame. He lifted a hand to touch his bleeding nose, then his mouth twitched as a grin fought its way to his lips. "My wife's gonna be tickled pink to see this, Summerfield," he said. "She's been wanting to do it herself for quite a while now."

Gideon stared down at the sidewalk, trying to get a grip on his ragged emotions. "Where is Honey, sir?"

"Kansas." With one hand, Race held a handkerchief to his profusely bleeding nose while his other hand slid into his breast pocket to withdraw an envelope. "The train will get you to Hutchinson. I've written directions and drawn a map to get you the rest of the way. There's a few dollars in there, too."

"More than a few," Gideon said, eyeing the contents.

Race shrugged. "Buy my daughter a wedding ring."

Gideon smiled for the first time in months. "Yes, sir."

"And do me a favor when you get to Kansas, will you, Summerfield?"

"If I can."

Race sighed. "Tell my wife you broke my damn nose, and then put her on a train and send her home to me."

* * *

"Don't fuss over me so, Mama." Honey lifted her chin a notch as Kate worked the last frog closure on her cape.

"I'm not fussing, Honey. And as long as I can't talk you into staying in here where it's warm, I'm making sure you'll be warm enough on one of your blasted treks through the fields." Kate pulled the final stiff braid through its loop. "There. At least you won't be catching your death out there. How's your arm feeling this morning?"

They had been in Kansas nearly a month now—Honey and her mother and Uncle Isaac—and in all that time, Kate hadn't gone a single day without quizzing her daughter about some aspect of her recuperation.

Honey gave her an exasperated sigh now, then launched into a well-practiced litany of well-being. "My shoulder's fine, Mama. Only a little stiff today. I can wiggle my fingers to beat the band. See." Poking her hand from the depths of her cloak, Honey demonstrated. "My breathing's fine. My heart's ticking like a Swiss watch. And my baby's fluttering in my tummy like a butterfly."

Kate's mouth curled down. "Then you should stay inside and not go traipsing off all by yourself."

Laughing as she fit her long hair beneath the hood of the cloak, Honey said, "Aren't you the lady who climbed in a wagon and hit the Santa Fe trail when you were carrying me?"

"I didn't have much choice," Kate snapped.

"Well, I do have a choice, Mama, and I choose to go out for my morning constitutional now." She reached for her mother's hand and squeezed it. "I'll be fine. Stop worrying."

How could she not worry? Kate thought as she watched her daughter walk out into the cold of a brittle November cornfield. How could she not be eaten away with worry for Honey and for herself as well?

What had she been thinking, walking out on Race the way she had, throwing that ultimatum in his face? "Honey's going to Kansas to have her baby, Race. I'm going with her, and I won't be coming back until you do what you have to do to get that Summerfield man out of jail."

Blast his stubborn hide, he'd let her go, too. Kate hadn't expected that. Neither one of them had backed down, not even at the train station when tears had pooled in Race's beautiful eyes and her own hot tears had streamed down her cheeks.

"Two damn mules." That was what Isaac had called them. Two damn, hard-headed mules.

And Honey was just as mulish. "He'll come to me as soon as he can." Her faith in the man was unshakable. But Kate wasn't all that sure. In her head she believed Gideon Summerfield was a decent and honorable man, while her heart warned her that that same decency and honor could very well make him walk the other way when and if the prison doors opened, believing Honey was better off without him.

"Another damn mule," Kate muttered, swiping a tear from the corner of her eye.

"You railing at Horace again, Miz Kate?"

Kate turned to Isaac Goodman's broad grin. "I thought you were out in the barn, Isaac."

He held his hands to the wood stove. "Gettin' cold out there."

Kate shrugged. "It's cold everywhere."

"Yup. All the mules need to be growing thicker coats now that winter's settling in." He lowered himself into the rocking chair by the fire. "I only hope I live long enough to see you all come to your senses."

Kate's voice was little more than breath. "I hope so, too, old friend. I hope so, too."

Honey made her way carefully over the frozen, uneven ground between the rows of dead cornstalks. The sky to the west was leaden, promising snow, and a chill wind lifted the hem of her cloak. The mask of hope she wore for her mother's benefit was gone now, and her shoulder ached from the wet cold.

She'd been able to hide her physical pain. If she hadn't, her mother would never have allowed her to make the trip back to Kansas. Honey wondered, though, just how long she'd be able to conceal the other pain, the one that kept searing her heart like a knife held in a fire.

Part of that pain was for her brother Zack, who had disappeared the day he had shot her by mistake. It was a heartache for her mother, made worse by the fact that her father refused to search for him. "Let him go," he'd thundered. "If he didn't have the decency to stay long enough to find out if his sister was living or dead, then let him go to blazes where he belongs."

Much as she ached for Zack, Honey ached for Gideon more. What if her father remained stubborn and intractable in his refusal to help with the parole he'd once promised? Or, if he did use his influence in Missouri to arrange the parole, what if her mother was right when she hinted that, despite love, Gideon might choose not to come? What if he didn't come?

Honey lifted a clenched fist toward the darkening sky. "What if?" she cried. "What if everything went right for a change? Is that so much to ask? I always thought I was doing things all wrong, but then I finally went and did something perfect, something so right."

Tears welled in her eyes, blurring the heavens, turning to wet brine on her lips.

"I...I don't know how to fix this. I've tried and I've tried. I've spent my whole life trying. So hard." Her voice fell to a whisper as Honey gathered her cloak around her and went to her knees. She bowed her head. "I'm tired of trying so hard. Please...please let me just accept. Give me patience. Let me just fold my hands and wait."

When she answered the knock on the door, Kate's hand flew to her mouth and she uttered a choked little cry.

Gideon met her surprise with a warm, lopsided grin. "I'm supposed to give you a message from your husband, Mrs. Logan. He said to tell you that I did you a favor by busting his nose—purely by accident, mind you—and he sorely needs you to come home."

She laughed as tears sprang to her eyes. "Welcome, Gideon. Welcome home."

"Thank you, ma'am." Hard as he tried to steady his gaze on Kate Logan, his eyes moved to scan the room behind her, hungering for the sight of Honey. Instead he saw an elderly man, rocking back and forth, grinning to beat the band.

"Now we got us a true Missouri mule to add to the family," Isaac said. "I surely hope I live long enough to see the consequences of this. Yup. I surely do."

"Where is she?" Gideon asked softly, returning his gaze to Kate.

"Out walking," Kate said, pointing over his shoulder. "Honey's just about worn a road through all that corn."

Gideon stood there a moment, speechless, until Kate put her hands on his shoulders and turned him toward the field.

"Go on," she said. "You two have lost too much time already. Besides, I've got some fast packing to do if I'm going to make the afternoon train. And I do plan to be on that train."

Gideon's breath caught in his throat when he saw Honey sitting on the frozen ground between the corn rows. Her cloak riffled around her in the wind. The hood had blown back, allowing the wind to toss her beautiful dark hair. Her hands were folded in her lap. Her head was bowed. And she was crying.

Ah, God. He had caused that pain, those tears. The sight tore at his heart and his immediate instinct was to run in the opposite direction rather than risk hurting her more.

But he stood there, dry-mouthed, hardly able to breathe. "Angel." It was all he could say.

She lifted her head, blinked as if she couldn't believe her tear-bright eyes.

Gideon summoned a grin as he sauntered toward her. "You 'bout done crying?"

"About." Honey swiped the back of her hand across her wet cheek.

He folded his legs and sat beside her. "Don't stop on my account now. Get it all done, Ed, honey, 'cause it's the last time you're going to do it."

Her tears came faster then, cascading over one another down her face, pooling in the corners of her smile. She tried to speak, but between the tears and the width of her smile, she couldn't manage anything but a wet croak.

Gideon slipped his arms around her, lifting her onto his lap, rocking her, nuzzling his face into the wet wool of her cloak. His hand slid under the folds of the fabric and found her warm belly. "We made a miracle, bright eyes. The two of us."

"I told you, Gideon. I told you dreams can come true." She sniffed, snuggling into the warmth of his chest.

He raised his head to gaze at the cornstalks. Close enough, he thought. Next summer they'd be green and he'd bring Honey and the baby out to hear the wind moving through the broad, glossy leaves.

"Guess you're going to make me prove myself as a farmer now," he said. "I only hope I remember half as much as I've forgotten."

"I'm sure there are plenty of men at the grange who will be happy to help."

His mouth tightened. "Well, don't count on my being too welcome there, bright eyes. One small farmer with one bad past doesn't count for much, sweetheart. But we'll get by. I'll do right by you, Honey. I swear."

Honey wiped away the last of her tears. "Your bad past is over, Gideon. And in case you hadn't noticed, mister, your small farm takes up better than half the county. Most of those grange members are your tenants, and they're going to be worrying about *your* opinion of *them*."

He tipped her chin up, grinning as he gazed into her eyes. "Hell, bright eyes. You mean I wasted all those years robbing banks and trains when all I had to do was marry a rich girl?"

"Well, if you get bored with farming, Gideon, we can always raise our own outlaw gang. Do you think half a dozen would be enough?"

"That might take a while, Ed, honey," he said, his brow furrowing in mock solemnity. "Take a lot of loving, too."

Honey grinned as she snuggled close. "In that case, I say the hell with the farm. Let's just have us a whole dozen little desperadoes."

* * * * *

Harlequin® Historical

WOMEN OF THE WEST

Don't miss these adventurous stories by
some of your favorite Western romance authors.

Coming from Harlequin Historical every month.

Don't miss any of our **Women of the West!**

WWEST-1

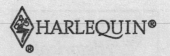

HARLEQUIN®

CHRISTMAS ROGUES

is giving you everything you want on your Christmas list this year:

- ☑ -great romance stories
- ☑ -award-winning authors
- ☑ -a FREE gift promotion
- ☑ -an abundance of Christmas cheer

This November, not only can you join ANITA MILLS, PATRICIA POTTER and MIRANDA JARRETT for exciting, heartwarming Christmas stories about roguish men and the women who tame them—but you can also receive a FREE gold-tone necklace. (Details inside all copies of Christmas Rogues.)

CHRISTMAS ROGUES—romance reading at its best—only from HARLEQUIN BOOKS!

Available in November wherever Harlequin books are sold.

Harlequin Romance ®

New from Harlequin Romance
a very special six-book series by

MIDNIGHT SONS

DEBBIE MACOMBER

The town of Hard Luck, Alaska, needs women!

The O'Halloran brothers, who run a bush-plane service called **Midnight Sons,** are heading a campaign to attract women to Hard Luck. *(Location: north of the Arctic Circle. Population: 150—mostly men!)*

"Debbie Macomber's *Midnight Sons* series is a delightful romantic saga. And each book is a powerful, engaging story in its own right. Unforgettable!"

—Linda Lael Miller

TITLE IN THE MIDNIGHT SONS SERIES:

HARLEQUIN PRESENTS®

Don't be late for the wedding!

Be sure to make a date in your diary for the happy event—
the sixth in our tantalizing new selection of stories...

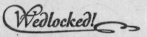

Bonded in matrimony, torn by desire...

Coming next month:

THE YULETIDE BRIDE by Mary Lyons
(Harlequin Presents #1781)

From the celebrated author of *Dark and Dangerous*

A Christmas wedding should be the most romantic of
occasions. But when Max asked Amber to be his
Yuletide Bride, romance was the last thing on his mind....
Because all Max really wanted was his daughter, and he
knew that marrying Amber was the only way he'd get
close to their child!

Available in December, wherever Harlequin books are sold.

LOCK7

Pick up the phone—along with five desperate singles—and enter
the Harrington Agency, where no one lacks a perfect mate. Only
thing is, there's no guarantee this will stay a business arrangement....

For five fun-filled frolics with the mate of your dreams, catch all
the 1-800-HUSBAND books:

Coming to you only from American Romance!

HARLEQUIN®

I N T R I G U E®

WHO IS THIS

Woman of Mystery

They say what makes a woman alluring is her air of mystery.
Next month, Harlequin Intrigue brings you another *very*
mysterious woman of mystery—Joyce Sullivan. We're proud to
introduce another writer to Harlequin Intrigue, as
the Woman of Mystery program continues.

And not only is the author a "Woman of Mystery"—
the heroine is, too!

Laurel Keighley is hiding—from haunting memories of
Christmas past...and a sexy stranger with the power to
influence Christmas present.

Don't miss

#352 THE NIGHT BEFORE CHRISTMAS
by Joyce Sullivan
December 1995

Be on the lookout for more "Woman of Mystery" books in
the months ahead, as we search out the best new writers,
just for you—only from Harlequin Intrigue!